Betrayal of the Chosen

Tournament of the Gods Book #2

By Timothy L. Cerepaka

An Annulus Publishing Book

Annulus Publishing, Cherokee, Texas, 2016

Published by Annulus Publishing

Copyright © Timothy L. Cerepaka 2016. All rights reserved.

Formatting by Timothy L. Cerepaka

Contact: timothy@timothylcerepaka.com

Cover design by Elaina Lee of For the Muse Design

ISBN-13: 978-0692652015

ISBN-10: 0692652019

Acknowledgements

I would like to thank my uncle, James Wilhite, for helping me get this manuscript into publishable shape. I'd also like to thank the rest of my family for supporting me while I wrote this novel. You guys rock.

Chapter One

WHEN BRAIM KOTOGS rose, yawning and stretching, from his bed this morning in his room in the inn, he had not expected to find a large package on his dresser. It was a plain package, square and wrapped in featureless brown paper, but there was something about it that made Braim hesitate. He didn't sense any magical energy emanating from the package, but he didn't see any labels on it or anything, either, so he didn't know if it was from a friend or not.

Brushing back his red bangs, Braim got up and walked over to the package cautiously. The wooden floor was cold under his bare feet, but he barely paid attention to that. The room was dark, with the only real light being the sun's rays peeking through the closed shutters of his room. Outside, he could already hear the sounds of the city of World's End; people walking, vehicles moving, and what sounded like blustery wind blowing through.

But right now, Braim was focused on the package. He held his wand at his side, ready to use it should the package prove deadly, even though there was nothing to suggest that there was anything bad about this package.

Except for the fact that it somehow got in my room without explanation, Braim thought. *Yeah, there's* definitely *nothing suspicious about that.*

Braim stopped a few feet from his dresser and eyed the package carefully. He noticed that one of the corners was ripped, showing a red tip, but all that told him was that the box was red, which was hardly useful information, in his opinion. He considered going and waking up the innkeeper, a minor spirit— also known as a katabans—named Mishak, and asking if he knew anything about the package or its contents, but Braim decided that he didn't really need to do that. The package didn't seem very threatening to him. It was just mysterious. And because he couldn't sense any magical energy from within, he decided that whatever it might be, it probably wasn't harmful.

Still, Braim didn't touch the package himself. Raising his wand, he applied a little bit of telekinesis to make the package float in the air. He then carefully ripped the brown packaging off using that same telekinesis, although it wasn't as careful as he'd like, mostly because he specialized in necromancy and not telemancy.

In seconds, the floor beneath the floating package was littered with plain brown packaging paper, while the package itself floated before him. It was red, as he had suspected, and just as plain as the paper that had covered it. He turned it around, but still saw no labels on it.

Whoever packaged this box is either unimaginative or trying to hide something from me, Braim thought. *Probably the first.*

Another application of telekinesis and the package's lid fell off. He then tilted the package just enough so he could see its contents. Unfortunately, it had packaging paper in it that made it impossible to tell what was inside it, though he managed to remove that quickly enough in order to see what was underneath it.

To his surprise, it was some kind of bracelet. Due to the low light conditions of his room, Braim couldn't exactly make out all of the details of the bracelet, so he removed the bracelet from within, tossing the box aside. He then floated the bracelet into his hand, which he looked down at with curiosity.

His first impression was that it was ancient. It was made of some kind of ancient metal and covered in markings he couldn't read but which he recognized as being from an ancient language. He turned it over his hand, but saw nothing to indicate it's nature.

Just an old piece of jewelry, Braim thought. *That's a weird gift to give someone.*

Braim looked down at the box on the floor, but didn't see a card or anything else that could have explained what the bracelet was supposed to be or who had given it to him. He also wondered why it was so old and who it might have belonged to in the past.

Not sure if I should try it on, Braim thought. *It doesn't look harmful, but just because it doesn't look harmful doesn't mean that it is safe.*

But Braim was curious, so he took the bracelet and slipped it on his wrist. The bracelet was a tight fit, but once it was on, it was very snug and secure. He twisted his arm over to see if the bracelet's appearance had changed when he put it on, but it looked the same as it always did.

Braim stood there for a couple of minutes, expecting something to happen, but the longer he stood there, the more obvious it became that the bracelet was not going to do anything to him. It seemed to be nothing more than an ancient piece of jewelry, and not even a very pretty one at that.

Do I have a fan or something who sent me this as a gift? Braim thought. *But if that's the case, then why isn't there a note or card from them explaining to me what this is and why they gave it to me? They can't be* that *shy, can they?*

Those questions made Braim uneasy. He supposed that receiving a mysterious bit of ancient jewelry wasn't as bad as being attacked by a four-armed half-god wearing a mask that resembled the face of a baba raga, but he had had enough mysterious experiences in his short return to life so far to last the rest of it and was not in the mood to have any more.

So Braim tried to remove it, but the bracelet stuck fast to his wrist and would not budge.

Uh oh, Braim thought. *Okay, not a problem. Let's just use some magic to remove it.*

Braim pointed his wand at the ancient bracelet and focused on using telekinesis to remove it. He narrowed his eyes and concentrated hard, imagining in his head that it would simply float off his wrist and back into the box from which it came.

But as soon as Braim used his magic, the bracelet tightened around his wrist. Not only that, but when it tightened, he suddenly felt as tired and worn out as if he had not slept at all. He staggered forward and then fell to his hands and knees. He could barely keep his eyes open. His thoughts became sluggish and his body became weak.

Unable to stay awake any longer, Braim fell face-first onto the floor, his last thought being, *I knew I shouldn't have put on that bracelet.*

Chapter Two

PRINCESS RAYA MANA'S first thought, upon entering the shop on World's End with a sign written in a language she couldn't read, was that the katabans had terrible taste in fashion. And she thought this as a half katabans herself.

In fact, the only reason Raya had entered this shop at all was because she had seen a very nice dress on display in the front window. It was red, her favorite color, and was made of a beautiful silk that she had never seen before in her life. The hem flowed even more beautifully, looking more like water than thread, and it even had the symbol of Grinf—a hammer wreathed in fire—etched into the right shoulder. What's more, it looked like it would fit her perfectly.

The only problem was that Raya had no idea what the price was. She was hardly price-conscious. As Princess of Carnag, there was nothing that she could not afford. If she wanted something, she could always ask her parents to get it for her and they would, no matter the price.

But Raya was on her own here in World's End and had only a limited amount of funds that her parents had given her before she came here. She didn't really know the exact amount—somewhere around a thousand coins, though they were written out on about fifty pieces of paper for ease of carry—but she decided that she would be able to afford that dress no matter how much it cost.

Yet if Raya hadn't wanted that dress so badly, she would have stepped right out of this shop and never visit again. The assortment of clothing looked normal enough, such as dresses and skirts for women and shirts and pants for men, but they were in such gaudy, contrasting colors that Raya just didn't understand how anyone could possibly wear them and not feel (and look) like a complete fool. There was a men's suit, for example, that was hot pink and lime green, while a women's dress seemed to be trying to cram every color of the rainbow onto its surface and not in an elegant way, either.

Not only that, but the shop was cramped. It had looked rather wide-open on the outside, but the clothes were practically crammed against each other in its tiny space. There was a thin path between the racks of clothing that went from the door to the counter at the other end, but even for Raya—who was hardly a large girl—it was slow-going. The place was hot as well, like all of the windows were closed. Raya would have thought that the owner of this place might have used magic at least to cool it down, but either the shopkeeper didn't know how or just didn't care about making sure that his shop offered the best experiences for his customers.

Additionally, the fabric on the clothes was unlike any fabric Raya had known back up north. Clothes that looked silk felt coarse and rough. One dress even felt like it had been covered with spikes (which she barely managed to avoid cutting her fingers against when she tried to touch the dress). She wondered whether this was a special fabric made by the gods or if the katabans made it themselves.

6

Then there was the smell. It wasn't bad, exactly, but it was odd because it smelled more like freshly-cut grass or seaweed than clothing. Every single piece of clothing in the shop seemed to give off that smell, which made Raya wonder if the shopkeeper had intentionally sprayed his clothes with it. Did that smell appeal to the katabans who lived here or something?

I thought that World's End, being the Throne of the Gods, would have far *more upscale shops than this place,* Raya thought with a grimace, slowly making her way to the counter near the back. *And just where are all of the customers and employees? Is today a slow day for them or something?*

Finally, Raya reached the counter, which was made of gold and ruby, which was in rather stark contrast to the rest of the shop's ordinary wooden flooring. Underneath the counter, Raya saw a hodgepodge of shoes—high heels, hiking boots, leather shoes, and so on—through its glass front, but she didn't see a price anywhere. Nor was she interested in finding out how much they cost. She wanted one thing, and one thing only, and she was going to get it.

But unfortunately, there was no one at the counter to answer her questions. She looked to the left and to the right, but didn't see anyone anywhere. She saw a door at the back of the shop, perhaps the office, but she didn't want to have to go all the way to the back of the shop just to get someone who could tell her how much that marvelous red dress cost.

That was when Raya noticed a tiny bell sitting on the counter. It was a rather pretty bell, made out of silver, which Raya assumed was what she needed to ring in order to summon whoever the shopkeeper was. Of course, the bell might have been for sale, but Raya saw no price on it, so she assumed that it wasn't.

Raya grabbed the bell and shook it. It made a pleasant little tingling sound. In fact, it was so cute that Raya almost wanted to keep the bell for herself.

But there was no response. Raya looked around the shop again and still didn't see anyone else in here. She wondered if perhaps the shopkeeper had gone out to lunch before reminding herself that it was actually mid-morning and therefore not yet lunchtime.

Besides, do katabans even have *lunch?* Raya thought. *Maybe they work all day long without eating anything.*

As it was, Raya hated waiting, especially in a shop like this. She turned around and made her way back to the exit, this time faster than usual because she was used to the shop's layout by now.

But, despite her disappointment in the shop's customer service, Raya could not help but look at the red dress on display in the window. Even from behind, it looked fabulous and she could even see a path to it through all of the clothing. So Raya made her way to the red dress, deciding that she would at least get the pleasure of touching it even if she couldn't own it.

In a couple of minutes, Raya reached the window display. She stopped and looked up at the red dress, imagining herself wearing it and impressing everyone else.

Especially Carmaz, Raya thought with a smile. *I don't know what kind of clothes he likes on a woman, but even a man like him would be knocked out by that dress.*

Oh, how Raya wanted it. She would have given anything in the world to have it, paid any price. She had tons of nice dresses back home, of course, but this was a dress on World's End, which meant that it was unique, maybe even better than all of the other dresses back on Carnag. She reached out and brushed her fingers against the hem. It was soft and smooth, exactly what she looked for in a dress.

Raya looked over her shoulder. She still didn't see or hear anyone. There were no employees or customers in sight. And a quick glance out the front window showed that the streets of World's End were as empty as King's Desert this morning.

No one will know, Raya thought, clutching the hem of the dress, *if I take it. Not stealing. This is of course not stealing. It's just taking something that this shopkeeper clearly can't sell. I mean, if he could sell it, then logically I shouldn't have even seen it in the window. I doubt the katabans who live here even like it, so if I take it, the shopkeeper won't be losing any sales.*

It had been a while since Raya had taken something, but she knew that if she was quick, she could take the dress and get out of here in minutes.

But just as Raya tightened her grip on the hem of the dress, a soft voice behind her said, "Hello, young lady. How may I help you?"

Raya almost whirled around and punched the voice's owner, but she restrained herself. Instead, Raya let go of the dress's hem and, turning around, put the sweetest smile on her face that she could.

Standing behind her—almost too close for comfort—was a katabans who looked like a kindly old man. He had a shock of gray hair and wore a funny orange and gray suit, a color disaster to Raya's eyes. His eyes were green and black. Literally, one eye was green and the other was black. It made it hard for Raya to look him in the eyes, though she was grateful for that, because she was pretty sure that the katabans would have seen her desire to take the dress if she had looked him straight in the eyes.

"Oh, er, I was just interested in this, uh, dress," said Raya, gesturing at the dress behind her and trying not to look too guilty. "It's very pretty and I thought it might fit me well."

The katabans looked over her shoulder at the dress and then nodded. "Yes. I think it would fit your body splendidly. It is almost like that dress was made for you, if I do say so myself."

Raya giggled a little, though it was more out of nervousness than anything. "Oh, that is so sweet of you. Who made the dress?"

"I did," said the katabans, jabbing his thumb at his chest proudly. "I made every bit of clothing in this shop."

Raya looked around at all of the dresses and suits and pants. "Really? How did you do that?"

"Through hard work and magic," said the katabans. "I come from a long line of katabans tailors who have made clothing for our fellow katabans. I make clothes for all genders and body types, but I specialize in making beautiful dresses for beautiful women like yourself."

"You certainly do a good job of that, if that red dress is as good as it looks," Raya said.

"Actually, it *isn't* as good as it looks," the katabans said. "It is better. It is an Anwan original."

"Anwan," Raya repeated. "Is that your name?"

"Yes, ma'am," said the katabans tailor, nodding. He gestured at the shop they stood in. "And this shop is called Anwan's

Tailoring. I sell and repair clothing for katabans. I can also make custom orders. I run the whole shop by myself. I don't have a single employee to help."

"That sounds like a lot of work for one man," Raya said. "Er, katabans."

Anwan must have noticed her slip, however, because he said, "Man? Are you by chance human?"

Raya didn't like the way Anwan said the word 'human.' Nor did she like how he leaned forward when he said that, as if he was going to eat her there and then if she answered wrongly.

But Raya didn't see any way she could lie about her species to him, so she said, "Actually, I'm half human. My father is human, while my mother is a katabans."

Anwan rubbed his large chin, like he was thinking about what she'd just said. "Father a human, mother a katabans ... young woman who looks human ... and that outfit you're wearing is part of the Tournament uniform that the gods ordered me to make for the Tournament last month ..."

Raya looked down at the clothes she was currently wearing. They were indeed a simple blue tunic and pants, very practical, though also incredibly boring. She only wore them because she didn't have any of her old dresses from home and because Alira, the Judge of the Tournament, demanded that all godlings wear them. Otherwise, she wouldn't have left these folded up in the drawers of her dresser back in her apartment.

"Wait, so you made these uniforms?" said Raya, looking back up at Anwan in surprise.

"Yes, ma'am, all one hundred of them," said Anwan, nodding. He then pointed at her. "And let me guess, you are Princess Raya

Mana, daughter of Hanarova, correct?"

Raya started when Anwan mentioned her mother's name. She could only say, "Well, uh, yes, that's correct. I'm the Princess of the House of Carnag and next in line to become Queen should anything happen to my mother. But how do you know my mother's name?"

Anwan's kindly smile quickly turned into an angry scowl when she asked that question. She noticed how he jammed his hands into his pockets, which made her worry that he was going to pull out some kind of weapon on her, but the tailor only drew a thin string from his pocket and began to play with it in his hands.

Then Anwan's scowl vanished, though when he spoke, he sounded very restrained. "Everyone on World's End knows Hana. In the old days, your mother was a servant of the Mechanical Goddess, the Goddess of Machines. Do you know her?"

"Mother has mentioned the Mechanical Goddess to me before," Raya said, "though she doesn't like talking about her days from before she met Father."

"Well, sometimes older people have their reasons for not wanting to talk about the foolishness of their youth, Raya," said Anwan. "But you see, I knew Hana when she was not much older than you. Quite the feisty girl, she was. I never imagined that she'd fall in love with and marry a human. It's unheard of among katabans. Not that there's anything wrong with that, of course," Anwan added hastily.

Raya frowned. She could tell that Anwan hardly approved of her parents' marriage, despite his insincere (and rather awkward) attempt at a save. He was clearly just trying to avoid offending her so she wouldn't take her business elsewhere (which didn't mean much, seeing as she didn't know of any other tailors in the city).

But Raya typically liked avoiding confrontations, too, so she said in a casual voice, "No offense taken. I am just surprised to run into someone Mother knew in her youth. Did she work for you?"

"No, she didn't," said Anwan, shaking his head as he continued to play with the little string in his hands. "She was a regular customer, at least until she went to work for the Mechanical Goddess. Then she spent all of her time on Stalf and I saw her maybe once a year at most. Last time I saw her was at the end of the Katabans War some thirty years back, after Jakuuth Grinfborn and his followers were locked away beneath World's End for their crimes."

"Perhaps I can reunite you with Mother after the Tournament is over," Raya said. "I could even make you the royal tailor of the Carnagian Royal Family. I—"

"No," said Anwan, shaking his head again. "I mean, that is a kind and generous offer, Princess, but I prefer to continue the work of my family here on World's End, rather than move up north to live among humans. But maybe I will come visit some day, if your mother approves."

Raya could tell that Anwan had rejected her offer for other reasons, but at the moment, she found that she could not gather the strength to care. Her mind was still on the dress, which she was going to get now that Anwan was here to tell her the price.

So, changing the subject, Raya said, "Well, Mr. Anwan, I would like to buy that dress in the window. Just how much does it cost?"

"Five hundred crimsonite," said Anwan without hesitation.

Raya frowned again. "Five hundred what?"

"Crimsonite," Anwan repeated. "It's the currency we katabans use on World's End to exchange for goods and services. Did your mother never tell you about it?"

Raya rubbed her arm, feeling a little embarrassed. "Well, no. We use coins up north. Everyone does."

"Ah," said Anwan. "I understand. Yes, of course humans would not use crimsonite. Even we katabans only use it for certain goods and services. Other goods and services, you see, we barter or trade for. We katabans are not as close to money as humans are."

"I see," said Raya. "Well, what is the current conversion rate of crimsonite to coins?"

Anwan stroked his chin. "You know, I have no idea. I've never had to convert human money into katabans money, mostly because I've never had any human customers before. And to be honest, I am not sure I want human money. It is completely worthless here on World's End."

Raya's eyes widened. She looked at her purse and pulled out a fistful of money and waved it in Anwan's face. "Are you telling me that this is all worthless? That I have no more money than the average street beggar? Is that what you're telling me?"

Anwan stepped back, though he didn't put away his piece of string. "I am sorry, Princess, but I can't take your money. I wish I could, but from a business standpoint, you have to understand that it makes no sense for me to do so."

"But ..." Raya was at a loss for words. She looked at the money in her hands, which was little more than glorified paper at

14

the moment. She had always been taught that money could buy anything and that if you had money, then there was nothing you could not do.

Thus, hearing Anwan tell her that it didn't matter how much money she had, that he wouldn't take any of it, was like being slapped in the face and pushed into the mud. She could not comprehend it.

"I am deeply sorry, Princess, but without knowing the conversion rates between crimsonite and coins, I can't give you the dress," said Anwan. "Perhaps you have something that we could barter for? Or trade?"

Raya shook her head to snap herself out of her existential crisis. She put her money back into her purse and looked up at Anwan. "Trade?" She said the word like she had never heard it before, which was partly true, as she had never had to trade to get something she wanted before.

"Yes, trade," said Anwan, nodding. "For example, perhaps you have another dress of equivalent value that you could bring here and give me in exchange for the dress in the window. I might just take anything you give me, seeing as I don't have any human clothes here and would greatly appreciate the opportunity to study the work of human tailors and dressmakers."

Raya thought about that. She looked over her shoulder at the red dress in the window and then looked back at Anwan. She was tempted to simply walk out the shop and go elsewhere, but she found that she simply couldn't say no to that dress. After all, if Raya refused his offer, then there was a very good chance that someone else would come and buy it before she did. If that happened, then she would be quite miserable.

"All right," said Raya. "I have some dresses back in my apartment that are human-made. But I can't bring you them right away. I have to head to the Stadium in order to watch the next sub-bracket challenge. I only stepped in here because I thought I'd have enough time to get the dress, but I definitely don't have time to run back to my apartment and then return here and then go to the Stadium afterwards."

"That is perfectly fine," said Anwan. "I'll hold the dress for you while you are away. I doubt I'll sell it anyway. No one around here seems to want it, so I can hold it for you without much trouble."

Raya smiled, already forgetting her earlier crisis. "Thanks. I don't know exactly when I will be back, but it will definitely be before the day is over."

"Very well," said Anwan. "My shop is open until late in the evening, so you'll have plenty of time to get back here and make the trade."

Raya nodded. "Then I need to get going right away. But I promise I'll be back with a human-made dress even better than this one. For sure."

Chapter Three

CARMAZ KORVA WALKED alone through the streets of World's End, keeping his head down and his hands in his pockets. He felt tired and sluggish, given that he hadn't slept much last night. Nonetheless, when the first rays of the sun had peeked through his window, he had gotten up, dressed, had breakfast, and headed out to the Stadium.

And he had to go there. Today was the day of the Human God Sub-Bracket Challenge. He did not know exactly what that would entail, but seeing as he was in the Human God Sub-Bracket, that meant that he had to be there whether he wanted to or not. Alira had specifically told him to be there early, along with the other challengers in that sub-bracket.

She didn't say which route through the city he had to take to get there, however. So Carmaz had decided to take the longest route he knew of, which would take him about ten minutes longer to reach the Stadium than it normally would. To add to the time, Carmaz walked at a slow pace.

The streets of World's End seemed empty this morning. He saw no merchants hawking wares or children playing in the streets or individuals running errands around the city. Carmaz knew very little about katabans culture and understood even less, but from what he had gathered from his stay here, most katabans only stayed in World's End in between missions given to them by the gods. He suspected that most of the katabans were currently out in the rest of the world, doing whatever it was that the gods had told them to do. Perhaps some were even keeping an eye on the Void to make sure that it wouldn't cross its boundaries again.

In any case, the absence of the people made World's End feel more like a city of ghosts than a city of gods. There weren't even any gods out right now, though Carmaz was all right with that, considering how he wasn't a terribly big fan of the gods. Besides, he liked the silence and solitude, as it meant that he didn't have to worry about someone asking him any dumb questions about himself.

Or the grief I'm feeling, Carmaz thought.

It had only been a week since his best friend since childhood —and his best friend in the whole world—Saia had been killed by the Void. Yet it seemed like much longer to Carmaz. It was almost like he was living a second life now. The first had lasted nearly thirty years and had included Saia. The second had just started a week ago and without Saia.

Despite having come to terms with the fact that Saia's death had indeed happened, Carmaz still found it hard to believe. Several times over the past week, Carmaz would wonder what Saia would say about this or what Saia would do in this situation, only to remind himself that Saia was dead and thus unable to have an opinion on anything.

And none of the other godlings had been particularly helpful in aiding him in dealing with his grief. Raya was still determined to seduce him (a fact he found bizarre, considering how brusquely he had treated her, but he supposed that he never did understand the opposite sex very well), Tashir had given him a long rant about the importance of strength in a warrior, Malya had given him a hug and told him she was there if he needed to talk with her (a gesture he did appreciate, though he still found it hard to talk with someone like her, who was essentially still a stranger to him), and Yoji had been worse than useless, telling Carmaz all the 'facts' that modern mages knew about depression and how to combat it (facts which seemed utterly useless to Carmaz at the moment, however true they might have been).

As for Braim, Carmaz had made a point of avoiding the mage ever since Saia's death. It wasn't necessarily that he hated Braim or anything. Truth of the matter was, he thought Braim was a good guy.

The problem was what Carmaz intended to do with Braim. He always felt guilty every time he thought about the deal he had made with the Ghostly God shortly after Saia's death, but he always pushed the guilt away, because he didn't think he was doing anything wrong.

What's wrong with wanting to bring your friend back to life? Carmaz thought, turning down an alleyway that he knew would increase his walking time by five minutes at least. *I know Braim doesn't want anyone studying him like a wild beast, but he doesn't understand that understanding how he came back to life is for the greater good. If we could somehow learn how he did it, then we could also use it to bring back other people, not just Saia.*

That was the deal he had made with the Ghostly God. Carmaz would help disqualify Braim from the Tournament and let the Ghostly God get him and study him to understand how his resurrection had occurred. Carmaz had already put stage one of his and the Ghostly God's plan into action last night.

Assuming everything went according to plan, Braim should be opening that box, putting on that bracelet, and losing his power at this very moment, Carmaz thought, glancing up at the pinkish morning sky visible between the massive skyscrapers on all sides. *Then it's the Ghostly God's turn to start the next phase of the plan.*

Carmaz didn't like the idea of working alongside any god, especially a southern god like the Ghostly God, but he was a practical person and therefore saw no reason to let his own personal biases get in the way of bringing Saia back to life. As long as that task was accomplished, Carmaz was willing to do anything that the Ghostly God asked him to do—well, as long as it moved him closer to his goal of resurrecting Saia, anyway. The only thing he wasn't sure about was the bracelet's origin. The Ghostly God had been very vague about where he had found it, but Carmaz hadn't pushed the issue because he figured there were all kinds of magical artifacts in the world that could do all sorts of strange things and this was simply one of them.

Now Carmaz was normally not the kind of person to even think about cheating death. Having grown up on Ruwa, he probably had an even greater understanding of death than most of the other godlings or most people in general. He had seen many people die over the years there. In fact, death was so common on Ruwa that he barely even thought much about it.

That was before *I met Braim and discovered that resurrection is indeed possible,* Carmaz thought. *And if it is possible to bring back those who died, then maybe it is also possible to return Ruwa to its original glory.*

That was how Carmaz had managed to reconcile his desire to resurrect Saia with his desire to win the Tournament and use his new godly powers to help his people. If he resurrected Saia, then Carmaz could show him to the Ruwans and give them hope that life could be improved.

Back on Ruwa, most of the villagers stopped supporting me when I told them that I was going to become a god, Carmaz thought. *They didn't believe I'd be any better than Skimif or any of the other gods. But once they see Saia brought back to life, they'll have no choice but to support me and believe in the possibilities of the future.*

Until then, Carmaz would have to do without their support. He felt the gold Ruwan coin in his pocket, the one that the young girl Frissa had given him before he left. It was the only reminder of home that he had now, seeing as Saia was dead now. He hadn't thought much about the coin since receiving it, but he kept it by his side regardless. It was one of the few things that kept him going nowadays and it would keep him going until he won the Tournament.

It wasn't long before Carmaz arrived at the Stadium. The massive building looked the same as it always had, even though it had been consumed by the Void only a week ago. He pushed the doors open and entered the lobby, where he found all of the godlings gathered. It reminded him of the last sub-bracket challenge last week, only this time, there were slightly fewer people due to the deaths that the Void had caused.

Carmaz did a cursory glance of the godlings, but he didn't see either Raya or Braim anywhere. He was grateful for that until he heard a familiar feminine voice shout, "Carmaz!" causing him to look to the side to see Raya running up to him in excitement.

She almost hugged him, but Carmaz moved out of the way just in the nick of time, causing Raya to go staggering forward with her arms out. She almost fell flat on her face, but she managed to catch herself, and then stopped and turned to look at Carmaz with a smile on her face.

"Hello, Raya," said Carmaz without any enthusiasm. "How are you?"

"Great," said Raya, without missing a beat. "Doing just fine. How about you? Are you ready for the next challenge?"

Carmaz found Raya's happiness odd. She had been right in the midst of the Void during its initial attack and had even passed out trying to escape from it, yet here she was acting like all was right with the world. It made Carmaz wonder if Raya was really that happy-go-lucky or if this was how she coped with trauma. Especially after learning that Raya had witnessed the death of Abacos, one of the original Steeds of Hollech, but again, she seemed entirely unaffected by it, as if she had not been through a severely traumatizing event fairly recently.

But he didn't mention it. Instead, he said, "As ready as I can be without actually knowing what the challenge is going to be, yes."

"Good," said Raya. "I know you'll do perfectly. In fact, I *demand* that you do perfectly."

Carmaz quirked an eyebrow. "Demand? Are you demanding *me* to do perfectly or are you going to demand Alira to judge me leniently?"

"Both, obviously," said Raya. She then looked around and frowned. "Where's Braim? I haven't seen him all morning. Did he sleep in or something?"

Carmaz folded his arms over his chest and gave a very convincing fake shrug. "Who knows? I haven't spoken to him since Saia's death, so I have no idea what he's been up to since then."

Raya looked a little troubled, and Carmaz understood why. Both of them had heard about how Diog, the God of the Grave, had attempted to murder Braim in order to 'correct' his 'unnatural' existence. It was well-known that Diog had ordered a half-god known as Ragao to kill Braim a couple of times as well. Right now, both Diog and Ragao were unable to harm anyone, but the possibility that someone else might have harmed Braim was still quite real.

And Raya doesn't even suspect that I might have had a part to play in it, Carmaz thought, keeping his facial expression neutral in order to make sure that Raya did not suspect that he had a part to play in Braim's lateness.

Then Raya shrugged and said, "Oh, well. Braim probably got sick or something. Or maybe he's just lazy. If Alira gets angry, she can get angry at him. I want nothing to do with it."

Carmaz nodded. "Same. Besides, I doubt Alira would call off today's challenge just because Braim is late. There's no reason to, not when all of the other godlings are here and ready to participate."

"Exactly," said Raya, "though I'd be quite disappointed if this challenge was delayed due to Braim's lateness. I'd probably slap him upside the head for laziness if that happened."

Again, Carmaz nodded, even though he didn't quite share her sentiments. All Carmaz hoped was that the Ghostly God was doing his part of the plan and that nothing had gone wrong. If it had, then there was a very good chance that he and the Ghostly God would be caught.

The Ghostly God is smart, if insane, Carmaz thought. *He's the one who came up with the plan, so I doubt he will mess it up.*

At that moment, an unfamiliar voice said, "Hey, are you Carmaz Korva?"

Carmaz and Raya turned to see a short and stout man walk out of the crowd of godlings. Carmaz was pretty sure he had never seen this man before, who had long, shoulder length black hair and dark skin to go along with it. He also had a necklace around his neck, which had a hook symbol hanging from it, though Carmaz wasn't sure what the symbol meant.

"Um, yes?" said Carmaz, not sure how to respond to this man's question.

The man stopped and held out a hand to Carmaz. "My name is Samvan Curos. I'm in the Human God Bracket, just like you. Pleased to meet you."

Carmaz, still not sure of this man's identity or intentions, nonetheless took the man's hand. It was hard and sweaty, though Carmaz wasn't disgusted by it because that described the hands of most Ruwans back home, though he didn't expect to feel such a tight and powerful squeeze as Samvan's fingers practically ate his own.

"Nice to meet you," was all Carmaz could think to say when he and Samvan finished shaking hands.

Samvan nodded in response, then looked at Raya and said, "And you're Princess Raya, right?"

Raya puffed out her chest. "The one and only."

Samvan nodded at her as well, but it was a very brief nod. He then returned his attention to Carmaz and said, "Carmaz, I just wanted to thank you for saving Alira from the Void. Rumor has it that you were the one who woke her up so she could teleport you and everyone else out of the Stadium during the Void's attack."

"I did do that, yes," said Carmaz. "But why are you thanking me? It wasn't particularly heroic. I just did what we needed to do to survive."

"Well, I wanted to thank you on Alira's behalf, of course," said Samvan. "I'm not actually her official spokesman or anything, but I can tell she was thankful for what you and the others did last week. I also wanted to thank you on a personal level."

"Personal level?" Carmaz said. "Are you friends with Alira or something?"

"No," said Samvan with a wistful sigh. "Not yet. She doesn't like to socialize with us godlings much. I've tried talking to her, but she just sort of blows me off. I'm kind of used to it, because most women treat me that way, but I thought that she might be at least a little bit more tolerant than most."

"Are you telling me that you actually like her?" said Carmaz, though he was quite sure that he had missed something at some point and was misunderstanding Samvan's words. "As in, in *love* with her?"

"Oh, it doesn't matter," said Samvan, waving off Carmaz's question. "What matters is that I thanked you for saving her, which gives me more chances to get to know her. I wish I had a better way to thank you, but this is all I can do for now."

Carmaz exchanged puzzled looks with Raya, who looked

rather disgusted by Samvan. He understood that feeling. While Alira was by no means an ugly woman, he found it hard to believe that anyone could actually love her. He didn't see what Samvan saw in her, but decided that he'd rather not know. It was just one of those things that he'd prefer to be ignorant of.

Changing the subject, Carmaz said, "So, Samvan, what is that symbol on your necklace supposed to represent?"

"This?" said Samvan, grabbing his necklace and holding it up. "This is the symbol of Hona, Goddess of Prisons and Prisoners."

Raya stepped back. "You aren't a prisoner yourself, are you?"

Samvan laughed as he let go of his necklace, which fell against his chest. "No, no. I was actually a prison guard before Tinkar showed up and told me that I am supposed to participate in the Tournament. Almost all prison guards in the world worship Hona. She is the one who makes our prisons strong and gives us the strength we need to keep prisoners behind bars."

"Oh," said Raya. "Are you a mage, then?"

"Nope," said Samvan, shaking his head. "My sister is, but I'm not. I'm just a normal old mortal. I've always wanted to learn magic, but I've never had the discipline for the subject. Besides, I've found that I can beat prisoners just as well with my club and fists as I could with magic. Don't fix what isn't broken, in my opinion."

"I don't know any magic, either," said Carmaz. "Don't need it, don't want to learn it."

"Hey, looks like we have something in common," said Samvan with a chuckle. "Maybe the three of us could form a magic-less humans club or something. Most of the other godlings seem to know some magic, so I think we non-magical humans got to stick together, you know?"

Carmaz didn't feel particularly threatened by the magic of the other godlings, so instead he said, "What do you think the Human God Sub-Bracket Challenge is going to be? Any hints from Alira yet?"

"She's as tight-lipped as always," said Samvan with a sigh. "I really do wonder about her sometimes. I mean, how does she expect any of us to win the challenge if she doesn't tell us about it until the last minute? Makes no sense at all if you ask me."

"She probably thinks that anyone who is destined to win will be able to figure it out on their own," said Carmaz, shaking his head. "Of course, whether that logic actually works or not is another question entirely."

"Well, it worked out for me," said Raya, gesturing at herself. "I managed to win *my* sub-bracket challenge with ease."

"Only because half of the other Hollech Bracket challengers were killed by the Void," Carmaz said. "If the Void hadn't attacked, who knows whether you would have won or not?"

"Of course I would have won," said Raya. She looked at Carmaz as though he had offended her. "Are you doubting my abilities? I'm one of the best godlings around. And I will prove it in the actual Hollech Bracket Challenge, whenever that is supposed to be."

"If you say so," said Carmaz with a shrug. "But personally—"

Samvan suddenly shushed both Carmaz and Raya, causing Carmaz to look at him and say in annoyance, "What?"

Samvan pointed toward the front of the crowd, which was when Carmaz noticed that all of the other godlings were now looking in that direction. He and Raya followed Samvan's pointing finger until they saw Alira lowering down from the ceiling on her stone platform.

Alira looked the same as she always did. Tall, wearing silver robes, with blonde hair tied in a tight bun and severe-looking glasses that revealed even more severe-looking eyes. She carried the thick Rulebook in her arms, which looked too heavy for a woman of her size to carry comfortably, but Alira held the Rulebook without showing any strains in her body.

But Alira did appear tired nonetheless. Even from a distance, Carmaz could see the bags under her eyes and how her neatly-done bun had a few loose hairs here and there. She no longer looked as cool and collected as she had the first time Carmaz had seen her.

It is probably due to our experience with the Void, Carmaz thought. *It never occurred to me to wonder how she reacted to it. Last I remember, Alira was angry and had gone to speak with the gods about it. I wonder what they told her. Maybe she is just stressed out from almost being killed, though now that I think about it, can Alira be killed at all? She's technically not a goddess ... I think.*

Actually, Carmaz wasn't sure *what* Alira was, exactly. She was clearly stronger than most mortals, but he had a feeling that she was not quite as strong as the gods. She seemed to be a truly unique individual. In fact, she *was* unique, seeing as she had been created specifically for the Tournament. He didn't even know the full extent of her powers and abilities, though that was probably intentional, as Alira struck him as a private individual who never revealed more to anyone than they needed to know.

Carmaz stopped thinking about all of that when Alira cleared her throat and spoke in her usual matter-of-fact, authoritative voice.

"Good morning to you all," said Alira, looking down over all of the godlings with her severe eyes. "I see that not all of you have made it this morning, but that is fine, because not all of the godlings are needed to attend this event. The Tournament will go on, regardless of who does or doesn't show up."

Now that struck Carmaz as odd. Alira had seemed very adamant about *all* godlings watching the last challenge. He had expected her to talk about sending someone to go and check up on the few that were not here, yet instead Alira acted as if it was not a problem. He supposed it probably wasn't, really. With Diog, Ragao, and the Void currently not in any position to harm anyone, chances were that the few godlings who were not present were not in any danger. Except for Braim, but Carmaz told himself that the Ghostly God was probably not going to harm Braim during his experimentation on him.

Or maybe she knows why they couldn't show up and just wants to get on with the Tournament and doesn't want the rest of us to worry about it, Carmaz thought. *That's always a possibility.*

Carmaz looked at Samvan. Samvan was hanging on Alira's every word. He seemed absolutely entranced by her voice and her appearance. Carmaz decided that Samvan had very strange taste in women.

"Today is the start of the Human God Sub-Bracket Challenge," Alira said. "With that said, will each Human God Bracket challenger please step over to the left side of the lobby, while the rest stay to the right?"

Samvan was the first over to the left side of the lobby, in front

29

of the door that would take them into the Stadium field. Carmaz followed right behind him, as well as eighteen other people who Carmaz didn't know or recognize. They lined up to the door, which was currently closed, while the rest of the godlings lined up before the door on the right side of the lobby, which was also closed.

Then the doors opened and both lines began walking through the doors. Carmaz looked over his shoulder to see Raya waving at him rather happily, but he soon lost sight of her when he entered the room into which he and the other Human God challengers were walking.

It was a room large enough to hold all twenty of them. There were two doors directly ahead of the group, emblazoned with images of humans on them. The right door had a generic man on it, while the left door had a generic woman on it. They looked 'generic' because they did not have any specific features to nail them down to any particular race, though Carmaz supposed that made sense, seeing as the Human God was the god of all humans, not just those of a particular race or ethnicity.

To the left and to the right were hallways that turned out of sight. Raya had once described this room to Carmaz. According to her, those hallways led to other sets of doors similar to the one before them, which acted as entrances for the other godlings to take to enter the Stadium field. Carmaz wondered if he was going to get to go through the other doors or if he was going to get to go through the ones in front of him, though it didn't really matter to him either way.

It was only after the door behind them closed shut—seemingly of its own free will—that Alira appeared before the group. She adjusted her glasses with the bottom of her hand and then drew out a thin deck of cards, with colors ranging from yellow to blue to green and beyond, from her robes, which she held up for the group to see.

"Welcome, challengers, to the Human God Sub-Bracket Challenge," said Alira. She almost tripped over that last word, which Carmaz only noticed because Alira usually had perfect pronunciation. "As always, keep in mind that all of the rules written in the Rulebook apply and that breaking any of these rules for any reason is grounds for instant disqualification from the Tournament. You must compete fairly and without cheating. In fact, do not even consider cheating. The rules do not allow me to disqualify people who merely think about cheating, but I do frown upon it highly and would think less of those who do."

Carmaz tried not to look guilty. He was certain that helping the Ghostly God keep Braim out of the Tournament was against the rules, even though he had not read the Rulebook (mostly because he couldn't read). But Alira didn't know about that, nor did she seem to suspect Carmaz of having cheated. He glanced at Samvan, who was still looking at Alira like she was the only person in the world worth listening to.

"Allow me to explain today's challenge to all of you," said Alira. "And I want you all to listen very carefully, because we are on a strict schedule and I do not want to have to say this again. Understood?"

All of the challengers nodded, Samvan nodding with far more enthusiasm than the rest of them combined.

"All right," said Alira. "This first challenge will be a duel between the two competitors. The member of each pairing will be given access to a variety of weapons and be allowed to pick just one to take with them into the field. You may pick any weapon you like. There will, however, be no killing in this duel. You may harm your opponent, but killing your opponent is grounds for instant disqualification from the Tournament and expulsion from World's End. The winner will be whoever successfully disarms their opponent first."

Carmaz frowned. While he wasn't against fighting—it was actually something he was good at, despite not having taken any formal training classes—he wondered why this was the first challenge. He didn't quite see what this had to do with humanity, unless the point was that humans were more violent than other species and therefore required a fighter to rule them.

Though now that I think about it, that's not exactly an inaccurate description of humanity, Carmaz thought.

He looked at the others standing around him. Some, like Samvan, looked eager to start fighting, while several others looked a little hesitant at the idea. He suspected that most of them didn't know much about fighting or were not good at it. There was one young woman—closer to his age than to Raya's—who was rubbing her hands together eagerly, as if she couldn't wait to start fighting.

Alira held up the thin deck of cards a little higher. "To determine which pairings will go together, I have assembled a deck of twenty cards, with ten different colors between them. When I give these cards to everyone, you must find the challenger whose card is the same color as yours. For example, if you get a purple card, then you must find another challenger with a purple card, who will be your opponent for this challenge."

Carmaz was already familiar with the way the pairings worked, mostly because Raya had told him about it before. He thought it was kind of a silly way to pair challengers up, but he knew better than to voice that opinion of his aloud, otherwise Alira might just kick him out of the Tournament for disrespect. Granted, she hadn't done that so far, but he figured that if Alira was anything like the gods, then she had a strict limit for the amount of disrespect she tolerated from mortals such as himself.

Alira threw the cards into the air, but rather than flutter to the floor, the cards spread apart and flew to their respective challengers. Carmaz caught one of the blue cards, and as soon as he did, the eager young lady from before was at his side. She carried a blue card in her hand, same color as his, which she shoved into his face.

"Looks like the two of us are challengers," said the young lady. Her voice was rather shrill, which made Carmaz wince. "Name's Eria. Yours?"

"Carmaz Korva," said Carmaz, pushing the young lady's card out of his face. "What's your last name?"

The young lady stared at him. "What?"

"Your last name," said Carmaz. "You said your name is Eria. Eria …?"

Eria didn't seem to understand his point at all, so Carmaz decided to drop it.

"So, Eria," said Carmaz, "where are you from?"

Eria rubbed her big nose and said, "Kikasa. More specifically, I am a graduate of the Kikasa Military Academy. One of only two women graduates."

She said that with some pride, though Carmaz didn't know

what the Kikasa Military Academy even was. But he noticed a tattoo on her left shoulder that resembled a steel sword.

"Notice my sword tattoo?" said Eria, gesturing at her shoulder. "Got it in the Academy. I worship Atikos, the Goddess of Healing and Steel. The steel sword is one of the many symbols that represent her and the one that the Kikasan military tends to like best."

"I see," said Carmaz. "I'm from—"

"Ruwa," Eria finished for him. She smiled. "Everyone knows about you, because you were the one who saved Alira and all. The only thing I don't know is what kind of job you held there."

Carmaz found that he didn't feel comfortable with the idea of strangers knowing his name and homeland (and probably other things as well) without him first telling them. Eria may have been a fellow godling, but to him she was still a stranger and he didn't like strangers knowing a lot about him before he met them.

But Carmaz didn't show any discomfort. He simply said, "I didn't have any real job on Ruwa. Jobs are very scarce. I just did whatever was needed to survive. I hunted food, helped repair or build new buildings, fought off any wild animals that attacked, and so on. Nothing special."

"Oh, right," said Eria. "Ruwa is sort of a hellhole, isn't it? I'm surprised that anyone still lives there. Why don't they just leave?"

Carmaz forced himself not to slap Eria silly for that suggestion. "Because very few ships ever come to Ruwa. And of those few that do, they're mostly pirate ships that don't take passengers except as slaves."

"Oh," said Eria. "Well, I also just remembered that the other nations of the Northern Isles have an agreement not to trade with

Ruwa due to its disastrous situation. That probably isn't helping."

Carmaz looked at Eria in surprise. "I didn't know about that."

"You mean no one told you?" said Eria. "I thought *everyone* know about it. Then again, I only know about it because my brother, who is a Kikasan politician, told me about it once, so that probably doesn't speak well of my knowledge of international politics, heh."

So it's not just the gods that have abandoned us, but other people as well, Carmaz thought. Anger rose up within him, but he forced it down because he knew that getting angry at Eria for something that she didn't have any control over would do him no good. Besides, he suspected that she was analyzing him for weaknesses. As a soldier, she was probably very good at fighting and he had no reason to suspect that she was not trying to figure out how to beat him before their duel began.

"So anyway, I'm really looking forward to this duel," said Eria. "I was worried that the first challenge might be some sort of debate about issues plaguing humanity or whatever, but a duel is more up my alley. How about you?"

Carmaz folded his arms over his chest and shrugged. "I don't care what the challenge is. All I know is that I will do my best to win it."

"That's what I wanted to hear," said Eria, slapping Carmaz on the shoulder with more force than he thought someone of her size should have been able to use. "I just know that our fight will be great if you have that attitude. I'm the same, really. It's how I was one of only two women graduates from the Kikasan Military Academy."

Carmaz nodded, but before he could respond, Alira's loud

35

voice rang in his ears, "It appears that everyone has found their partner. Now I want everyone to head down the hallways on either side and stand in front of whichever set of doors they find. Once everyone is situated in front of their doors, then I will tell you when to enter the field."

Carmaz wanted to go to the two doors in front of the group, because those were the closest, but Samvan and his partner—a tall, thin man who didn't look like much of a fighter—had taken those spots already.

Eria grabbed Carmaz's arm and quick pulled him into the left hallway, which was the closet to them, and said, "Here. We can take these doors."

Carmaz blinked, not having realized that Eria had just pulled him here so fast. He looked at the doors in front of them. They resembled the first set of doors in the main area, complete with the carvings of the generic men and women in front of them. Eria took her place in front of the door with the man on it, while Carmaz stood in front of the one with the woman on it. The other godlings streamed past them, each pair taking up a different set of doors until soon everyone had found their set.

Then, without warning, the doors in front of Carmaz and Eria opened and Alira's voice rang out through the hallways: "Challengers! Step through the doors, pick your weapons, and let the duels begin!"

Chapter Four

BRAIM AWOKE WITH a start. He was sweating and breathing hard, like he had just had a terrible nightmare. His senses were all confused and he had no idea where he was, at least until his senses returned to normal and he could think straight.

Darkness. That was what he saw. Darkness everywhere. His immediate reaction was to think that this was the Void, that the Void had somehow gotten him again, and that maybe it actually was going to kill him this time. He reached for his wand, only to discover that it was nowhere near him.

But then Braim took a moment to feel the darkness (as much as one *could* feel the darkness) and he realized that this wasn't the darkness of the Void. The darkness of the Void had a malevolent, intelligent quality to it, like someone standing just outside of the corner of your eye waiting to strike when you least expected it, but this darkness felt like regular old darkness. He sensed no malicious intelligence controlling it, though the room he lay in was cold nonetheless.

Of course, knowing that he wasn't in the Void only comforted him slightly, because that still didn't explain *where* he was or how he got here. It didn't look like his room. Even at night, his room never got *this* dark, mostly because of the lights of the city peeking through the cracks in the curtains.

Nor did it smell like his room, either. Braim's room normally smelled of partially-melted candle (from the candles he occasionally lit at night whenever he got up to do his business) and zap fish soup, which was a food he often ate in his room.

This place smelled like dust and mist. It smelled old, as if he was inside an ancient, decaying house. It reminded him of a graveyard, though Braim doubted that this was Diog's castle that he was in.

Braim looked down at his body. The darkness was too black for him to see, but he could feel that he was still wearing his clothes at least. He could even move, though he hesitated to do so without being able to see where he was and his movement was somewhat limited due to the straps he felt around his body. He felt a hard stone slab underneath him, very different from the bed he had been sleeping in earlier.

How long have I been out? Braim thought. His stomach suddenly growled. *And where's breakfast?*

Braim tried to sit up, but unfortunately he could not due to the straps keeping him down. He struggled against his straps, but they would not budge.

Wait, what am I doing? Braim thought. *I don't need physical strength to break out of these. I can just use my magic. Don't have my wand, but I can still use magic even without it.*

So Braim focused hard on snapping the straps with his telekinesis. He was not an expert in telemancy, but he was good enough at it to be able to use it to perform simple tasks like this.

But whereas Braim usually felt the magical energy rise within him whenever he cast a spell, right now … he felt nothing at all. It

38

wasn't that Braim didn't know how to do it, because he did. Nor did it have to do with his hunger. It was just that he couldn't feel his magical energy at all.

"What the hell?" said Braim aloud, mostly out of habit. "Why —"

"Looks like the bracelet still works," said a familiar deep voice from somewhere within the shadows.

At that moment, a pale, hideous glowing green face loomed out of the darkness with a grin full of crooked teeth. Braim immediately recognized him for who he was.

"Ghostly God," said Braim, his voice tense. "What are you doing here?"

"This is my mansion," said the Ghostly God, waving around at the shadows with one hand. "Or the basement of it, actually, one that I rarely use, but which will suit my current purposes perfectly."

"Current purposes?" Braim said. "Are you saying that *you're* the one who put that box in my room with the bracelet?"

"I didn't put the box there personally," said the Ghostly God. "But I did help plan where it would be placed."

"So you created the bracelet, too?" said Braim. He could now feel the bracelet still wrapped around his wrist, although it didn't feel as tight as it did before.

"Wrong," said the Ghostly God. "It isn't even a Martirian creation. It was created by the inhabitants of the world known as Harnum, which existed before Martir, and is surprisingly hardy, considering how many eons it has been since Harnum's fall. I just used it because I knew how useful it could be."

Braim furrowed his brows. "Bracelet from Harnum ... hmm, I

think I remember Darek telling me about that once."

"Yes, Darek would know, seeing as he was the one who owned the bracelet for a while there," said the Ghostly God. "Of course, since he is still under contract to serve me for another eight years, I ordered him to give me the bracelet, which he did. I of course did not tell him why I needed it, but he didn't ask. He can be a good servant when he wants to be."

"It doesn't matter where that bracelet came from," said Braim. He nodded at the straps holding him down. "These straps are too tight. Mind loosening them up a bit for me?"

"No," said the Ghostly God. "I'm not a fool, Braim Kotogs. You will have to try harder than that to trick me into freeing you."

"Then I'll just break out on my own," Braim said. He paused, and then added, "Somehow."

"Somehow?" said the Ghostly God. He chuckled. "Let's see: The straps are too thick and tight for you to snap through sheer physical strength alone, and you no longer have any magical powers, so you can't use magic to free yourself, either."

Braim's eyebrows rose in surprise. "Wait, I don't have any magical powers anymore?"

The Ghostly God's grin became even more chilling. "Did I forget to tell you? That's what the bracelet does. It takes away your ability to perform magic. I am still not entirely sure how it works—Harnumian technology shouldn't be compatible with Martirian physics—but I am the God of Ghosts and Mist, not the God of Technology, so I am simply going to 'roll with it,' as you mortals might say."

Braim was pretty sure that no mortal on Martir actually said that, but that was irrelevant compared to the revelation that the

Ghostly God had just sprung on him. "This can't be right. Once you learn how to use magic, it's impossible to lose that ability."

"Didn't Darek tell you about the time he lost his own magical power?" said the Ghostly God. "And by this same bracelet, too. I suppose it was a rather embarrassing turn of events, which is probably why he never mentioned it to you."

Braim wanted to believe that the Ghostly God was lying, but deep down, he knew he wasn't. It was the only reasonable explanation as to why he couldn't use magic anymore and why he couldn't feel his magical energy, either. It was an unnerving feeling, almost worse than the darkness in the back of his mind that kept tugging at his attention, but there was no point in denying it any longer.

"Why'd you do it?" said Braim. He cracked a smile. "This isn't some sort of weird joke or something on your part, is it? I mean, I know you gods tend to have a different sense of humor from us mortals, but this really isn't that funny."

"I find humor pointless, so I can assure you that this is not some kind of joke," said the Ghostly God. "I really did kidnap you and take you off of World's End, just like what my brother Diog did, only I did it a thousand times better. Of course, I am a southern god, so it goes without saying that we do things much better than our northern siblings."

Braim suppressed a shudder. "Are you going to eat me?"

The Ghostly God rolled his eyes. "Of course not. Why would I do that?"

"Because you southern gods like to eat humans," Braim pointed out. "That's kind of why the whole Godly War happened at the beginning of time."

41

"I'm not hungry at the moment," said the Ghostly God, patting his stomach. "Even if I was, I wouldn't eat you. I've tasted your kind before. Absolutely terrible. The Loner God keeps telling me that Nikons like yourself taste delicious, but I personally think that your kind are dry and brittle."

Braim had no idea whether to take that as a compliment or not. So he said, "Then why'd you kidnap me at all? Just for the thrills?"

"Thrills bore me," said the Ghostly God. "But I thought you'd already know why I kidnapped you. I haven't been exactly secretive about my desire to study you and find out how you came back to life, you know."

"And I haven't exactly been secretive about my desire to not be studied like a dead lizard," Braim said. He looked down at his straps again. "I'm starting to think that the two of us could have come to a more agreeable arrangement about the matter."

"You would never have agreed to be studied, no matter how 'agreeable' the arrangement," said the Ghostly God. "That's why I had to do this. Not by myself. I had some help from one of your fellow godlings, though I won't tell you who."

"Was it Raya?" Braim asked. "Because she doesn't like me all that much."

"As I said, I'm not going to tell you," said the Ghostly God. "What matters is that I am going to find out what makes you different from other humans. I will try to keep you alive, but keep in mind that sometimes sacrifices must be made to further the knowledge of everyone."

"So why don't *you* make the sacrifices, then?" said Braim. "Because I'm pretty sure that that would be better than forcing

42

someone else to make the sacrifices for you."

"It doesn't matter who makes the sacrifices," said the Ghostly God. "What matters is that I am not denied the knowledge that I seek. And believe me when I say that this knowledge could be revolutionary if I get it from you."

The Ghostly God reached out with one metallic hand, causing Braim to say, "Hold on there. What about the other gods? And Alira? They'll notice I'm missing again and will send someone to go look for me."

The Ghostly God's hand paused about halfway to Braim, as if the Ghostly God had not considered that. But then the god's smile became far more wicked than before and he said, "You think I'm stupid enough to leave behind a trail for the other gods to follow? When I kidnapped you, I left behind a corpse that I altered to resemble you. I then told Alira and the others that you are extremely sickly and that you just need to rest without interruption for the rest of the day, which is all the time I will need to find out what makes you tick."

"What are you going to do to me, exactly?" asked Braim. He was trying to distract the Ghostly God with questions until he could come up with an escape attempt. "Dissect me?"

"If necessary, yes," said the Ghostly God. "But in truth, I don't think I'll need to do that. I believe that your unique nature is due to both your body and your soul. There is something different about you that cannot be found through means as simple as dissection."

Then the Ghostly God wrapped his cold metal fingers around Braim's forehead. He tightened his grip around Braim's forehead, putting so much pressure on it that Braim was certain that his head was going to explode.

"Instead, I am going to put you in the Mind Chamber," said the Ghostly God. "And this will be interesting, because I have never put a human in the Mind Chamber before, so I will get to see its effects on humanity as well."

Braim opened his mouth to ask what the Mind Chamber was, but before he could do so, he suddenly felt like he was falling through a deep pit. The Ghostly God's grinning face vanished into the shadows above him and soon was completely lost from sight.

Braim found himself lying on his back in a cave. He sat up, which made him realize that he was no longer being held down by the straps on the stone table, and then looked around the cave. He didn't see the Ghostly God anywhere, which made him wonder where the Ghostly God was. The pressure from the Ghostly God's hand, however, was still present on his forehead, which made it hard to concentrate.

The cave itself was pretty normal-looking. It had stalagmites and stalactites and the air was somewhat damp. It was also incredibly cold, but Braim didn't mind it so much because he was used to the cold by now. He scrambled to his feet and felt his pockets for his wand, but he could not find his wand or anything else that he usually carried around in his pockets.

Is this supposed to be the Mind Chamber? Braim thought, looking around at the ordinary cave. *When he told me about it, I was expecting something a lot scarier. This is ... pretty ordinary-looking, to be honest. The Spirit Lands were scarier than this.*

Then Braim heard a low, rumbling growl from somewhere in the back of the cave. He turned to face it, but the cave stretched out so far into the darkness that he couldn't see the end of it. It seemed like the cave just stretched on forever and ever, with no exit in sight. The place had a slight, bloody smell to it, though Braim saw no bloodstains anywhere.

But that low, rumbling growl still emitted from the back. Braim didn't know what kind of animal could make that sound. It might have been a fearsome baba raga or perhaps a great gray shark (though now that he thought about it, that second option was unlikely considering how great gray sharks only existed underwater, which he was not at the moment). Whatever it was, Braim didn't know if he should run, or stay and find out what it was first.

"Welcome to the Mind Chamber, Braim Kotogs," said the Ghostly God, whose bodiless voice seemed to be coming from everywhere at once. "What do you think about it so far?"

That low rumbling growl made Braim hesitate, but then he said, "Boring. There's nothing in here."

"That's because you just got here," said the Ghostly God, sounding amused. "Besides, I haven't shown you the true horrors of the Mind Chamber just yet. I wanted to give you a moment to see where you were before I unleashed the true horrors of the Mind Chamber upon you."

"What *is* the Mind Chamber, anyway?" said Braim, looking around again. "This doesn't look like a chamber in my mind or anything. It's just a cave."

"The Mind Chamber is a place I created to punish disobedient or slacking katabans servants," said the Ghostly God. "Most gods tend to use corporal punishment to punish their servants, but I prefer to punish them mentally. It is much, much harder to handle mental assault than it is to handle physical assault … and mental damage takes far longer to heal than physical damage."

"So are you going to torture me, then?" said Braim, folding his arms across his chest, trying to ignore the low rumbling growl still coming from the darkness. "Is that it?"

"No," said the Ghostly God. "Instead, I am going to test you. My current hypothesis is that the unique relationship between your soul and your body lies within your mind. If I can discover what makes your mind different, then I will be that much closer to understanding how you were able to return to life."

"I'm not sure if that will work," said Braim. "What kind of tests could you possibly do that would help you figure that out?"

"I'm not going to tell you because I want it to be a surprise," said the Ghostly God. "If I tell you ahead of time what kind of mental tests I have set up for you, then you will be able to prepare for them. I want you vulnerable and ignorant. Your reactions— and the data I thus collect—will be much more genuine and therefore useful for my research purposes."

Braim rolled his shoulders. "Then what's up with that low, rumbling growl I keep hearing? Is that you?"

"Of course not," said the Ghostly God. "That is the first test, actually. Good luck."

"Good luck?" Braim repeated. "Good luck with what?"

But the Ghostly God did not answer, which made Braim suspect that he was no longer there. Of course, the Ghostly God was probably watching Braim's progress from the safety of his mansion, but Braim still had no way of contacting him.

Relax, Braim, Braim told himself. *The Ghostly God probably isn't going to kill you. He just wants to figure out how you came back to life. That's all.*

Of course, as soon as Braim thought that, he realized that the Ghostly God hadn't said anything about leaving Braim undamaged. But Braim tried to keep an upbeat attitude about it. The way he saw it, he might very well be able to escape the Mind Chamber so long as he was smart about it.

Every place has an escape route, Braim thought. *I can't see the exit now, but there is probably one somewhere along the line. I'll just find it and use it to get out of here with no problem.*

That was when Braim heard it. Following the low, rumbling growl was what sounded like wet footsteps slapping against the ground. The sounds grew louder and louder, as did the growl, as if the source of those sounds was approaching Braim.

And when the monster stepped out of the shadows and into Braim's sight and he saw its appearance, Braim screamed.

Chapter Five

RAYA WAS BORED. She hadn't expected to be. She had expected to be engaged by the duel between Carmaz and that woman who called herself Eria, which was displayed on the vision bubbles floating before the watching eyes of the other godlings.

But even though Alira had already called for the duel to start, only a handful of the pairings had even began fighting. The others were still choosing their weapons from the vast array of weapons offered to them by a bunch of katabans weapons dealers who had agreed to give the godlings some of their weapons for the duration of the challenge. That included Carmaz and Eria. Well, Eria had already picked out her weapon, a double-bladed sword that looked rather nasty to Raya, but Carmaz seemed to be having trouble choosing his.

Come on, Carmaz, just pick something already and fight her, Raya thought with a scowl. *It's not that difficult. Just grab a sword and start stabbing her already.*

What made Raya's boredom so terrible was that she kept thinking about that dress that she wanted back in Anwan's shop. Anwan had agreed to hold it for her until the sub-bracket challenge was over and she could find one of her other dresses to trade, but Raya kept worrying that Anwan might grow tired of waiting and just decide to sell the dress to someone who had actual money. It made Raya wish that she had simply taken the dress, but she knew that there was no way in a million years that she would have been able to get away with that with Anwan right there, even if she did her best not to get caught.

Raya looked to her left and right. To her left was Malya, that kindly middle-aged woman who reminded her of a mother. Malya looked rather content and at peace with the current pace of things, simply sitting back in her chair with her hands folded over her lap. Her swords were leaned against the back of the seat in front of her, but Raya had no doubt that this woman could grab them in an instant if needed.

To Raya's right was Yoji, the young magical prodigy who was also in the Hollech Bracket and had been one of the winners of the Hollech Sub-Bracket Challenge last week. He was talking with Tashir, the shark-headed aquarian makhimancer, who was on his right, about something to do with magic or something. Raya didn't really know or care. She was just glad that Yoji wasn't trying to talk to her. It seemed like he always tried to fill her in on some useless trivia about the gods every time he saw her, even if she didn't ask him to.

Then Raya looked down at the rest of the godlings seated in the rows below her. Most of them were watching the few duels that had started, though she noticed a couple of the guys in the front seats were apparently making bets on who would win each duel (and from what Raya could see, they were betting quite a bit more money than she thought people like them would have).

That made Raya look at Alira. The Judge was mostly watching the duels, clearly keeping an eye out for the winner, but every now and then she'd looked at the godlings as if to make sure that none of them had run off without her knowing. Alira seemed far more fearful now to Raya than she had before the Void's attack, which made sense, because Raya herself occasionally had a hard time sleeping at night or going into dark places that reminded her far too much of the Void.

Right now, of course, Raya had nothing to be afraid of, or at least she shouldn't have anything to be afraid of. But she kept remembering how the Void had managed to engulf the entire Stadium with her in it just a week ago. She didn't think that that was likely to happen again—the gods and katabans were more aware of the Void's power now and had taken measures to make sure that it didn't pull that same stunt—but Raya still feared every now and then that those shadowy corners in the viewing box were the Void's shadows, just waiting to engulf her and the other godlings before they even realized it.

It didn't help that Raya kept feeling the Void's shadows crawling along her body. It was probably—hopefully—just her imagination at work, but Raya remembered how it felt to have the Void crawling up her body. She had felt so violated, but she had not actually spoken with anyone about this because she wasn't sure that anyone else would actually understand.

"A bit worried about something, dear?" said Malya, causing Raya to snap out of her thoughts and look at her. There was a concerned look on Malya's face. "You look worried."

Raya shook her head. "No. I'm just dreadfully bored by this challenge. Carmaz and Eria still haven't started their duel yet."

"They will in time, dear," said Malya. "But you seem to be worried about something else."

Raya felt a twinge of annoyance at Malya's perceptiveness. While she didn't hate Malya, she really was not in the mood to confide in her or anyone else. Besides, Malya was not royalty, as far as she could tell, and Raya had always made a point of never sharing important information with peasants unless she absolutely had to.

"It's nothing," Raya said. "Absolutely nothing. I'm fine."

Malya smiled a knowing smile. "When I was your age, I kept insisting the same thing whenever anyone asked me how I felt. But it was never true. I always was bothered about something, sometimes serious, sometimes not."

Raya crossed her arms over her chest, but it was hard to remain moody and angry toward Malya's rather calm attitude. "Well, you are clearly not royalty, so I'd prefer it if you wouldn't pretend like you understand me or what I'm going through."

"I was the same way toward my elders when I was your age," Malya said. She chuckled. "Then I realized that they understood me even better than I understood myself. Trust me, Raya dear, I likely do understand what you are going through right now, even if you don't think I do. And I don't have to be the daughter of the most famous king in the Northern Isles to understand how you feel."

Raya still wanted to avoid talking about it, but she now saw that Malya wasn't going to drop the subject no matter what. Raya hated these types of people. She intentionally avoided them back home on Carnag, because if there was anything she hated more than older people who thought they knew better than she, it was *talking* with older people who thought they knew better than she.

"All right," said Raya, slumping in her seat. "You win."

Malya looked quite pleased with Raya's admission of defeat, though she also managed to look as kindly as ever. "So what's bothering you?"

Without really looking at Malya, Raya said, "The Void."

"Ah," said Malya. "Well, I understand that. The Void is indeed a terrifying thing. We are lucky that it didn't kill us all."

"Yeah," said Raya. She shivered and rubbed her arms. "But I still hate it. I wish it didn't exist."

"We all do, Raya," said Malya. She glanced at the vision bubbles. By now, most of the pairings had picked their weapons and started their duels, though there were still no winners yet. "I have to admit, though, that I almost forgot that you were right there in the thick of it when it started. I don't think I ever learned how you escaped alive."

Raya shrugged. She *really* didn't want to talk about this, at least not with Malya. She'd be okay discussing it with Mother, but Malya wasn't Mother, no matter how motherly she may have acted.

But again, there was no way out of this, so Raya said, "Well, I —"

She was interrupted by a sudden cheering from the front row from a couple of burly guys who were pointing at the uppermost middle vision bubble. Raya saw a woman standing over a defeated man before the bubble popped out of existence.

"We have our first winner of the Human God Sub-Bracket Challenge," Alira announced. She pointed at the woman on the vision bubble. "Rinnye Cakan! She will be escorted out of the Stadium now to return to her quarters and rest. The other nine duels are still ongoing."

Raya didn't know who this Rinnye girl was, but the godlings sitting in the front row were whooping and hollering like she had just won the entire Tournament. It made Raya feel a pang of jealousy. Based on what she had gathered from the others, no one had cheered for *her* when she had won her challenge. Granted, that had been because everyone was still recovering from the Void's attack, but Raya still hadn't received as much praise for winning as she had wanted to even after the Void left.

As the cheering died down, Raya resumed her conversation with Malya, saying, "I opened a portal to the ethereal and escaped through it."

"Hmm," said Malya. "Well, I can't say I've ever done that, but I am amazed that you did."

"Well, it wasn't *impossible* to do, you know," said Raya. "I mean, that was the first time I've ever actually done it, but you do know I'm part katabans, right? That gives me certain abilities that full-blooded humans don't have."

"That must have been horribly traumatizing," Malya said. "I heard you were found unconscious on the streets after the Void was expelled. How did you get there?"

Raya had already explained this to a lot of people before, so she was reluctant to do so again. She hoped that Carmaz would pick his weapon already, but the vision bubble showed that he was very indecisive, because he was still picking up swords or other types of weapons, looking them over with interest, and then putting them back down and moving onto the next. Even Eria looked bored and impatient by now. Raya half-expected that woman to start attacking Carmaz just to relieve her boredom.

"I don't know," said Raya. "When I entered the ethereal, I lost consciousness due to the pain that the Void had inflicted on me. All I know is that someone probably picked me up and took me to World's End, but I couldn't tell you who."

"Well, it must have been a katabans of some sort," said Malya. "Only katabans can enter the ethereal, right? Do you know of any katabans that would like to rescue you?"

"I don't," said Raya. "Outside of my mother—who had no way of knowing that I was in trouble at the time—I don't know any katabans that would do that."

"You must have a guardian spirit protecting you at all times," said Malya. "All humans do, you know."

Raya looked at Malya in confusion. "Guardian spirits? What's that?"

"You mean you've never heard of guardian spirits before?" said Malya. "Well, I suppose it is something that only we Frianans believe, but that does not make them any less real than the gods themselves. At birth, all humans are granted a guardian spirit that follows them around and protects them from harm. Aquarians might have them, too, but I don't know for sure."

Raya looked around, but saw nothing except for Yoji, Tashir, and the other godlings seated in the rows below. "I don't see any guardian spirits."

"They rarely make themselves visible or known, even to their humans," said Malya. "But sometimes, when the circumstances are right, they appear as if from nowhere. I saw mine once when I was only six years old."

Raya, still rather skeptical, nonetheless found herself very interested in Malya's story, so she sat up straighter and more comfortably in her seat and folded her hands over her lap.

"Really? What did it look like?"

"He looked like a handsome man wearing a dark cloak," said Malya. "I didn't see much of him, of course, because it was midnight and raining, but he appeared to me and brought me back to my parents. You see, I had wandered off from our house at night for reasons I don't quite remember and the only reason I returned alive was because of my guardian spirit."

"Does your guardian spirit have a name?" asked Raya.

Malya nodded matter-of-factly. "Of course. I learned from speaking with a seer—a special type of mage on Friana that can see guardian spirits—that his name is Joff. Aside from that, however, I don't know much about him, except that he is always there and is always protecting me even when I can't see him."

Raya brushed some strands of blonde hair from her eyes. "How do you make your guardian spirit appear to you, then?"

Malya shrugged. "I honestly don't know. I've always been told that your guardian spirit only appears to you in your darkest hour, when the line separating life from death is at its thinnest. I don't know about that, though, because I wasn't near death when I was six, merely lost and afraid and confused, but that's what most seers claim, so who am I to argue with them?"

"How could I communicate with my guardian spirit?" asked Raya. "Is it even possible?"

"You need to find a seer," said Malya. "They're not exactly the most common type of mage, mostly because many mages are skeptical of the concept of guardian spirits, but there is a sizable minority of them living on Friana who offer their services to both rich and poor alike. Perhaps after the Tournament, I can introduce you to the one I've known for my whole life."

Raya wanted to roll her eyes, but she did not want to disrespect Malya, so she simply shrugged and said, "No, that's fine. I don't really believe in guardian spirits anyway. Even if I did, I don't care to know him or her or whatever it is. My guardian spirit, if it exists, will protect me no matter what, right?"

"That's typically how guardian spirits work, yes," said Malya. "But wouldn't you want to at least thank him for his help?"

"How do you know my guardian spirit, if it exists, is male?" asked Raya.

"Most are," said Malya. "Again, I don't know why, but most guardian spirits tend to be male. There are a lot of female ones, of course, but most people have male ones. Just the way it is."

"Well, no matter its gender, I really don't want to know it," said Raya, shaking her head. "All I care about is that it is doing its job, which is to keep me safe, and that it will keep me safe until I win the Tournament."

"Very well," said Malya. "But if you ever need to talk to your guardian spirit, I can connect you with a seer who will be able to do it for you for a very reasonable price."

Raya nodded, though it was only to be polite. In truth, she found the entire concept of guardian spirits to be ridiculous and was glad that her parents didn't believe in such superstitious nonsense. She had always known that people outside of Carnag believed in very silly things, but this had to take the cake for the silliest belief she had ever heard from another human being.

"Anyway, how do you feel now?" asked Malya. "Better?"

"Yes, I do," said Raya, "though I think it will take quite some time before I stop mistaking every little shadow for the Void."

"That's good to hear," said Malya. Then she looked at the

vision bubble and said, "Oh, it looks like Carmaz has finally chosen his weapon."

Raya whipped her head to look at the vision bubble displaying Carmaz and Eria. Carmaz had indeed picked out his weapon— some kind of sword, from what Raya could tell, though she wasn't much of a weapons expert, so she couldn't identify what type of sword it actually was—and now he and Eria stood opposite each other, studying each other for the fight.

Then Eria attacked.

Chapter Six

CARMAZ WAS AWARE of Eria's impatient foot tapping and sighing. He was aware that the katabans weapons merchant before him—a portly male with wolf-like teeth and long purple hair—was wondering what was taking Carmaz so long just to pick a simple weapon. And he was aware that the other godlings watching him through the vision bubbles were probably just as impatient and annoyed at his apparent indecisiveness as Eria and the merchant were.

But Carmaz took his sweet time anyway, going over the dozens of weapons offered by the merchant, all free for the taking. There were swords, axes, knives, brass knuckles, attachable claws, and many other types of weapons Carmaz had never seen before, much less known the existence of prior to the challenge. Part of the reason Carmaz had taken so much time to look at everything was that he wanted to see all of these weapons because most of them did not even exist on Ruwa.

The main reason, however, for Carmaz's delay was that he wanted to make sure that the Ghostly God had plenty of time to study Braim without interruption. If Carmaz won the challenge too quickly, then the possibility of the gods or someone else finding out that Braim had gone missing would increase dramatically. And that could not be allowed, at least until the

Ghostly God had figured out what made Braim work and returned him to World's End before anyone realized Braim was missing.

Every now and then, Carmaz looked around the field. It was not a very wide open area. It was shaped somewhat like a wedge, with the tip narrow and the bottom wide. There was plenty of room for him and Eria to fight, but it was still too confined for his liking. The temperature was pretty even, at least.

He also occasionally looked at Eria. She was holding her sword and looking quite bored, having picked out her own weapon literally ten seconds after they had entered the field. She hadn't even taken the time to look at all of them. Eria had only glanced at the vast array of weapons on the table, grabbed her sword, and walked away. It seemed a little too rash to Carmaz, but Eria was more experienced in weapons and fighting than he was, so perhaps she needed less time to decide what kind of sword she needed than he did.

But then one of the swords laid out on the table before him caught his eye. It had a golden handle and a silver blade, which wasn't too flashy in comparison to the bright red ax or the platinum knife, but Carmaz found that he liked how it looked and so picked it up to examine in more detail.

The sword was light in his hands, but Carmaz could easily imagine using it to cut through his enemy. Of course, he wasn't actually supposed to kill or maim Eria, but he thought it would be useful nonetheless, especially against Eria's own sword, which was wider and heavier than his.

"That the one you want?" asked the katabans weapons merchant. There was a hint of hope in his voice, of restrained relief, like he wanted Carmaz to have chosen his weapon but did not want to get his hopes up in case Carmaz had not.

Carmaz didn't know for sure how far along the Ghostly God was in his experimentation with Braim, but he decided that he had delayed the start of the challenge long enough.

So he nodded and said, "Yes, I'd like this blade."

"Then take the damn thing," said the katabans weapons merchant in annoyance. "But make sure not to break it. It is a very expensive weapon and ain't easy to replace."

"I will," said Carmaz as he stepped away from the merchant's table and turned to face Eria. He heard the *pop* of an ethereal portal opening behind him and glanced over his shoulder to see that the merchant had already left, along with his table full of weapons, and then looked back at Eria. "All right. Ready to—"

He didn't get a chance to finish his sentence because Eria dashed at him with her sword. She moved faster than Carmaz's eyes could follow, but Carmaz managed to raise his sword just in time to block her attack.

Even blocking the attack caused him to stagger, however, because Eria put more effort behind the blow than someone of her size should have been able to. Eria pulled her sword back and struck again, but Carmaz dodged it by jumping backwards. He held his sword in both hands, a warning gesture to Eria to not attack him again unless she wanted to get harmed.

"You move fast for someone who clearly hasn't had any sword training," Eria said, gesturing at Carmaz's hands.

"How did you know I haven't had any sword training?" asked Carmaz. "I never told you that."

"Easy," said Eria. "You're not holding your sword correctly, your stance is atrocious, and with the way you're blocking my attacks, you're just going to end up breaking or heavily damaging your sword before you can even touch me."

Carmaz bit his lower lip, though he still held his sword up. "And? Are you going to interrupt our challenge to give me a lesson in swordplay?"

"Of course not," said Eria. She raised her sword. "I just wanted to make sure that you knew exactly why I am going to beat you."

Once more, Eria ran at him. Already predicting her next move, Carmaz held his sword defensively, expecting her to raise her sword and bring it down on him, which he would then block by holding his sword above his head.

But then, without warning, Eria brought her sword down, forcing Carmaz to quickly move his own sword down to block the blow. He managed to do it in the nick of time, catching her blade before it could hit him, but Eria was now pushing hard against him, putting stress on his arms from the awkward way in which he held his weapon.

Hang in there, Carmaz, Carmaz told himself, struggling to hold back Eria's pressure, which seemed like too much for a woman of her size and stature to be capable of putting on. *Just hold her back as long as you can. Wait for an opening. Don't drop the sword.*

Easier said than done, especially with Eria's smirk annoying him. She clearly thought that she was better than him, that it was only a matter of time now before she beat him in front of everyone else and moved on to the next challenge.

But Carmaz didn't allow himself to give up, not when he remembered the reason he was fighting. He pushed back against her with all of his might, actually causing Eria to stagger back. He then followed it up with a slash, but Eria recovered quickly and jumped backwards out of his reach.

Now, however, Eria's smirk was one, replaced by a smile that was far friendlier, if a bit hungry.

"Oh, so you're actually fighting *back* now," said Eria. "I admit I didn't see that coming. But I guess even beginners like yourself can sometimes get a lucky shot in when you try."

"Luck has nothing to do with it," said Carmaz, panting from the effort. "Where I come from, those who give up die, while those who keep struggling live. And I intend to keep struggling no matter what."

Eria tossed her sword from hand to hand as she said, "Inspiring words, but inspiring words have never won wars. Strength and skill, however, have, and I have plenty of both."

Again, Eria dashed at Carmaz. Carmaz tried to predict her next move, but the way she held her sword now was different from how she had held it before. She was holding it upside by the hilt, with the actual blade sticking out behind her. It seemed like an odd and impractical way to hold a sword, but Carmaz figured Eria had to have a plan, considering how experienced she was in swordplay, so he couldn't afford to take her lightly.

Then, without any warning whatsoever, Eria leaped to the side, causing Carmaz to look in the direction she was leaping. While she leaped, Eria swapped her sword from her right to her left hand and then slashed at Carmaz too fast for him to dodge or block.

Slash wasn't the best word to describe it, however, because Eria didn't hit him with the sword's edge. She slammed the flat of her blade into his gut, right in the area he had left exposed. It was like being hit with an iron bat, the blow knocking Carmaz's breath from his lungs and causing him to stagger. He tried to slash at her, but Eria just jumped out of his reach again, a playful smile on her face.

"I'm impressed," said Eria, holding her sword in a more familiar way again. "Most people tend to go down the minute I hit them like that, but you managed to stand your ground. Guess you Ruwans are made of sterner stuff."

Carmaz panted hard. He wasn't sure how Eria had managed to hurt him so badly with one blow like that. It didn't make sense how someone as thin as her could even hit that hard, but Carmaz had to admit that his knowledge of swordplay was limited to the times he'd seen pirates back on Ruwa hack apart their enemies, so Eria was probably utilizing some kind of hidden technique that allowed her to hit him harder than her body weight should have allowed her to.

She's not even a makhimancer, Carmaz thought, wincing at the pain in his gut where the flat of Eria's sword had crashed into. *Thank the gods.*

"Don't have anything to say?" said Eria, again tossing her sword from hand to hand. "That's fine. I'm not interested in conversation anyway. I'm in this Tournament to win it, so let's resume, shall we?"

Eria ran at him again. When she was within reach, she slashed at him once more, but this time Carmaz blocked it. He then slashed at her again, but Eria just dodged it by moving to the side and then swinging the flat of her blade at his exposed side.

The blow sent Carmaz staggering to the side—it had hit him

even harder than the last blow, and this time he was pretty sure that he had heard something crack inside him. But Carmaz ignored the pain to swing his sword at Eria, though by the time he did, she was once again outside of his reach.

Regaining his balance, Carmaz looked at Eria. His hands were sweaty and his clothes felt hot and heavy now, even though they were made out of a light material. Despite having only been hit twice, Carmaz felt like he had already been wrestling a swamp tiger all day and was certain that the next hit would be his last.

Eria, on the other hand, looked energized and ready to fight all day and well into the night. He didn't even see any sweat on her. Carmaz wondered where she got all of that energy from, but decided that it didn't matter. He needed to end this quickly, before Eria could get another devastating blow in on him, as he believed that her next blow would take him out. That meant he'd need to end the duel in one hit, which seemed like an impossible feat to him, because he hadn't managed to hit Eria even that many times yet.

But I can't let this duel go on any longer, Carmaz thought. *My body can't handle any more blows from her. I'll collapse the second she hits me again.*

Then Eria dashed at him once more. Carmaz almost didn't register it in time because he was distracted by his thoughts and pain. And by the time he did, Eria's sword was already within reach of his body. He lowered his sword to block her incoming blade, but he was too slow. The flat of her blade struck him in the stomach again, in the same spot as before, only this time even harder, and he gasped in pain. He staggered backwards, hanging onto consciousness through sheer willpower alone, as Eria stood up and smirked at him.

"You fought well for an amateur," Eria said, "but that technique I kept hitting you with is called the Trinity Knockout. Three hard blows in the right areas of the body can knock out even the toughest bruiser, without having to cut through skin or bone. Should be any minute now before you—"

Carmaz—still finding it hard to think straight through the pain —ran at Eria as fast as he could. He still wasn't nearly as fast Eria. He had, however, taken advantage of her penchant for banter in the middle of combat and caused her to not react in time.

He swung the flat of his blade at her hands. His sword struck, sending Eria's sword flying out of her hands. It landed blade first into the earth. Eria reached for it, but then Carmaz placed the tip of his sword at her neck, causing her to freeze.

Panting hard, feeling the sweat roll down his temples, doing his best to ignore the pain where Eria had struck three times, Carmaz said, "I think ... I think I win."

He could see Eria thinking hard about how she could get out of this situation as the winner, but then she sighed and said, "Can't disagree with that."

Relief flooded Carmaz's soul, but he didn't lower his sword from Eria's neck until he heard Alira's voice ring out through the field: "We have our second winner of the Human God Sub-Bracket Challenge: Carmaz Korva!"

Chapter Seven

BRAIM HADN'T STAYED still long enough to see the monster that had stepped out of the shadows. He had only seen its appearance for a brief second—pale-skinned, dragging behind it strange, slimy appendages, two large, deformed dead eyes—and had run.

It wasn't even a conscious decision on his part. Braim had run based purely on instinct. He knew that because it had not entered his conscious mind to do so, mostly because his conscious mind knew that there wasn't anywhere that he could run to.

But even as Braim ran as fast as he could, he heard the low rumbling growl of the monster and that unnerving slapping sound again. The entire experience reminded Braim vividly of a nightmare, only he was pretty sure that this was real and that if the monster got him, he wouldn't just wake up in his bed with a rapid heartbeat and sweaty body.

What does this challenge even prove to the Ghostly God? Braim thought as he ran. *How does this tell him anything about my nature? Starting to think he's just scaring me for his own sick thrills.*

Overwhelming fear propelled Braim down the dark, seemingly endless tunnel, and he was not one to argue with fear in situations where it made sense. And despite running faster than he had ever run in his life, the monster sounded like it was always one or two steps behind him, which prompted him to run even faster.

Up ahead, Braim suddenly saw a light. It was tiny, but the closer he got to it, the brighter it became.

An exit, Braim thought in relief. *Thank the gods. Well, all of the gods except for Diog and the Ghostly God, anyway.*

Now of course Braim didn't know what lay beyond that light. It could have been even worse than the monster, but Braim decided he would cross that bridge when he got there. For now, he just had to keep running.

But time seemed to slow around Braim, making his every step feel like he was running underwater. The growling and slapping of the monster behind him also sounded slower, but rather than reassuring him, it only increased Braim's terror. He forced himself to run even faster, but with time slowing, it didn't matter how much effort he put into increasing his speed, because he was just going as slowly as before.

Then Braim suddenly emerged from the tunnel and his speed returned to normal. But he wasn't prepared for the sudden return to his normal speed and he tripped and fell flat on his face onto soft green grass.

Braim ordinarily would have just lay there and take it easy, but he remembered that that monster was still chasing him, so he pushed himself off the grass and looked over his shoulder. To his surprise, however, he saw that the cave mouth had completely vanished, like the cave hadn't been there at all. And, of course, there was no sign of the monster itself, a thought which should have filled him with relief but which only made him that much more terrified.

Where is it? Braim thought, scrambling to his feet and looking around warily. *It's got to be around here somewhere, probably lying in wait and ready to kill me when I least expect it.*

Yet Braim didn't see the monster anywhere. In fact, Braim couldn't think of an environment more inappropriate for a monster such as that than the one he currently found himself in.

Braim stood at the top of a small, grassy hill. At the foot of the hill was what looked like a miniature village, with cute little cottages with red roofs lined in neat rows. Braim didn't see any people to go along with the village, but he didn't dare go down to investigate, because he was pretty sure that the village was nowhere near as peaceful or as cute as it looked. The only thing he liked about it was the scent of fresh bread wafting up through the air toward his nose, as if someone was baking, although he didn't see where that wonderful smell was coming from.

Braim looked up at the sky, which was blue and without clouds, and shouted, "Hey, Ghostly God! What the hell was that all about?"

There was no answer. Braim should have expected that, but all that did was confirm his fear that there was something wrong with that village and that he didn't dare go down it if he didn't want to get involved with whatever it was.

On the other hand, Braim didn't see anywhere else to go. Aside from that tiny little village, he saw no other settlements anywhere. No roads or paths, either. Not even a tiny little dirt road leading to nowhere. Just green grass and blue sky for as far as the eye could see.

Still not going down there, Braim thought, taking a step back.

I'll take my chances with the endless green grass than with whatever horrifying thing is down there in that village.

But then Braim felt movement under his feet, causing him to look down, expecting to see some kind of monster lying underneath his shoes.

Instead, Braim saw that the hill itself was moving. He found it hard to retain his balance, despite his best efforts, and as a result tripped and went tumbling down the hill. He came to a stop right in front of the village's gate, which was small enough him for him to fit his fist through if he cared to try.

Braim sat up and looked over his shoulder at the hill. It had returned to its original stillness, but he was sure that it would start moving again if he tried to climb back up it. Not that he felt inclined to do so, because Braim preferred to walk on ground that was actually solid and wouldn't move at the drop of a hat.

Guess I'll just have to go through this damn village, Braim thought as he stood up and dusted off his pants. *Wonder if the houses are going to come to life and try to kill me.*

Going through the village looked like it would be difficult because all of the houses were bunched together and the streets were very narrow. At least there weren't any people or animals for Braim to step on, though he had a feeling that the tiny village had much worse than tiny people or animals hiding within it. That smell of freshly-baked bread, however, was stronger than ever, which meant that there had to be at least one person in here. After all, bread didn't bake itself.

Preparing himself for the worst, Braim took one step over the tiny village gate and rested his foot between what looked like a fruit stand and someone's house. He didn't take another step in because he was fully expecting something really bad to happen, like maybe miniature villagers would stream out of their houses and start attacking his foot with tiny swords and knives.

But the tiny village was as quiet and still as always. The scent of freshly-baked bread was also still present.

So Braim, without letting down his guard, took another step in, placing his other foot between a windmill and a generic-looking temple. This time, he figured that the buildings themselves would have to attack him. It was the worst thing he could think of. After all, he was now firmly within the village's boundaries, which would make it harder for him to fight back if he was attacked.

Yet the village did not do a thing against him. It almost made Braim think he was paranoid. Maybe there was nothing truly terrifying about the village after all. The Ghostly God might have decided to give Braim a break from the terror. That would explain the delicious bread he smelled. Perhaps the Ghostly God knew that Braim loved that smell and so had somehow provided it to make Braim feel better.

Braim snorted. *Yeah, right. Because the Ghostly God cares so much about my personal well-being. That's why he kidnapped me and is forcing me to go through his personal torture chamber for bad reasons.*

Braim took another step forward, resting his foot between the village's tiny clock tower and a large mansion that might have been where the village's mayor stayed, if it had one. With no response from that, Braim took another step forward, and another, until he soon reached the other side of the town without any difficulty.

As soon as Braim stepped out of the village, he allowed himself to breathe. He hadn't realized it, but during his whole trip through the tiny village, he had been holding his breath. He let it out because he felt safer now, even though there was nothing dangerous about the village.

False alarm, I guess, Braim thought, wiping the sweat off his brow. *The Ghostly God must have done it that just to scare me. Still don't see how it is going to help him understand how I came back to life, though.*

Shaking his head, Braim decided to keep walking forward, but before he did, that scent of freshly-baked bread filled his nostrils again. He looked over his shoulder at the tiny village and started when he saw movement.

Streaming from the village were some of the tiniest villagers Braim had ever seen. They looked like they had been carved out of wood, like toys for young children, but their resemblance to actual people was uncanny. It was like a master carpenter had designed them, but the result was so terrifying that Braim wished that an amateur had designed them instead.

Even stranger was how they all looked alike. They did not wear actual clothes. Instead, their clothes were painted on their bodies, and they all wore the same outfit. The outfit consisted of green pants and a black shirt, with no variation in design at all between them from what Braim could tell. It was like they had been mass-produced in some of the factories that Braim had heard about that existed on islands like Carnag and Shika.

Each one of the tiny villagers carried in their arms loaves of bread that were even tinier than they were. The scent of freshly-baked bread that Braim had smelled the entire time he had been in

71

the village came from those loaves, which he would normally find pleasing under ordinary circumstances, but which he now found absolutely terrifying, even though none of the villagers behaved very threateningly.

Yet it was perhaps the villagers' eyes that most stood out to him. Like their clothes, their eyes were clearly painted on, though unlike their clothes, there was some small variation between them, though Braim only saw brown or black eyes. Regardless, the eyes could move. Braim could see them looking at him as they walked, but it was impossible to tell what they were thinking or if they were thinking anything at all.

Stepping backwards, Braim reached for his wand before remembering that he did not have it, and that even if he did, he couldn't use it against them because he didn't have his magical abilities anymore.

Calm down, Braim, Braim told himself. *These wooden dolls, or whatever they are, are just as unarmed as you. They're creepy, yes, but nothing that you can't handle even without magic.*

Then the villagers stopped several feet away from him. Braim froze, mostly because he wasn't sure what would happen next. He prepared himself, however, for whatever they were going to do, because he had the strongest feeling that these villagers were not planning to do anything kind to him.

Several seconds passed as Braim and the villagers stared at each other. Braim didn't want to make the first move because he was certain that the villagers would be able to counter it, but it seemed like the villagers might be thinking the same thing about him, because they made even less movement than he did.

Are they waiting for something? Braim thought. *Maybe*

they're waiting for the Ghostly God to tell them what to do. I wonder if the Ghostly God told them to throw freshly-baked bread at me. If so, that would be weird.

Braim chanced a look over his shoulder. He saw nothing for miles ahead, save for rolling hills and tall grass. Then he looked back at the villagers, but they had not moved an inch from where they stood.

The silence was starting to wear on Braim, who finally said, "All right. What's so dangerous about the bread?"

The villagers didn't respond. As a matter of fact, they were so still that Braim now suspected that they had returned to their usual stillness (or at least, what Braim *hoped* was their usual stillness, though he couldn't be sure that these tiny villagers were not always alive).

"Can't talk?" said Braim. "Or just don't want to?"

Their silence was as continuous as a flowing river. At this point, Braim was tempted to start walking all over them and kick them around and stomp on them, but he suspected that the villagers were far more dangerous than they appeared, so he decided against doing that.

But Braim didn't want to continue this pointless stand-off, either, so he said, "Well, I don't want any of your baked goods, if that's what you're trying to give me. I'm just going to walk away now and be on my way."

Still no response, so Braim took one step backwards—just one —when the villagers suddenly began singing.

'Singing' was perhaps not the right word for it. It sounded more like the clacking of little wooden blocks against each other. They weren't even 'singing' on key or any song that Braim recognized (which, admittedly, wasn't very much, seeing as he had forgotten most of the songs that he used to remember in his first life). There seemed to be a rhythm to it, but it was impossible to follow.

Braim turned around to run, but stopped when he saw another group of tiny wooden toy villagers standing behind him. They were not only physically identical to the first group of villagers, but sang in exactly the same way.

The tune—if it could be called that—went *click, clack, click, clack, clack-clack-clack, click* over and over. Braim looked to the left and to the right for an escape route, but he noticed that he was surrounded on all sides now by even more of those tiny wooden villagers.

And every last one of them was singing that same awful, ear-gratingly bad song. Braim covered his ears with his hands, but even that did little to block out the singing of the strange villagers.

"Stop … singing …" said Braim through gritted teeth. "Cut it out …"

But none of the villagers even slowed their tune. In fact, Braim was starting to think that they couldn't hear him at all. That made sense. After all, they didn't seem to have ears on their heads, and if they did, they probably couldn't hear anything (which might have explained why they were so awful at singing).

Braim, however, suspected that this song was being sung exactly as it was supposed to. He could feel its awful, boring, repetitive tune slamming against his eardrums, making it impossible to think clearly.

If these stupid villagers won't stop singing on their own, then

I'll make *them stop singing,* Braim thought.

Still covering his ears, Braim ran toward the singing villagers, who didn't seem at all alarmed at his running toward them. Either they were too stupid to see what he was about to do or they were so confident in their own self-defense abilities that they didn't see the need to be worried. In any case, it was very satisfying for Braim to kick the first line of villagers away, sending them hurtling through the air, though those ones continued to sing even as they landed on their fellow villagers.

Though the villagers were numerous, Braim found them easy enough to kick apart. One solid kick caused one of the villagers to blow apart into pieces, while another sent three of them flying. Their freshly-baked loaves of bread also flew upon being hit, landing on the dirt or hitting other villagers in the head, which disappointed Braim somewhat due to how delicious the bread smelled, but he ignored it because he valued his own survival more than well-made baked goods.

As for the singing, most of them still sang even as Braim kicked his way through them. Part of Braim had to admire the creepy little things for their tenacity in the face of adversity, but another part of him thought that they were utterly stupid for not ceasing their singing long enough to save themselves.

They aren't even trying to move out of the way, Braim thought as he kicked and ran, knocking down at least a dozen villagers with every kick. *Guess they must not have any sort of actual survival instinct or something.*

That was when Braim felt a sharp, stinging bite on his left ankle. He stopped running long enough to look down and see that one of the tiny villagers was biting his ankle. Its facial expression hadn't change at all, but now there was some of his blood covering its mouth and it was gnawing at him with surprising ferocity.

Braim shook his leg hard enough to send the tiny wooden villager flying. The villager's teeth hadn't sank into his ankle very deeply, so it flew off without trouble, but Braim would have bet all of the wealth in the Northern Isles that he saw a blood-soaked smirk on the face of the tiny villager when it launched off his leg.

Then he felt another stabbing sensation, this time in his right ankle, and saw that it was another one of those villagers biting him. This time, he didn't even hesitate to kick it off so hard that its head split from its body.

Braim grimaced at the pain in his ankles, but he didn't have time to focus on them because he now noticed that all of the villagers were baring their sharp teeth at him. Not only that, but many of them were still singing that same awful song from before, which continued to beat at Braim's ears—and perhaps his very sanity—despite his best efforts to ignore it.

Now Braim still had the advantage of strength and height over the villagers, but the pain in his ankles told him that it made much more sense to run than to risk letting these little monsters kill him.

So Braim ran forward in a burst of speed, knocking over or kicking aside any villagers unfortunate enough to be in his way. He felt the villagers biting at his ankles, but so far none of them had any success, which Braim intended to keep that way for as long as he could.

'As long as he could,' unfortunately, only turned out to be about a few seconds, because not long after Braim started running, he felt more sharp wooden teeth bite into his ankles. The sudden, unexpected pain sent him falling to the ground face first, the villagers in front of him scattering to avoid being crushed by his fall.

The sudden fall onto the ground stunned Braim long enough for the villagers to immediately pounce on him with their tiny yet sharp teeth. He felt them tearing apart his clothing and skin, even biting directly into his bone, ripping through muscle and flesh as though it were paper. He punched and kicked and rolled, but it was all useless, especially when the villagers began gnawing off his fingers. Blood soaked through his clothes and made him feel hot and sticky.

The last thing Braim saw, before he completely passed out from the blood loss, was one of the villagers ambling up to his face, smirking at him, and then lunging for his eyes.

Chapter Eight

WATCHING CARMAZ WIN had been the most exciting thing to happen to Raya today. She had sat practically on the edge of her seat during the entire duel, becoming so absorbed in the fight that she didn't even notice when she almost fell off her seat onto the floor. She had gasped in horror and sighed in relief whenever any exciting turn of event happened, either gasping whenever the tide of battle seemed to turn against Carmaz or sighing whenever Carmaz got the upper hand.

In fact, Raya had wanted to go down and congratulate Carmaz on his victory after Alira had declared him the winner. Unfortunately for her, Alira had said that the godlings were not supposed to go down to the Stadium lobby until the rest of the sub-bracket challenge was officially over. It seemed like a terribly unfair rule to Raya, but at this point she had come to expect that from Alira, who claimed to follow the Rulebook strictly yet always seemed to be able to 'find' a brand new rule that probably wasn't actually in there whenever it was most convenient for her.

Raya, then, found the rest of the duels rather boring. Samvan ended up winning his duel, even though his weapon, a club that looked very capable of bashing in someone's skull, broke. His opponent was a far less graceful loser than Eria. He stomped on his weapon and then stormed off while leaving behind a trail of curse words that Raya had never even known existed. Nor was she certain that she even wanted to know that they did.

But one thing Raya could say about the duels was that, after Samvan's victory (which made him the third victor in the Human God Bracket), the other duels ended in a timely manner. Alira called out each winner as they occurred, which was followed by their respective vision bubbles popping, until soon all of the bubbles were gone, revealing a blank stone wall in front of which they had been floating.

That was when Alira gave the godlings permission to leave. So Raya, of course, was the first one out and the first one down into the lobby, where she saw all ten of the sub-bracket winners. She immediately spotted Carmaz, who looked as hot and sweaty as he had on the vision bubble, standing next to Samvan, who was talking with him about something that Raya couldn't hear and didn't care about.

Raya dashed over to Carmaz, but she stopped a couple of feet from him, rather than try to hug him as she did before. While Raya would have liked to do that, she knew how fast Carmaz could dodge her hugs, so she decided to play it a little safer at the moment.

"Congratulations, Carmaz," said Raya, spreading her arms wide. "You did an amazing job back there on the field. You were absolutely fantastic."

Carmaz looked embarrassed for some reason, while Samvan said, "Did he? I didn't get to see his duel with Eria."

"He did," said Raya, nodding. She clasped her hands together and sighed. "It was the most amazing duel I have ever seen in my life. I didn't know that Carmaz was so good with a sword."

Carmaz just shrugged. "I didn't do anything special. It was mostly dumb luck on my part."

"Nonsense," said Raya. "You won using your own abilities as a sword fighter. I will not allow you to deny it."

Carmaz looked away from her to the ten losers, who were apparently being escorted out of the Stadium by the Soldiers of the Gods. "Where are they being taken to?"

"Alira said they're going to be sent back to their home islands," Samvan said. He looked around anxiously for a moment. "Where is Alira, by the way?"

"Still up in the box, last I saw," said Raya. "Why?"

"Because, uh, I want to know the time of the next sub-bracket challenge, obviously," said Samvan in an unconvincing voice. "I heard there's supposed to be another one today."

"Really?" said Carmaz, looking at Samvan in surprise. "Two sub-bracket challenges in one day? I thought they were spread out a week apart."

"That was the original plan," said Samvan, scratching his chin. "But rumor has it that the Void's attack on the Stadium last week caused the gods to urge Alira to pick up the pace. They want to fill in the remaining holes in the Pantheons and they want to do it right away."

"I see," said Carmaz. "The gods think that the completed Pantheons will help them fight against the Void if it should attack again, right?"

"That's what the rumors say," said Samvan. "Of course, they could be wrong, but that's what I've heard and I think it's true. The gods are just really scared right now."

"No doubt about that," said Carmaz. His voice became harder. "The Void is merciless and will keep coming at us until it succeeds in killing every last one of us. I hate to say this, but I think only the gods can fight it."

Raya shivered involuntarily when they mentioned the Void. Their mention of the Void had caused Raya to remember how she had felt when the Void had touched her, memories that she immediately blocked so she could focus on the situation at hand and not allow depression to affect her.

"I sure hope so," said Samvan, rubbing his hands together anxiously. "I just hope that this sped up schedule isn't causing Alira any undue stress. I mean, she's the Judge of the Tournament and all, so she needs to have as clear a mind as possible in order to make correct judgment calls, you know?"

Raya had no trouble telling that Samvan had certain other motives for his worry over Alira's health. She knew his kind, the kind of guy who wouldn't give up on a girl he liked even if there was no realistic way that they could ever end up together. Those men—a few of whom Raya had known in her life, even before she grew into a woman—were always disgusting in her eyes, though Samvan didn't seem nearly as lecherous as some of the men she had known.

Still, Alira's completely out of his league, Raya thought. *I wonder if I should tell him that or if I should let Alira have the honors. I will let him figure it out on his own. Right now, I have far more important things to worry about, such as congratulating Carmaz.*

So Raya said to Carmaz, "But really, Carmaz, who cares when the next sub-bracket challenge is going to be or how quickly the

Tournament is moving along? What matters is that you won and are now on your way to becoming the new God of Humans. Isn't that exciting?"

"Yeah, I guess," said Carmaz. "I'm really looking forward to using that power to help my people. Alone."

The amount of emphasis that Carmaz put on that last word did not go unnoticed by Raya. She folded her arms and said, "But what if, say, one of the other gods wants to help?"

"They won't need to," said Carmaz. He jerked a thumb at his chest. "Especially if the gods in question happen to be quite new themselves."

Raya huffed and, without another word, turned and stormed out of the Stadium lobby through the front doors. She heard Samvan calling for her to come back, but Raya didn't listen. She just stomped out onto the streets and began making her way to her apartment. She had the path from the Stadium to her apartment memorized, so she simply allowed her feet to carry her there so she could devote her conscious though to how stupid Carmaz was.

Raya didn't understand why Carmaz kept rejecting her advances or why he seemed so against the idea of them being together. It brought to mind something Mother had once told her, about how you should always avoid falling in love with someone outside of your class because they would never love you back (of course, when Raya thought about how Mother had been a lowly katabans servant before marrying Father, who had been the prince of a powerful nation in his youth, she wasn't sure if that was the most accurate marriage advice in the world).

I'll just go straight to my apartment, grab one of my dresses, and then go back to Anwan's Tailoring and trade it in for that nice red dress, Raya thought. *Shopping for nice things always manages to take my mind off stupid men like Carmaz. Besides, Carmaz just got out of that no doubt stressful challenge. Perhaps if I give him time to cool off, he'll be more accepting of my advances and encouragement.*

Of course, Carmaz always rejected her advances even when he was well-rested, but Raya preferred to think that he was just tired and needed some rest and maybe a good meal. Carmaz was, after all, a reasonable man, and there was no way that any reasonable man could keep rejecting her, at least not for very long.

Thus, with a smile on her face that she had not thought she'd ever wear again, Raya continued on the path back to her apartment, already imagining how fabulous she would look in her new red dress once she got it.

Half an hour later, Raya was walking down the street again, this time with one of her dresses in her arms. It was a simple white dress, the simplest and plainest dress she owned, though its trim was embedded with tiny golden stones that glittered in the light of the afternoon sun. Raya had picked this dress to trade away because she really didn't like it as much as the red dress. This one had always been her least favorite, so she didn't think she was losing much by trading it away. Besides, she suspected that Anwan didn't know much about mortal clothing styles, so he would probably be happy to have even the plainest of mortal clothing in exchange for his red dress.

The streets of World's End were more active now than they

were earlier in the morning. This slowed Raya's progress somewhat, as she had to walk past the katabans people that walked along the streets. Most of the katabans looked at her with curiosity as she passed, though Raya did her best to ignore them. All she wanted to do was go into the shop, get her dress, and get out.

The problem was that Raya just didn't feel comfortable around most other katabans, despite being half katabans herself. It was probably because Raya had been raised almost exclusively among humans, but that didn't still didn't change her feelings about them. She knew that most of the katabans on World's End didn't hate her or bear any ill will toward her at all, but she still liked to keep eye contact with strange katabans to a minimum whenever she walked the streets of World's End.

In fact, Raya didn't even let herself relax until she saw the sign for Anwan's Tailoring (which, while written in Godly Divina, was recognizable thanks to its distinctive logo of a needle going through a spool). And she didn't let herself breathe until she pushed open the door and stepped inside, where she let out a sigh of relief.

Safe, Raya thought.

Then Raya looked up and shouted, "Mr. Anwan! It's me, Princess Raya. I have the dress I want to trade in."

Raya stood there and waited for Anwan's response, but all she received was silence from within. She stood on her tiptoes to see over the tops of the clothing, but she didn't see Anwan anywhere at all in the tiny shop. She glanced at the window displays. Her red dress was still there, for which she was grateful, because she had worried that Anwan might have sold it off to someone else while she was away.

But I can't get my dress until Anwan comes out and agrees to make the trade, Raya thought, glancing at the dress in her arms with a scowl. *I hope I don't have to wait long. I'd rather not go another hour without that dress in my arms.*

So Raya walked deeper into the shop, looking this way and that for any sign of Mr. Anwan. She saw no sign of his appearance anywhere. It was as though he had mysteriously vanished off the face of the earth. That would be a problem if true, because then Raya would not be able to get her dress at all.

He has the most awful customer service, Raya thought, pushing aside some coats to see if Anwan was hidden behind them, though she only saw more clothes. *I walk in—twice in the same day—and he isn't here* both *times? He must not expect to receive a lot of customers, otherwise he would have been here waiting for me even if I hadn't agreed to come and trade with him.*

When Raya reached the counter, she looked for the bell to ring to summon Anwan, but unfortunately it seemed to have mysteriously vanished because it was nowhere in sight. That annoyed her greatly, to the point where she was considering just turning and walking out of the shop right there and then and never coming back until the Tournament was over, if even then.

I am the Princess of Carnag, Raya thought with a scowl. *I could understand this blatant unprofessional behavior if I were a simple peasant girl, but I am royalty and expect to be treated as such.*

Raya looked to the door behind the counter, the one that she assumed led into the back office. There was a good chance that

Anwan was in there, perhaps figuring out what taxes he owed to the city or something like that (though Raya didn't know if World's End even had taxes), but Raya wasn't sure she wanted to knock on the door and see if he was in there. It seemed like too much effort to her, especially because she shouldn't have had to do that at all to get his attention.

Then Raya looked over her shoulder to the display windows at the other end of the shop. That beautiful red dress—which reflected the sun light from outside wonderfully—was completely unguarded, she noticed. What was to stop her from trying to take the dress and leave before Anwan arrived?

No, I couldn't get away with that, Raya thought, shaking her head. *Anwan might not catch me, but there are more people out in the streets now and they might see me taking the dress without Anwan's permission. I could, of course, just lie and tell them that Anwan gave it to me for free, but that could only work for so long before Anwan notices and then tells everyone that I took it from him without proper payment or compensation.*

Raya normally had great confidence in her ability to get away with this sort of thing without anyone noticing, but the more she weighed the pros and cons of taking the dress, the more she realized that, at least in this case, taking that dress would be a stupid move.

With a deep sigh, Raya walked around the counter to the back of the shop, toward the old wooden door that she assumed was the entrance to the shop's office. She did not hear anything on the other side of the door, but perhaps that meant that Anwan was taking a nap. But even if he was just resting, that only succeeded in making Raya respect him even less than she already did.

Seriously, how has this katabans stayed in business for as long as he has with such awful customer service? Raya thought as she brushed aside a large, flowing green and purple dress that reminded her too much of poisoned fruit. *Does he treat every customer this way or am I the exception?*

When Raya reached the office door, she raised one of her hands and knocked on it quite loudly, saying as she did so, "Mr. Anwan, are you there? Hello?"

But there was no response at all. Raya placed her ear against the surface of the door, hoping to hear Anwan snoring, but all she heard on the other side was complete silence.

Pulling away from the door, Raya scowled again. *Did he go out to lunch or something? I bet he's actually in there. He didn't seem to like Mother much, so he's probably trying to avoid doing business with me because I'm her daughter. Well, I'm not going to leave this shop until I get the dress I want.*

So Raya grabbed the doorknob and turned. She expected it to be locked, but much to her surprise, the doorknob turned without a hitch. It didn't even make any noise, which she found slightly creepy before she realized that it was probably well-oiled.

Raya pushed the door open and poked her head inside the office. A light stone embedded in the ceiling showed her a tiny room—almost like a closet—with files of paper and a tiny desk with a chair behind it. The air was stale and hot, mostly due to the lack of windows in the room, and there was hardly any room for movement. Papers—probably boring things like bills and receipts —were scattered over the desk, along with a jar that had several different writing utensils sticking out of it. On top of the papers were some thread and yarn, but it looked less like the beginnings of a new dress or shirt and more like something Anwan might have fiddled with in his spare time or when he was stressed out about something (such as losing potential customers such as herself).

Aside from that, however, Anwan was nowhere to be seen, even when Raya stuck her head in a little further and looked more closely at the room's interior. Not that that meant much. The room was too small for anyone as tall as Anwan to hide in.

So he really must *be out to lunch, then,* Raya thought. *Or maybe he had to make a delivery to another one of his customers. Or maybe—most likely—this is just his way of saying, 'I want nothing to do with you. Go away.'*

Those thoughts would have been enough by themselves to make Raya close the door, stomp out of the shop, and never even think about returning to this place, had Raya not noticed something odd on the desk.

Peeking out from underneath a stack of what Raya presumed were bills (though she couldn't read the language they were written in, so she couldn't tell) was the handle of what appeared to be a knife. It stood out to Raya because of its unique handle, which looked almost bone-like under the light, yet was very clearly metallic.

Raya had only ever seen knives with that kind of attention to detail back among the nobles of Carnag and especially Shika. Back home, learning how to use a knife for self-defense was a popular pastime among Carnagian and Shikan nobles. Raya herself knew a thing or two about using knives in self-defense, though she wasn't as good at it as others and she didn't care to spend much time learning about it. In addition to using knives for self-defense, many nobles saw knives as a status symbol, which was why it was not uncommon to hear about a noble paying hundreds, if not thousands, of coins for a custom knife made out of the very finest materials available to mortals, such as gold and silver.

So how could Anwan possibly own a knife as nice-looking as that? Raya thought. *His business may be successful, but I sincerely doubt that he's making enough money to afford significant luxuries like this.*

Raya looked over her shoulder, just in case Anwan had somehow sneaked up on her without her knowing. The katabans tailor was nowhere to be seen, so Raya decided that it was safe to step inside and check out that knife. Just for a moment and then she would put it back where it belonged. Or perhaps, if it was nice enough, she'd take it and pretend not to know what anyone was talking about when the taking was discovered and someone asked her if she knew anything about it.

Stepping into the tiny, cramped office, Raya grabbed the knife's handle and pulled it out from under the papers covering it, sending a handful of papers falling to the floor. She raised the knife up to her face and looked it more closely than before.

The knife was less of a knife and more like a very short sword. The edges were jagged but clean, which either meant that it rarely saw use or Anwan was good about cleaning it regularly. It was much heavier than it looked, though Raya managed to hold it with one hand, and its handle felt wrong in her grasp, though she assumed that that was because it had obviously not been designed for her hands.

But the handle's metallic texture reminded Raya of something that she had seen once while visiting Castle Shika a few years ago. Prince Sanar, the Prince of Shika, had once shown Raya the Shikan Royal Family's collection of Void metal chains. Void metal was a type of metal said to be from the Void itself, but that wasn't what made Void metal so unusual. What made it unusual was that it was completely unlike any other type of metal in Martir and was so strong that not even the gods could break it.

At the time, Raya hadn't cared much about it because she found that sort of thing boring. The only reason Raya even recalled it now was because she had had a huge crush on Prince Sanar at the time (a crush which had since vanished when she learned that Sanar's interests leaned in the other direction) and hung on his every word as he explained what Void metal was.

The question, then, was why Anwan owned a knife made of that very rare, hard-to-find substance. Granted, World's End was right next to the Void, so perhaps this knife somehow escaped the Void and washed up on one of the beaches of World's End. Yet for some reason that struck her as unlikely, probably because Void metal was too heavy to float.

Now that I think about it, did Prince Sanar tell me how anyone actually got Void metal in the first place? Raya thought. *Did the gods take it from the Void or what?*

Whatever the case may be, Raya felt ill just by holding the knife. It was probably just her imagination, but she was starting to feel exactly how she had felt last week when the Void had caught her. Yet now that she found this knife, she wondered what other interesting treasures that Anwan might be hiding in his office.

"Princess Raya?" said a familiar voice behind her that made her jump and almost drop the Void metal knife. "What are you doing in my office?"

Raya turned around to see Anwan standing in the doorway of the office. He wore the same orange and gray suit from before, though the expression in his eyes was nowhere near as friendly. He was looking at her with suspicion.

"Oh, uh, hello, Mr. Anwan," said Raya, putting on her cutest, most winning smile. "I was just—"

"Looking for me?" Anwan finished for her.

"Yes," said Raya, nodding. She looked at the knife and said, "I am so sorry for touching your things like this. I was just so curious. Let me put it down."

"No," said Anwan, shaking his head. He held out his hand. "Give it to me and I'll put it up where it belongs. That thing shouldn't be left out where anyone can find it anyway."

Raya didn't trust Anwan with the knife, but she handed it back to him handle first anyway. Anwan took the knife, which he then sheathed into the knife sheath attached to his belt that Raya had not noticed before. Raya wondered if Anwan always carried the knife and she just hadn't noticed it the first time she met him or if this was a new development.

Anwan stepped aside to allow Raya to leave his office, which she did without complaint, because the lack of proper ventilation made it a very uncomfortable place to be. When Anwan closed the door behind her, he turned to face Raya, though his eyes were far less hostile than they were mere seconds ago.

"I must apologize for my entering your office like that without your permission," said Raya, folding her hands behind her back in a way that she knew would make her appear very innocent and sweet to most people. "I was just so eager to trade for that fabulous red dress that I was very impatient. It's a big vice of mine that Mother is always castigating me for."

Anwan smiled, though Raya didn't like his smile one bit. "I completely understand, Raya. When I was your age, I was always so eager to do business with others that I sometimes forgot my manners. It has been ages since I last made a mistake like that, but I still remember it very well. I take no offense to your actions, especially since you have not actually harmed any of my products or property."

Raya almost let out a sigh of relief, but she hid it because she didn't want Anwan to think that she felt any guilt. She was already under the impression that he was watching her carefully, much more carefully than she liked, which meant that she would have to be just as careful herself in order to avoid arousing his suspicions unnecessarily.

"Well, I am glad that we have that little misunderstanding out of the way, then," said Raya. She glanced over her shoulder at the front of the store, where the red dress still stood in the display window. "Before we move onto business, would you mind telling me where you were? Were you out to lunch or something?"

Raya looked back at Anwan. The tailor stroked his chin for a moment before saying, "I was in the back checking on some tailoring supplies. I just got so caught up in my work that I didn't realize there was anyone in my shop until I remembered that you were supposed to be returning to trade for the red dress."

"Ah," said Raya. She held up her white dress. "Well, here is the dress that I would like to trade for the red one. How does this look?"

Anwan carefully took the white dress out of Raya's hands and looked down at it. Then he held it by the shoulders, allowing the full dress to fall before him and giving him a complete view of the entire thing, which he turned around once.

"It looks very nice," said Anwan, without looking at Raya. "Very nice. A little different from katabans clothing, but I am sure I can figure out how to reproduce it with just a few nights of study." Then he looked up at Raya. "Exactly how old did you say this dress was?"

"Three years old," said Raya, holding up three fingers. "And I've kept it in perfect condition all that time."

"It's condition is indeed near pristine," said Anwan, nodding. "Very beautiful for a human dress. But I can actually see some katabans sewing techniques in here. Why is that?"

Raya frowned. She was not much of an expert on sewing, so to her, her dress just looked like a dress, but she said, "Well, I do remember Mother overseeing the creation of that particular dress. Perhaps she instructed the tailors how to sew the dress with katabans sewing techniques?"

It was amazing how fast Anwan's expression changed. One moment, he had the look of a curious artist studying a new style in the hopes of improving his own; the next, he was shoving the dress back into Raya's unwilling arms.

"Hey!" Raya protested. She tried to push the white dress back to him, but Anwan wouldn't take it. "I thought you wanted this dress?"

"Sorry, but I just realized that I don't want it," said Anwan, shaking his head. His tone was polite but strained. "And as a business owner, I have every right to turn down whatever deal I want without having to state my reasons for it."

"But what about the red dress?" asked Raya, glancing over her shoulder at the dress in the window at the front of the shop. "Can I still have it?"

"Have it? Gods no," said Anwan, shaking his head. "And don't even *think* about bringing another one of your dresses here, either. I don't want to do business with you ever again. I will simply sell the dress to a katabans woman who can appreciate its beauty and value better than any human woman could."

"Human woman?" Raya repeated. "But I'm part katabans. Doesn't that mean anything to you?"

"Please leave," said Anwan, pointing to the storefront. "Now. Before I call the Soldiers of the Gods and ask them to take you away."

"But I—"

"Now!" Anwan roared.

Raya—still not entirely sure what had just happened here—turned and ran around the counter to the front door. She dashed out into the street, and as soon as she did, she heard the door slam shut behind her. Looking over her shoulder, Raya saw Anwan's angry face in the door window before he turned and stomped away back deeper into his shop.

What the hell was that all about? Raya thought, her heart beating quickly from the sudden excitement. *What did I say? Oh well. At least I can still look at the red dress in the window.*

Then Anwan appeared in the window, took down both the dress and the mannequin it was displayed on, and then vanished back into the shop itself.

What a jerk, Raya thought. She looked down at her old white dress, which was now a lot more wrinkly due to Anwan's

94

mistreatment of it. Now *what am I supposed to do with this dress?*

Raya decided to head back to her apartment. Or possibly go to the Stadium instead. It was possible that the next sub-bracket challenge was about to begin, though she believed that she would have been summoned back to the Stadium already if that was the case.

I don't want to do either, though, Raya thought. *I want that dress. And I want it before the next sub-bracket challenge.*

Unfortunately, Raya did not see any way that she could get that dress now. For reasons known only to the gods, Anwan had completely changed his opinion about her. He now saw her as a threat, as something to be kept out of his business at all costs. It was not a feeling Raya was used to, mostly because she had been so accepted and loved by everyone as a child.

This is unacceptable, Raya thought with a scowl, stepping back to allow a couple of chatting katabans to walk by her without walking into her accidentally. *I am the Princess of Carnag. No businessman, even one as experienced and old as he, has any right to deny me what I want. He must accept my deal or else.*

Of course, Raya currently had no way to enforce the 'or else' part of her threat. Although she was indeed royalty, here on World's End, most of the katabans did not treat her any differently from the other godlings and the gods had never even spoke to her. That was almost enough to make Raya decide to forget about the dress and just go back to her apartment and maybe take a nap before the next sub-bracket challenge started, if there was time for one.

Raya turned to head back up the street and do just that when an idea occurred to her. She looked at Anwan's Tailoring again, but now the shop looked a lot darker and more foreboding than it had before.

Then she looked around the street she was standing in. There weren't as many katabans around here as there had been moments ago. She spotted a single male katabans who was cleaning the streets with a broom, but the area was rather empty aside from him.

Why can't I just ... take the dress? Raya thought. *Just break into the shop, take the dress, and leave. And I can do it before Anwan even realizes that I'm there. Just got to make sure to avoid leaving any clues or hints, hide the dress in my apartment, and keep it there until I have to go back to Carnag or win the Tournament.*

The small part of Raya that had always disliked her tendency to take things without asking for them (what some might call a 'conscience,' although she thought of it an as annoyance) told her that it was too dangerous to attempt to take it now. Anwan was still in his shop, after all, and there was no telling what kind of trouble she'd get into if she was caught.

But I've never been caught before, Raya thought. *Never. Not even once. Why should this be any different? Besides, I like to think of it as properly punishing a peasant who does not understand how to deal with true royalty like myself. Perhaps if I take the dress, he'll think twice before rejecting the offers of other human women like myself in the future.*

The only problem was coming up with a plan to take the dress, and to take it in good time, too, because the next sub-bracket challenge was probably going to come up sometime soon and she didn't want to be summoned back to the Stadium while in the middle of taking the dress.

Luckily for her, however, all of her old taking instincts were coming alive and she could already see the beginnings of a great plan percolating in the back of her mind.

Even before she finished her plan, Raya was already walking over to the katabans street cleaner, who she knew would play an important part in her plan, a sweet grin on her face as she imagined just how wonderfully her plan would go off. She was certain that it would not fail.

Chapter Nine

CARMAZ WAS USED to pain. Back on Ruwa, pain was an essential fact of every day life. The pain of hunger, the pain of thirst, the pain of untreated disease, the pain of broken bones ... the more Carmaz thought about it, the more surprised he was at how he had managed to survive all that pain well into adulthood. Most children on Ruwa did not live very long, and even those who entered adulthood often did so with some sort of severe disability or disease that sometimes rendered them crippled for life.

Maybe it was my destiny as a godling that kept me from suffering the fate that claimed so many of my peers, Carmaz thought. He grimaced. *Or maybe I just got lucky.*

But despite all of that pain, Carmaz was certain of one thing: None of it compared to the pain from the blows that Eria had landed on him during their duel.

True, when the duel ended, Carmaz had told Eria what a great opponent she was and how he had appreciated their duel. Which was perfectly true, because he had truly found Eria to be a challenge and now had a new respect for her that he hadn't had before.

But Carmaz tried to pretend that his injuries were not as severe as they actually were. He had put on a brave face after winning the duel, especially in the lobby where he had had to deal with more of Raya's not-so-subtle flirting, but unlike the other sub-bracket challenge winners, had not stayed to received congratulations from the others. He had managed to sneak out of the lobby when no one was looking and return to his apartment, where he collapsed on the sofa and tried to drift to sleep in order to forget about his pain.

Not that that did him much good. While lying down did mitigate the pain somewhat, it was still there and it still hurt. Carmaz probably should have gone to a katabans doctor or healer to get his pain dealt with, but he didn't know how informed that the doctors and healers on this island were about human health. Besides, he didn't feel anything broken in his body, so he figured all he needed was some rest and then he would be fine.

If only I could *rest,* Carmaz thought.

The pain was what kept him awake. He tried to change his position on the sofa, but it didn't matter because he still felt the pain no matter what position he lay in. He sat up, feeling the pain in his stomach and at his side where Eria had hit him hard.

It will probably just be temporary, Carmaz thought, wincing as he felt his bruised stomach. *Hopefully.*

But despite the awful pain he had experienced, Carmaz was actually very happy. He had won the sub-bracket challenge in his bracket. It meant that there was now only one last challenge for him and the other nine people in his bracket, just one final challenge between him and the title of God of Humans. He had no idea what that final challenge was going to be, but after this one, he was sure that he could handle whatever Alira had in store for him and the others.

And I will *win,* Carmaz thought as he fished out the golden Ruwan coin from his pocket and rubbed it between his fingers. *For Ruwa and for Saia.*

Speaking of Saia, Carmaz wondered how the Ghostly God's study of Braim was going. He had heard nothing at all from the Ghostly God since Braim's disappearance (which most of the population of World's End was still in the dark about, to his knowledge), but that was fine because he didn't want to hear anything from that particular deity until he had some actual findings to share.

But how much longer do we actually have until everyone realizes that Braim isn't just feeling sick and that he is actually missing? Carmaz thought. *And how long will it take for them to notice that the Ghostly God is missing as well and connect the two disappearances together?*

Carmaz didn't have a high opinion of the gods, but he didn't think they were stupid. They must have known that the Ghostly God had shown a little too much interest in Braim. They may not immediately connect the dots, but sooner or later one of them would, and it wouldn't be long after that that Carmaz's connection with the Ghostly God would be exposed as well.

Alira will probably kick me out of the Tournament if she finds out what I did, Carmaz thought, *even though Braim will be returned in time to compete for the Skimif Sub-Bracket Challenge.*

Just then, there was a knock at the door of his apartment. Carmaz, thinking that it was probably Raya, didn't get up. He hoped that whoever it was would just leave him alone, because right now he was in no mood to talk to anyone else.

But then that single knock was followed by a series of far more incessant knocks that sounded like it was an emergency. Still Carmaz tried to ignore it, until he heard a voice on the other side say, "Open up, Carmaz. I know you're in there. I have some news to share with you."

Carmaz recognized the voice as belonging to Tashir. Tashir was one of the few other godlings who he liked and respected, despite his own inhibitions toward aquarians. He respected the makhimancer's strength and ability. Even so, Carmaz still didn't want to talk with anyone. He just wanted to sit on his sofa and rest until the pain went away, but when Tashir mentioned the word 'news,' Carmaz decided to get up and let him in.

Gathering what little strength he had left, Carmaz deposited his coin back into his pocket, stood up from his sofa, and made his way to the door. He undid the lock and pulled open the door to find Tashir standing in the doorway. The aquarian makhimancer carried both of his swords sheathed at his side, but otherwise seemed to be far more at ease than he normally was.

"Come in," said Carmaz, stepping aside and gesturing for Tashir to enter.

"Thank you, Carmaz," said Tashir as he stepped over the threshold, allowing Carmaz to close the door behind him. "I was sent by Alira to tell you the news about the time of the next sub-bracket challenge."

"All right," said Carmaz, wincing at the pain in his stomach. "When is it?"

"According to Alira, the time of the next sub-bracket challenge is in three hours, later this afternoon," said Tashir. "It is the Spider Goddess Bracket, so that means that I will be competing in this one."

Carmaz walked past Tashir over to his sofa and sank back down into it. Then he looked at Tashir and frowned. "I forgot that you are in the Spider Goddess Bracket."

"No surprise there," said Tashir. "You've been under some terrible stress recently that has no doubt affected your memory. I have seen it happen to soldiers after they return from war. Their memory is poorer than it was before they left, though they usually learn to cope."

Tashir did not sound like he was trying to sympathize with Carmaz. He was simply stating a fact. If anything, Carmaz thought that Tashir was perhaps not-so-subtly attempting to make Carmaz get over his pain and grief as quickly as possible.

Carmaz nodded. "Do you have any idea why you were chosen to participate in the Spider Goddess Bracket? What do you and spiders have to do with each other?"

"I cannot say for certain, but I have always been interested in arachnids," said Tashir. "Prior to becoming a makhimancer, I considered becoming a biomancer specializing in the study of arachnid life. I gave up on that, however, when my people went to war and they needed every man they could get, so I had to learn makhimancy to help the war effort."

"Wasn't the Spider Goddess also the Goddess of Sleet?" said Carmaz. "What does that have to do with your talents or interests?"

"I have no idea," said Tashir, shaking his head. "We never get sleet underwater, though it can be very cold down there at times. In any case, I have long since come to accept my destiny. But whether I will or will not succeed, I do not know, seeing as I do not know what the next sub-bracket challenge will be. I have faith in my blades, however, that I will succeed."

Carmaz nodded again. "Is that all the news you have for me?"

"No," said Tashir. "There is more: the gods have made a verdict on Diog. They are going to place him underneath World's End with Void metal shackles to prevent him from escaping."

Carmaz raised an eyebrow. "I didn't know the gods could imprison each other like that."

"It is not a regular occurrence, from what I understand," said Tashir. "And it is not going to be permanent, either. Diog is simply going to remain in chains underground until the Tournament is over and the winners are ascended. They do not want him interfering with the Tournament again."

"Makes sense," said Carmaz, though he was actually thinking, *Is that what they will do to the Ghostly God once they find out what he is doing to Braim?*

"I agree," said Tashir. "But I find it hard to believe that a northern god tried to kill a mortal. It is typically the southern gods who would attempt to do such terrible things to mortals. Very depressing indeed."

"Yeah," said Carmaz. "But I've never had a very high opinion of the gods anyway. I always knew you could never truly trust them."

"I have to admit that I agree with you," said Tashir. "You may not know this, but we aquarians tend to be less loyal to the gods than you humans. We still worship them, of course, but it is easier to be a heathen in aquarian society than it is in human society, or so I understand from my discussions with the other human godlings."

"Then why are you even here?" said Carmaz, gesturing around the place, though he was trying to indicate the entire island. "Why didn't you just remain at wherever you come from?"

"Because I have no choice," said Tashir with a shrug. "When Tinkar came to my home and told me that it was my destiny to compete in the Tournament of the Gods, I knew I could not deny his demand. So I let him take me to World's End." Then Tashir looked at Carmaz with a questioning gaze. "The better question is, why are *you* here? You seem to like the gods even less than I do."

Carmaz bit his lower lip, but then said, "Because I want to help my people. They've been downtrodden for so many years that I think this is the best chance I have of restoring Ruwa to its former glory. That's why."

"A noble goal," said Tashir. "Attaining godlike power in order to use it to help your people. What about Saia?"

Carmaz tensed. "What about him?"

"Are you not fighting for him as well?" asked Tashir. "Don't you wish to avenge his death?"

Carmaz rubbed his stomach, trying to ease the pain, as he said, "Yes, I would like to, but I don't think I can. The Void isn't just some random killer on the street. It's a powerful force of nature that even the gods can barely stand against. Even if I win and become a god, there's a good chance I won't be able to do much against the Void."

"I see," said Tashir. "What about Braim Kotogs?"

Carmaz froze where he sat, but only briefly. He then returned to a more natural position, hoping that Tashir hadn't noticed his reaction to Braim's name. "What about Braim? Is there something

I should know about him?"

"No," said Tashir. "I was just wondering if you had spoken to him about what the afterlife is like. After all, Braim was once dead himself, so he might at least be able to tell you what Saia is doing now."

Carmaz tried to behave as casually as possible. Rubbing his side, Carmaz said, "I haven't spoken to Braim about that yet. It never occurred to me to do so, actually. I've just been so busy and distracted that I never thought to ask him what the afterlife might be like."

"Well, I would suggest that you do so," said Tashir. "That way, you can get some closure on this tragic turn of events."

"That's fine, Tashir," said Carmaz, keeping his tone friendly and civil, though he found it harder to do because he kept expecting the conversation to take a turn for the worse. "Maybe I'll ask him later when he's feeling better."

"I understand," said Tashir. "I was just trying to understand your motivations. But I see that you have answered my questions to my satisfaction, so I will leave now."

"Why?" asked Carmaz. "Isn't there any other news to share with me?"

"No," said Tashir, shaking his head. "At least for the moment. I have to leave because I want to train for the sub-bracket challenge. Based on the last two challenges, I have no doubt that it will be quite difficult, so I am going to take advantage of however much time I have left before I must compete."

"All right," said Carmaz. "Makes sense. The door's unlocked, so you can let yourself out. I'll be at the Stadium at the time of the event."

"All right," said Tashir. Then he glanced at Carmaz's hand, which he was rubbing his side with. "Have you had a healer look at your bruises?"

"It's fine," said Carmaz. "Eria didn't break anything vital. I'm going to be perfectly fine."

"Strength is an admirable trait in anyone, but sometimes you have to admit that you are wounded and need help," said Tashir. "I know what it is like to be hit with the flat of a sword. It is not usually as painful as being stabbed, but it can still hurt and leave serious damage depending on where and how hard you were hit."

"As I said, I'm going to be fine," said Carmaz. "I appreciate the concern, but I just need some rest. I mean, if I was in any serious trouble, I think Alira would have had someone heal me after I beat Eria."

"I suppose so," said Tashir. "But Alira has never struck me as a woman who actually cares about us all that much. She doesn't seem to know much about medicine and healing."

"Who cares?" said Carmaz. He pointed at the door. "Anyway, the door is right there, so if you want to leave, you can."

Carmaz didn't mean to sound so rude, but he couldn't help it. He just wanted to be alone at the moment, mostly because he was afraid that the conversation might go into the wrong direction if Tashir stayed around.

Tashir looked at Carmaz with a surprised expression, but then gave Carmaz one last nod and turned and left the apartment, closing the door behind himself as he did so. When Tashir was gone, Carmaz slumped in his sofa and let out a sigh of relief.

Good thing he didn't suggest we go visit Braim together or whatever, Carmaz thought. *Thought for sure that he might mention that the gods had found out that Braim was missing, but he didn't, so I'm safe for now.*

Carmaz then looked up at the ceiling. Part of him wondered again how the Ghostly God's study of Braim was coming along, but another part of him was too tired to think about that, so he stretched out onto the sofa in the most comfortable position that he could and soon drifted off to sleep.

Chapter Ten

A WAKEN, BRAIM," SAID the Ghostly God's voice, which sounded distorted through Braim's ears. He felt the god's cold mental fingers shake him. "Come on. I know you aren't dead yet. Or rather, you have not died again."

Braim opened his eyes. He blinked several times, each blink showing him the Ghostly God's ugly pale face grinning down on him. Braim looked around and did not see either the strange monster or the tiny villagers anywhere. In fact, he saw that he was lying on the same flat stone table from before he was put in the Mind Chamber, in the same dark basement of the Ghostly God's mansion. It was still too dark to see anything, but Braim was certain that he was back in the basement because it smelled as old as ever.

It took Braim another second to realize that his eyes were whole. They did hurt a little, but he could still see, which was something he was thankful for, although his gratitude vanished when he looked into the Ghostly God's face.

"What … what happened?" Braim said, looking around wildly. "How did I get back here? How long was I out? I thought I was in the Mind Chamber about to get eaten by a bunch of tiny villagers."

The Ghostly God pulled out an ancient-looking notebook and

a pen and quickly scratched something down on it. Then he looked up at Braim and said, "Tell me, what else did you see down there? What were these tiny villagers like?"

Braim blinked several times again, only this time in confusion. "Didn't *you* make them? They were in the Mind Chamber, after all, so didn't you put them down there?"

"The Mind Chamber's effects are ... unpredictable," said the Ghostly God. He reached over and tapped Braim's forehead with the bottom of his pen, which didn't hurt, but it was annoying. "It takes what dwells within the deepest parts of your mind, your darkest fears, and combines them with your imagination to create a horrifying spectacle that is normally enough to cause great mental anguish in the viewer."

"So I'm afraid of tiny wooden villagers carrying trays of freshly-baked bread?" said Braim. "That's weird."

"It is probably symbolic, although of what I cannot say," said the Ghostly God. "Tell me, did the villagers suddenly turn violent?"

"Yes," said Braim, nodding. "They all grew these really sharp fangs and then started eating me." Then Braim paused and thought about what the Ghostly God had just said. "Wait. Are you telling me that I was never in any actual trouble at all? That it was all in my head? Including the tiny wooden villagers that tried to eat me alive?"

"Physically, yes, you were never in any real danger," said the Ghostly God as he wrote in his notebook, though what he could be writing Braim had no idea. "But mentally you were in rather severe danger. I am no expert on mortal psychology, but it is a well-known fact that mental scarring is often far worse and far more difficult to heal than physical scarring. Had things gone slightly differently, you could have awoken as a raving madman that even my sister, Hamin, Goddess of the Mind, would have had a hard time repairing."

The Ghostly God spoke rather nonchalantly about putting Braim's sanity at risk, though that didn't surprise Braim, considering how the Ghostly God seemed to treat mortals like slightly more intelligent (but still quite disposable) animals.

"But I think you are, mentally-speaking, much hardier than most mortals," said the Ghostly God, still without looking up at him. "You didn't even wake up screaming. That is either a testament to your natural strength or to the strength that you gained upon returning to life. Further testing will be needed to determine why you handled the horror so well."

"What kind of testing are we talking about here?" said Braim. He gulped. "Another trip to the Mind Chamber?"

"No," said the Ghostly God. He finished scribbling in his notebook and looked up at Braim. "The Mind Chamber, I believe, has already shown me all that it is capable of showing me from you. Unless you want to go back into the Mind Chamber?"

"No," said Braim, even before the Ghostly God finished speaking. "I really don't."

The Ghostly God actually looked disappointed by that before he shrugged and said, "Very well. The Mind Chamber is generally meant for punishment rather than academic research anyway. I have some other methods to test on you that will, assuming all goes well, provide me with much fruit."

"Are you going to tell me what these are?" said Braim. "Just a sneak peek, at least?"

"I could, but it really wouldn't help you even if I did," said the Ghostly God. "I'm taking Alira's approach to this experiment. Rather than tell you outright what is going to happen next, I am simply going to drop you into the middle of it without explanation. I find that that method works best for getting that genuine reaction that I need."

The Ghostly God spoke so coldly that Braim decided there and then that he couldn't hope to reason with him. If this was how the Ghostly God treated him after he barely survived that psychological onslaught, then Braim would need to figure out another way to escape.

"But first, I must return to my study and get a new pen," said the Ghostly God. He raised and shook his in Braim's vision. "This one is running dry and I cannot take notes without a good pen. I will not be long."

With that, the Ghostly God dissolved into mist, which then evaporated in the air, leaving Braim alone on the stone table.

As soon as the Ghostly God vanished, Braim struggled against his bonds. Of course, it was a useless gesture. They were just as strong and thick as ever. It didn't help that Braim felt more tired than before, mostly due to the fact that he had been lying here on this table for only the gods-know-how-long without even a few seconds in which to stretch and exercise.

So Braim gave up after only a few seconds of trying, but then he started to think about other ways he could escape.

Think, Braim, think, Braim thought, looking around the dark basement for anything that could spark an idea in his head, though he could barely see anything due to the darkness. *You have to think. Come on. Use that brain of yours and figure out a plan of escape.*

That was easier said than done, because as far as Braim could tell, he was completely unable to escape on his own. Without his magical powers, he was worse than useless. No one knew he was here. And by the time anyone *did* realize that he was missing, Braim would probably be left a jabbering lunatic courtesy of one of the Ghostly God's experiments.

Maybe I'll just have to handle whatever the Ghostly God decides to do to me, Braim thought. *After all, if I can't get out of here on my own, then I'm completely at his mercy.*

That was when Braim heard movement somewhere in the darkness to his right. It sounded light and quiet, but in the utter stillness of the dark basement, it was extremely noticeable. Braim looked to his right, squinting in the darkness, but he still didn't see anything.

Maybe it was just a mouse, Braim thought with a sigh. *I bet this place has a rat infestation or something.*

Then Braim heard that sound again. It sounded like someone was walking toward him in the darkness., but he could not see them, whoever they were.

Can't be the Ghostly God, Braim thought. *He'd have announced his return if it was him. Besides, he doesn't have any feet, so he can't walk.*

Of course, that still didn't quite answer *who* it was. It might have been one of the Ghostly God's servants, perhaps coming down to check on Braim or possibly torture him. Or both.

That was why Braim was surprised when a light suddenly flared into existence to his right. It wasn't the brightest light in the world, but now Braim's eyes had adjusted to the darkness of the basement, the light blinded him briefly.

"Ow!" Braim said as he blinked several times. "Who's there?"

"You mean you don't recognize me?" said a familiar, rather shrill voice. "I would be offended if I actually gave a damn about your opinion. Too bad I don't."

It took Braim's eyes several seconds to adjust to the light. When it did, he got a good look at the owner of the voice that had spoken.

Standing in the darkness was a young female mage holding up a glowing wand, which was the source of the light. She had beautiful blonde hair and violet eyes, though her scowl took away some of her natural beauty. She wore old blue mage's robes that looked a touch too big for her, but she didn't seem to notice the size difference at all.

Braim recognized the girl right away, but he could not believe his eyes, because he had not seen her in a long time. "Aorja? Is that you?"

Aorja Kitano, a former student at North Academy and one of the first mages who Braim had met after he returned to life not long ago, rolled her eyes. "No, I'm Kano. Of course it's me. Who else *would* I be? Your mother?"

Braim could not take his eyes off her, even though he was sure that they were lying to him. "What are you doing here? How did you even know I was here? Is any of this real or is this another mind trick of the Ghostly God?"

"The Ghostly God hates me, so he'd never use me as a mind trick," said Aorja. "So yes, I am the real deal."

"That still doesn't explain how or why you are here," said Braim. "Isn't the Ghostly God aware that you're here?"

"Nope," said Aorja, shaking her head. "He's a little distracted right now by my friend, so I estimate we have about ten minutes before the Ghostly God deals with him and comes down here."

Aorja pointed her wand at Braim's straps, which immediately snapped apart. Braim sat up and stretched his arms and legs, but he didn't jump off the table right away because he wasn't sure he could trust her.

"Why are you saving me?" asked Braim. "I know we worked together back in the Spirit Lands, but I didn't think you actually liked me all that much."

"You're right," said Aorja, though she didn't seem to be paying much attention to him because she was looking around as though she thought that the Ghostly God was going to reappear any minute. "I'm only rescuing you because I want to spite the Ghostly God. I didn't even know you were here when I arrived."

Braim looked at Aorja in confusion. "Why do you want to spite him?"

"Because he left me to rot in prison after I helped him back in North Academy and I still haven't forgotten about that," said Aorja as she walked around the table, as if in search of something. "So I decided to come to his island and get back at him. I can't kill him—I'm still a mortal—but I can at least give him hell."

Braim swung his legs over the side of the table and slid onto the floor. Stretching his arms and legs, he said, "How did you even find his island? I thought he kept its location a secret from mortals."

"Because I went to it once when I was his servant," said Aorja. She stopped and then turned to face Braim again, the light illuminating her harsh expression. "I'm a Limitless, so it was easy

114

for me to teleport from the Northern Isles to here. I had to do it discreetly, though, as I am still not as powerful as the Ghostly God."

"Right," said Braim. "What took you so long?"

"First, I've spent the last three months on the run from everyone, because there's a huge bounty on my head because I am one of the few Rock Isle escapees who hasn't been returned to their cell," Aorja said. "Second, I've had to practice teleporting through solid objects. It's a difficult skill that most mages cannot do, but I managed to master it, which is how I teleported from the surface of the island directly into the basement of the Ghostly God's mansion. And finally, I had to come up with a good plan to make sure that the Ghostly God didn't kill me as soon as I got here."

"So what's your plan?" said Braim.

"Blow up his damn mansion," said Aorja, gesturing at the basement in which they stood. "I know a thing or two about creating magical explosions, so I should be able to do it without any problem."

"Oh," said Braim. "You aren't going to blow it up while I'm still here, though, right?"

"It depends," said Aorja. "Why should I take you with me?"

"Because I'm your friend?" said Braim. "Or at least an acquaintance who you knew for a little while?"

"As a general rule, I don't trust men, so you'll have to try better than that," said Aorja.

"It will mess up the Ghostly God's plans and make him angry," Braim said. He pointed at the table he had been strapped to moments before. "The Ghostly God kidnapped me because he wanted to learn how I came back to life. If you get me out of here, the Ghostly God won't be able to do that, which will really mess up his careful plans."

Aorja tapped her chin in thought. "Hmmm … if that's the case, then rescuing you would fit in with my general desire for vengeance almost perfectly."

"Also, the Ghostly God is not supposed to kidnap me," said Braim. "I'm one of the godlings in the Tournament of the Gods and we're not supposed to leave World's End. If the other gods know about what he's done to me, then he'll get in big trouble with them."

"That makes it even better," said Aorja. She smiled that crazy, sociopathic smile that she always showed whenever she was happy. "All right. I'll get you out of here, but don't think it's because I give a damn about your life. I'm only doing this because it will piss off the Ghostly God. Under other circumstances, I wouldn't even bother."

"Don't worry, beautiful," said Braim, giving Aorja the thumbs up. "I know you well enough to know that you don't have an altruistic bone in your body."

Aorja rolled her eyes, and then said, "Just let me set up the explosion spell and I will get us both out of here so fast that you won't even realize that we left."

Aorja then walked around the perimeter of the basement, waving her wand around. Sparks trailed wherever she waved her wand, but Braim didn't know what those sparks meant. He figured that they were probably the results of the spell she was casting, but Braim knew little about pyromancy or its associated magical fields, so he didn't say a word about it.

It took Aorja less than a minute to circle the basement and finish casting her spell. She then walked over to Braim with an exceedingly pleased expression on her face.

"Finished casting the spell," Aorja informed him in a voice that was much cheerier than normal. "Now let's get out of here before it goes off. It's going to be my biggest spell yet, so when it goes off, you'll be able to see it from World's End and North Academy."

"As long as I'm not in the middle of it when it happens," said Braim. Then he looked up at the ceiling. "Say, who is your friend that is distracting the Ghostly God, anyway? You didn't mention his name."

"It's Zeeree, of course," said Aorja. "Remember him? I don't think you actually spoke with him much."

"Name sounds familiar," said Braim. "But I don't remember exactly."

"Zeeree is my only real friend," said Aorja. "He's also a half-god, but he's a good half-god and the only being in the whole world that I trust."

"Now I remember," said Braim. "Wasn't he a complete idiot or something?"

Braim regretted those words when he found the tip of Aorja's still-glowing wand at his neck. Her eyes reflected her murderous intent, which almost made Braim think that Aorja was going to go back on her promise to free him.

"Zeeree may not be the most brilliant being in the world, but I won't stand back and let you talk about him like that," said Aorja, "at least while I'm around."

"Okay, okay, I'll keep my mouth shut about him," said Braim, holding up his hands. "As long as you can get me out of here alive, I promise I won't say even one more negative word about Zeeree from now on."

Much to Braim's relief, Aorja lowered her wand and said, "All right. But you say anything else about Zeeree again and I will leave you here when the mansion explodes."

Braim nodded and said, "So, are we going to get out of here now or is there something else you need to do first?"

"We can leave," said Aorja. She grabbed his arm. "Once we do, the spell will go off. It's a shame I won't get to see the Ghostly God's face when it explodes, but I guess you can't have everything you want in life, huh?"

With that, the world around them became darker than ever before. Then they reappeared in the middle of a dark, misty jungle that Braim had never seen before. Aorja immediately forced Braim to crouch down, however, and whispered, in a harsh voice, "Quiet. Don't make a move."

Braim did as Aorja commanded, though he did a cursory look around the place to see exactly where they had appeared. The ground was soggy and muddy under his feet, while the bushes in front of them and the trees around them were wet, which meant that it must have rained recently.

Then Braim almost jumped when he heard the roar of what sounded like a giant, followed by cursing from a familiar voice. Aorja, however, kept Braim down with one firm hand, saying, "Shhh! Do you want to be found?"

Braim shook his head, but before he could respond, Aorja pointed through a gap in the trees. Curious, Braim looked at where she was pointing.

Through the gap in the trees, Braim saw an ancient-looking mansion standing all by itself in a clearing. A rough, muddy path went up to its front steps, but the path looked like it hadn't been walked upon in years. The mansion itself appeared entirely abandoned, or it would have, had it not been for the two beings clashing outside it.

One was the Ghostly God. There was no mistaking the hulking, metallic, transparent figure who easily dodged the punches from his opponent, a much larger juggernaut of a being with rusted, metallic legs and a fat, green belly. Its fists rushed through the air like comets, but despite the ferocity with which it attacked, the half-god known as Zeeree could not land so much as one blow on the Ghostly God.

"Should we do something to help him?" Braim asked in a whisper, though in truth, all he wanted to do was leave.

Aorja shook her head. "No."

"No?" Braim repeated. "But isn't he your friend?"

"Yes, but he'll be fine," said Aorja. "Just wait a few more seconds now."

That was when Braim realized that Aorja wasn't actually looking at Zeeree's fight with the Ghostly God. Instead, her eyes were on the Ghostly God's mansion, though it did not occur to Braim right away why she seemed so interested in it.

By the time Braim understood why, however, the mansion exploded.

Chapter Eleven

RAYA STOOD BY herself in the alleyway between Anwan's Tailoring and whatever the building to her right was. She stood as silently as she could, focused on the side door that she had discovered when she had decided to do a little exploration of the building's exterior. What made this find so good was that the side door was not even locked. From what she could tell, it was simply another way to enter the shop, albeit one that wasn't as easy to find or notice as the one in the front.

But Raya didn't walk in just yet. She was waiting for the right moment to do so. She glanced at the streets, but did not yet see the street sweeper or Anwan. Waiting was excruciating for her, but Raya told herself to be patient. Father always used to gently reprimand her for her impatience, even though Raya was so used to getting what she wanted right away with no hassle.

I shouldn't have to wait very long, anyway, Raya thought. *The street sweeper seemed like a trustworthy fellow. He'll probably have Anwan out of the shop in no time.*

Earlier, Raya had spoken with the street cleaner, who couldn't speak mortal Divina very well, but apparently knew enough to understand and communicate with Raya anyway. He said his name was Yag (which Raya was unable to determine if it was his actual name or a shortened version of his full name) and that he had been sweeping the streets of World's End for as long as he could remember. He used a combination of magical and non-magical techniques to accomplish this task. Not that Raya had asked, but Yag had been so proud of his work that he had babbled on about it to her anyway.

And of course Raya listened and pretended to be interested and asked questions and made him feel important, like she actually liked him. Of course Raya found him repulsive. While Yag certainly was not lacking in the muscles department, his face looked like it had been smashed in by a rock and hastily repaired by an etimancer who didn't know what a normal human face looked like. He even smelled awful, like sweat and dust.

But Raya managed to look past that and made him think that she was possibly interested in him. She had waxed rather eloquently about his muscles and how he was clearly a very hard worker and how he was obviously popular with the women, at which point Yag had confessed that he usually worked too much to seek out female companionship and that even if he didn't, katabans usually required a blessing from the gods before they could seek out romantic or sexual partners.

Raya had never known that particular fact about katabans relationships, but that was fine because she didn't need to. She had simply said that she would be willing to have dinner with Yag once he got a day off, but only on the condition that he helped her with something.

A hard worker Yag may have been, but he clearly was not a terribly deep thinker, because he had agreed to do whatever she asked him to do in exchange for that dinner. He had agreed almost too easily, which had made Raya suspect briefly that he might be smarter than he let on, though she dismissed that theory the second Yag picked a large booger from his nose and flicked it away.

So Raya had explained the plan to Yag: He needed to enter Anwan's Tailoring and ask Anwan to come with him to his living quarters. His excuse was that he had a shirt that he had ripped terribly, his very favorite shirt in fact, and he needed Anwan's professional services to fix it. Yag would also explain, if asked, that the reason he didn't bring the shirt with him was that he could not carry it with him while he worked.

When Anwan agreed to go with Yag, Raya would enter through the side door, find the red dress, take it, and leave. Assuming all went well—and Raya saw no reason it shouldn't, because Yag was a useful fool who didn't question the orders that pretty women gave him and Anwan was a proud tailor who would never turn down an opportunity to put his skills into action— Raya would be in and out of the shop just in time for the next sub-bracket challenge. She probably would not be able to actually wear the red dress until the Tournament was over, but Raya was fine by that, because she just wanted to have it.

But if on the off chance that Raya *was* caught, well … she hadn't thought that through very well, mostly because she was so confident in her own taking abilities that she saw no reason to consider it. She supposed the worst that would happen was that the gods might get angry at her and she might not be permitted to step foot inside any shop on World's End ever again, but as long as she stayed in the Tournament, she would be fine.

Cheating may be against the rules in the Tournament, but that doesn't say anything about how you're supposed to behave outside *of the Tournament,* Raya thought with a smirk. *I can do anything I want and they can't kick me out of the Tournament for it.*

In truth, Raya really didn't see what she was planning to do as necessarily 'immoral' anyway. The way she saw it, Anwan had gone back on their deal, despite having led her to believe that he was going to trade the red dress for her white one (which she had thrown into the nearest garbage can because she didn't want it anymore and had nowhere else to put it). She saw herself as the victim of a malicious businessman who took advantage of her and denied her what she wanted.

Then Raya heard the bell from the front door of Anwan's Tailor tinkle and she ducked behind the garbage cans. Peering through the gap between them, Raya saw Yag and then Anwan pass the alleyway in which she hid. Yag carried his sweeper over his shoulder, while Anwan followed him with a box that might have contained his sewing equipment.

Raya smiled when she saw them pass. *Perhaps I really will have dinner with Yag after this is all over. I just hope that he can keep Anwan distracted long enough for me to find the dress.*

So Raya slipped out from behind the cans and pulled open the side door.

Or *tried* to pull it open. As it turned out, the side door was locked after all. Raya twisted and turned the knob, but the door wouldn't budge at all.

Raya almost cursed the door before she realized that Anwan had likely locked up the shop before he left so that no one could enter it while it was unattended. Likely he had locked all possible entrances. If so, that made Raya like him even less than she did now.

By the gods, Raya thought. *How am I supposed to get in there now?*

Raya tried to think about this from a logical point of view, rather than let her emotions get the best of her. The way she saw it, she needed to break the lock somehow or at least pick it. Raya knew a thing or two about picking locks, as she had done it as a hobby as a child, but she had not done that in such a long time (mostly because her status as royalty meant that there were no doors locked to her) and so didn't remember how to do it.

Raya observed the doorknob closely. She saw a keyhole in its center, but without a key, there was no way Raya could force it open. She needed to pick it, then.

But how do I do that? Raya thought. *I might be destined to become the Goddess of Thieves, but that doesn't mean I have a good lock pick on me at all times. I don't even have a bad one.*

Then another thought occurred to Raya: *Why not just open an ethereal portal into the place?*

The idea seemed logical enough. The ethereal was a second 'layer' within Martir that stretched over the whole world. Every part of the ethereal corresponded with some other part of Martir, which was how it was possible to use the ethereal to travel from one end of Martir to the other quickly. Using the ethereal seemed so obvious that Raya didn't know why she hadn't thought of it before.

But Raya, for all of her confidence in herself and her abilities, did hesitate. She remembered how she had had to draw upon all of her strength to enter the ethereal the first time and how she had fallen unconscious as a result. Raya had gotten lucky after her guardian spirit or whatever had saved her, but what if she lost consciousness again? She didn't know how to open an ethereal portal without wasting a lot of energy, after all. If she used a portal to enter Anwan's Tailoring, only to lose consciousness in the middle of her heist, then her entire plan would be ruined and it would be all her fault.

I must do it anyway, Raya thought. *I cannot pick this lock, so this is the only way that will let me get in there. Besides, Father always says that practice makes perfect, so I shouldn't be afraid of practice.*

That was easier said than done, however. Raya wasn't used to practice. She was used to succeeding without that much effort. Yes, Raya had had to put in some effort to learn some things, but by and large Raya had not struggled all that much in her young life and therefore was hesitant to try opening an ethereal portal again should she fail.

But the idea of not getting the dress was enough to propel her through her self-doubt and hesitation. Raya held up her right hand and tried to remember how she had opened an ethereal portal the first time. She recalled having to focus hard on opening the portal, so Raya put all of her focus on doing that. She imagined a portal opening before her, imagined seeing it burst into existence, just like it had in the first place.

Then Raya felt a huge portion of her energy zip out of her like a river flowing downhill. It made her stagger, but a second later, an ethereal portal opened before her. Despite her sudden weakness, Raya had enough strength in her to step into the portal, which vanished behind her with a rather weak *pop.*

Now Raya was in the ethereal for the second time in her life.

It was much colder than she remembered it being, causing her to shiver, but at the same time, Raya felt at home here. She looked up at the starry sky, which was unlike any sky she had ever seen, and at the pure white road that stretched on seemingly forever in both directions.

From what Raya could see, she was the only person in the ethereal at the moment, but she knew that katabans and gods alike traveled upon it often, so Raya didn't dilly-dally. She took a couple of steps forward, trying to determine where she should open the next portal, but it was hard to think because just opening that first portal had taken more out of her than she had anticipated.

The urgency of her mission, however, forced Raya to stop only a few steps away from where she had initially opened the portal and hold out her hand. A second later, another portal appeared, which surprised Raya, because she had not felt another loss of energy from this one. Maybe opening portals in the ethereal was easier than opening them in Martir.

In any case, the portal opened up and appeared to go into Anwan's Tailoring, so Raya wasted no time in stepping through the portal ... only for her feet to touch air.

Shocked, Raya stumbled through the portal and fell head first onto a rack of dresses, causing the rack to collapse underneath her rather noisily. Not to mention the fall hurt. While the dresses broke her fall, the fact was that she had not expected to fall and so found herself lying stunned on top of a bunch of katabans dresses.

How did that happen? Raya thought. She looked up at the ceiling of the shop, though the portal she had stepped through was no longer there. *How did I end up in the air like that?*

Raya tried to remember if Mother had told her about the ethereal messing up like that, but unfortunately Mother had never spoken with Raya very much about the ethereal or anything katabans related back home. She supposed that it probably had to do with her own lack of experience in the realm of portal usage more than anything, but even so, Raya felt incredibly embarrassed by this dumb mistake of hers.

But not embarrassed enough to lie there and waste time. Raya sat up and looked around at her surroundings to see exactly where she had ended up.

As it turned out, the problem had been the height from which she had fallen. Somehow Raya had ended up falling from a much taller height than she had planned. It made no sense to her, seeing as she had not gone up anywhere in the ethereal, but then maybe she had done something wrong. It wasn't as though Raya actually understood how the ethereal worked very well anyway.

In any case, Raya sat still and listened. She figured she was alone, considering how Anwan didn't have any employees and there were unlikely to be any customers in here with the doors locked and Anwan away, but she feared that her fall might have caused a lot of noise that could have attracted the attention of someone anyway. When she didn't hear anything, she allowed herself to relax.

Can't relax too much, though, Raya thought, looking at the dresses that she sat upon. *Once Anwan gets back here, he'll undoubtedly see the mess these dresses are in, maybe even know who did it. So much for stealth.*

Not sure how much time she had left before Anwan returned (Yag had promised to keep him busy as long as possible, but

Raya wasn't sure how much control Yag had over that situation), Raya stood up. Due to how soft the dresses under her feet were, however, Raya had to be careful about standing up in order to avoid falling over.

Raya stood in the left side of the shop, where the side door was located. From her current position on top of the dresses, Raya could see the front of the store. The red dress was still missing from the display window, but Raya already knew that. She was just checking to make sure that there was no one on the other side of the windows peering in. Thankfully, the streets outside appeared entirely empty at the moment.

Still, Raya stepped off the dresses and kept doubled over to make sure that no one would see her walking among the clothing set up all around the store. There was no point in sneaking into somewhere unseen only to end up being seen, after all.

The only question now was the location of the red dress. Raya had no idea where Anwan kept the dresses he took down from sale. A cursory glance around the shop showed her that the dress had not been placed among the others, which likely meant that it was being kept in the shop's storage room.

Where might that be, though? Raya thought, frowning when she looked around. *I know where the office is, but I don't know where the storage room is. Looks like I'll have to find it myself. Hopefully that won't be much of a problem, because this shop really isn't that big.*

Still keeping her head down, Raya walked amidst the clothing racks, making her way to the back of the store, where she believed the storage room was most likely located. Of course, Raya didn't know much about shops, but she knew that if she was running a business like this, then she'd put her storage room in the back away from the rest of the products that she was selling.

It was only about a minute later that Raya found another door in the back, this one hidden behind a lot of clothing that she had to push out of the way in order to access it. The door itself was rather unremarkable, made of plain wood and with a simple metal doorknob. It did not have any writing or pictures on it to suggest what it was used for, but Raya figured that it had to be Anwan's storage room.

It doesn't even appear to be locked, Raya thought with a smile as she reached for the doorknob.

When Raya laid her hand on the doorknob, however, she hesitated. She wasn't sure why. The door looked rather ordinary, but touching the doorknob had created a deep sense of unease in her that made her want to turn and leave, the dress be damned. And she almost did. The intense sense of unease was the most uncomfortable that she had ever felt in her entire life.

But then Raya reminded herself that she had vowed not to run, not when she had gotten this far. Raya may have been a lot of things, but she didn't give up that easily. She dismissed her sense of unease as being nothing more than her conscience trying to guilt her into leaving and Raya wasn't going to listen to it.

Raya opened the door and poked her head into a dark room. She squinted her eyes, wishing she could see better, but unfortunately there did not seem to be any light in this room. She was reminded vividly of the darkness of the Void, though this room's darkness was nowhere near as terrifying or unnatural as the Void's.

Then the room's light stone flickered on, allowing Raya to see that she had been correct: This was the shop's storage room. Granted, she did not see any sign that said so, but with all of the clothing set up in neat rows and piles away from the eyes of the general buying public, Raya had to assume that that was what the room was used for.

This room was a lot more cramped than the shop itself, though not nearly as cramped as Anwan's office. Clothes were either piled on top of each other or hung on racks. There appeared to be an equal amount of male and female clothing, as well as clothing that Raya couldn't identify the gender of, and it was quite hot in here, again due to a proper lack of ventilation. None of the clothing was dusty, however, which probably meant that Anwan took good care of them, which only made sense, seeing as he was the business owner and these were his products. The ceiling was low as well, though it was high enough for Raya to stand up to her full height in at least.

But Raya did not see the red dress that she so desperately wanted. Still, she knew it had to be in here somewhere, even if it wasn't easy to find, so Raya entered the storage room and closed it behind her as she did so. Then she started walking through the paths between the piles and racks of clothing, her head turning from side to side as she looked for that familiar red dress.

Come on, dress, Raya thought, stopping and pushing aside an ugly blue dress only to see a blank stone wall behind it. *Where are you? Anwan couldn't have hid you* that *well.*

Raya continued walking, but it was harder and harder for her to remain patient, because she was aware that the next sub-bracket challenge was going to be starting soon. It would probably start without her no matter what she did, but she figured that Alira would send someone to her apartment to get her if she did not show up on her own. Raya was still not afraid of being caught, necessarily, because she didn't think she'd get disqualified from the Tournament, but she still wanted to make sure that she got away cleanly with this taking.

The storage room, though more cramped than the actual shop, was much longer, almost like a hallway in its length. Raya found herself going deeper and deeper into the shop's storage room, discovering all sorts of strange clothing that was apparently meant to be worn by katabans. Raya did not stop and look at any of them for very long, but it was hard not to look at the dress that appeared to have been designed for a woman ten times as large as her, or the man's suit that had holes in the back that looked like they might have been designed for wings to fit through. And all of them were made of that same strange, itchy material that the clothes in the shop itself were made of, which prompted Raya to wonder once again why that material was apparently popular among the katabans, as she doubted it was very comfortable to wear.

Anwan's shop is a lot bigger than I thought, Raya thought after about five minutes of walking, with the end of the storage room still nowhere in sight. *If Yag doesn't keep Anwan distracted for long, I might have to leave early and try again another time. Unless Anwan manages to sell the dress to someone else at some point, that is.*

That was when Raya saw something reflecting the light from the ceiling at the other end of the room. It shone red in the light from the ceiling, which made Raya realize that it was that red dress that she wanted. Seeing it made Raya increase her walking speed until soon she was almost running. And she would have, but she advanced with more caution than necessary because that same sense of unease had returned over her, this time so insistent that she couldn't just ignore it.

Still, Raya reached the end of the storage room in good time. But it turned out to be for nothing, because when she stopped and looked at the red shining thing, she realized that it was a completely different dress. It was a lot smaller, for one, too small even for her, and its red was a much darker shade than the one she wanted. This particular dress might have been designed for a young girl to wear, but Raya was not that young, so she couldn't wear it even if she wanted.

Raya looked to the left and to the right. She saw nothing but other small dresses similar to the one before her on the left, but to the right, she found another closed door. It was completely black and appeared to be made out of solid stone. It looked rather out of place in the back of the storage room of a tailor's shop. There was nothing on it to indicate what it was, but Raya assumed that it must have been another part of the storage room or perhaps instead led to Anwan's workshop.

Maybe he thought I'd try to take the dress, so he went and hid it in here, Raya thought. *Or maybe he just has a bad habit of not labeling the doors of his shop.*

In any case, Raya thought that it was worth a look. She grabbed the handle and pulled, but the door was heavy and it didn't budge right away. She grabbed the handle with both hands and heaved and pulled, which was difficult even when she applied her full strength. It didn't help that she was still tired from opening those ethereal portals earlier, but she had no time to rest right now.

Eventually, the door began to move, until soon Raya had opened it up wide enough for her to enter. It wasn't opened all the way—it was much too heavy for her to do that—but now she could slip through without any problem. Taking her sweaty hands off the handle, Raya wiped them off on the nearby small red dress before peering through this other door. What she saw was completely unexpected.

Rather than open into another part of the storage room or Anwan's workshop, Raya found herself staring down a dark, stone staircase that stretched down far out of sight. It looked ancient, as if it had been placed here centuries ago by someone. The steps were chipped and dirty, while the walls were dusty and covered in grime. While Anwan's Tailoring was hardly the cleanest establishment that Raya had ever patronized, this staircase was far worse than the rest of the place.

What is this? Raya thought. Fear rose up her spine, though she tried to ignore it. *This doesn't look like something you'd find in a tailor's.*

Part of Raya wanted to close the door and leave. There was something wrong about this staircase and Raya wanted nothing to do with it. She almost stepped out and turned away, but again caught herself at the last minute. She was sure that the red dress was down there, though why Anwan would put it down there, of course, she didn't know.

He probably thought the staircase would scare away easily frightened people, Raya thought, smirking as she took one step onto the staircase. *I bet this is where he keeps his most valuable dresses and clothes. Of course he'd put the red one down here.*

Indeed, Raya now saw that the only problem that this presented to her was that she did not know the exact depth of the staircase. If it was too deep, she might not be able to get out in time before Anwan returned.

Then I'd better be fast, Raya thought.

She walked down the staircase one step at a time as fast as she could, but not too fast because the steps were steep and she didn't want to trip and fall. Raya also kept her ears open. While she didn't think there was anyone down here, she also didn't want to be taken by surprise by any traps that Anwan may have set for the unwary.

Soon Raya reached the bottom of the staircase, where she found yet another door, making Raya think that Anwan really liked doors for some reason. It was black as the door above, but made of a much lighter wood. It wasn't even locked, though Raya had to twist the knob a couple of times to open it, as though it hadn't been opened in a while.

When the door opened, Raya peered through the open door, but could not see anything at first due to the utter darkness. Then the light stone embedded in the ceiling activated, allowing Raya to see just what was behind this door.

It was a corpse lying on the floor in a circle of blood.

Chapter Twelve

A LOUD, INCESSANT series of knocks at the door awoke Carmaz from his slumber right away. He groaned involuntarily at the pain in his side and stomach. While it was not as bad as it had been earlier, it still hurt quite a bit and was impossible to ignore.

Nonetheless, he looked toward the door to his apartment, wondering who it could be, and said, in a somewhat tired voice, "Who is it?"

"Carmaz, it's Malya," said a familiar motherly voice from behind the door. "Are you up?"

Carmaz yawned, but winced at the pain in his stomach. "Yes. Why?"

"I need to talk with you about Raya," said Malya.

Carmaz groaned again, except this time because he didn't want to talk about Raya. He tried to make it sound like it was due to the pain in his stomach and side, however, which was easy because he really was in a lot of pain.

"Why?" said Carmaz.

"Because Raya has gone missing," said Malya.

"Missing?" Carmaz repeated. "What do you mean, 'missing'?"

"Could you please let me in?" said Malya. She sounded very worried now. "I'd rather tell you in the privacy of your apartment, if that is all right with you."

Carmaz didn't want to get up at all, but he forced himself to sit up, get off the sofa, and move over to the door. He undid the lock and, opening the door, saw Malya standing in the doorway. She had a worried expression on her motherly face, which made Carmaz feel a little sorry for her.

Stepping aside, Carmaz said, "Come in and explain the situation to me."

Malya entered, allowing Carmaz to close the door behind her, and then she said, "I went to Raya's apartment because I wanted to make sure that she knew when the next sub-bracket challenge is going to start, but when I went over there, I was told that Raya was not there and that no one knew where she was."

Carmaz returned to his place on the sofa, still rubbing his side where Eria had hit him, even though the pain was no longer as serious as it was earlier. "Last time I saw her, Raya stomped out of the Stadium lobby because she was annoyed at me. I thought she'd just returned to her room to sulk."

"Well, she didn't," said Malya. "I'm worried about her because no one knows where she is and the last time this happened she was nearly killed by a half-god."

Carmaz nodded, but said, "I think Raya will be fine. Diog and Ragao aren't a threat to anyone at the moment and the Void has so far not made any other moves. Raya can take care of herself ... sort of."

"I know Raya is a grown woman and all, but I am still worried for her safety," said Malya, rubbing her hands together anxiously. "I came to you because I thought you might know where she is."

"Sorry, but I can't help you there, seeing as I don't interact with Raya much outside of the Stadium," said Carmaz with a shrug. "Have you asked the Soldiers of the Gods if they know where she is?"

"No, but the Soldiers aren't protecting Raya anymore, so I didn't think that asking them would do us any good," said Malya.

"Well, I still think she'll be fine," said Carmaz. "I mean, I doubt that the gods would let one of the Tournament participants get into too much trouble on her own. She still has to compete in the final Hollech Bracket Challenge, after all."

"I suppose you're right," said Malya. "And as far as I know, Alira hasn't shown any concern over Raya's disappearance, either. Even so, I would still feel better knowing her exact location. Wouldn't you?"

Carmaz wanted to say, *I really don't care either way,* but he just shrugged and said, "It's not my biggest concern at the moment. Say, what time is it?"

"Middle afternoon," said Malya. "The next sub-bracket challenge is going to start soon. Tashir and the other challengers are training for it right now."

Carmaz sighed in relief. "Whew. I almost thought that I had overslept and missed it."

"Is that really your biggest concern at the moment?" said Malya, folding her arms across her chest. "Raya is missing and you are concerned that you almost overslept?"

Carmaz yawned. "Yep. But I didn't, so I don't have to worry about it anymore."

Malya looked rather offended by Carmaz's honesty, but he didn't see what the problem was. He thought he'd already made it clear by now that he didn't care much for Raya as a person. He didn't want her to die or anything, obviously, but he really didn't care if she was missing or not. The way he saw it, Raya was probably not in any real trouble at the moment, so why worry about her?

"All right, then," said Malya. "I think I'll just go visit Braim, then. I haven't gone to check up on him. Maybe Raya went to visit him."

Carmaz immediately stood up from the sofa. He tried to make it look natural, but he stood up so fast that Malya looked startled by his quickness.

"You know what? I don't think that will be necessary," said Carmaz, smiling at her in as friendly a way as he could. "Braim's feeling under the weather today, remember? We probably shouldn't visit him until tomorrow at least. I can help you find Raya instead."

"Oh, you will?" said Malya with a smile. "Oh, thank you. I knew I could count on you, Carmaz. You always did strike me as an honest young man. Perhaps that is why Raya likes you so much."

Carmaz continued to smile at her, but he was acutely aware, in that instant, of just how dishonest he was currently being. But he didn't dare utter a word about the real reason he didn't want Malya (or anyone else, for that matter) to go and visit Braim. He was just glad to see that Malya did not suspect him of being up to no good.

"Well, I try my best, Malya," said Carmaz. "Did the people at Raya's apartment say anything about where she might have gone?"

"All they told me was that she returned to her apartment and then left rather quickly, with a white dress in her arms," said

Malya. She shrugged. "I don't know what Raya might be doing with a white dress or where she might have taken it."

Carmaz tapped his chin, thinking about that for a minute. "Yes, that is strange, but Raya has always struck me as being a rather strange girl. Maybe she wanted to show it off to someone?"

"But who?" said Malya. "I at first thought that Raya might have been coming to bring it to you, but now that I can clearly see that she is not here, I am at a loss for where she might have gone."

"She's probably not at the Stadium," said Carmaz. "Raya is only there whenever there's a challenge. Besides, I don't think Alira would like if it Raya turned up there in a dress, rather than in her godling uniform."

"Perhaps Raya took the dress to a shop to sell it?" said Malya. "I have seen some places in this city that seem to sell dresses and clothing, but I can never read their signs because they're not written in a language I can read. But it still seems like a logical place for a young woman like Raya to go."

"I guess so, but that really doesn't help us because neither of us are very familiar with the clothing shops around here," said Carmaz. "Besides, Raya has never struck me as a very business savvy person. I doubt she knows the first thing about selling or trading, though she probably knows a lot about buying."

"Raya doesn't need to be a business savvy individual to make a deal with someone who is," Malya said. "Besides, I don't know what else she'd be doing with a white dress. Because she's the princess of one of the most powerful nations in the Northern Isles, I imagine she could fetch a high price for one of her dresses very easily."

"I agree," said Carmaz. "So where should we start looking?"

"We should ask around," said Malya. "Find a native of the city who knows all of the shops that buy dresses and their locations. But we must do it quickly, because the next sub-bracket challenge is going to start soon and I don't want to get on Alira's bad side by being late."

Carmaz didn't want to go out and search the entire city for Raya, but he had already agreed to help Malya find Raya, so he saw no way out of it.

Look on the bright side, Carmaz, Carmaz told himself as he and Malya walked over to the door of his apartment. *This way, you can at least ensure that the Ghostly God has more time to study Braim.*

It didn't take Carmaz and Malya long to find a katabans on the streets who was willing to talk to them and could speak in a language they both could understand. The 'willing to talk to them' part was the most surprising and difficult, however, because it seemed like all of the other katabans in the city did not like talking to mortals, even though both Carmaz and Malya were in line to become gods. Perhaps that was why they didn't like them. The katabans didn't like the idea of mortals becoming gods and thus ruling over them.

In any case, the katabans who was willing to speak to them seemed friendly enough. He told them that, while he had not seen Princess Raya around, he knew of the locations of several tailors who operated in the city. Not that that helped, since neither Carmaz nor Malya recognized the names of any of the tailors he listed.

So Malya asked the katabans to point them in the location of the nearest one, which the katabans told them was called Anwan's Tailoring. According to him, it was run by a famous katabans tailor known as Anwan, who was also one of the best on the island. After he gave them directions to the shop, Carmaz and Malya thanked him and went that way.

It didn't take the two of them long to find Anwan's Tailoring, which was located not far from the Stadium. It was a humble little storefront, very different from the massive buildings all around it. It certainly didn't look to Carmaz like a place that someone like Raya would ever step foot in. It just seemed too low class for Raya, but Carmaz didn't share that opinion out loud, because Malya was intent on checking out the place anyway. Besides, as long as it kept them away from Braim's room, Carmaz was willing to go with Malya just about anywhere at this point.

At first, it appeared like no one was in the shop, because when Carmaz peered through the front window, he didn't see anyone in there. All Carmaz saw was the strangest collection of shirts and dresses he had ever seen, none of which looked like anything Raya would like.

Carmaz looked at Malya beside him, who was also looking through the front window with both of her hands cupped over her eyes. "I don't see Raya or anyone else in there. I'm not even sure that the shop is open right now."

"Maybe the owner is in the back," Malya suggested, tearing her eyes away from the window to look at Carmaz. "Let's try knocking on the front door to see if they're open."

Seconds later, Carmaz was knocking on the front door of the shop, but he received no answer. And he made sure to check for the owner or any employees by looking through the window in the front door, but as before, he only saw tons of clothes wherever he looked. The shop seemed abandoned to him, which made him wonder if Anwan's Tailoring had gone out of business or something.

Carmaz turned to face Malya again. "Sorry, Malya, but I think this is a dead end. The door's locked and nobody's home, so we should probably head to the Stadium now before the next sub-bracket challenge starts and Alira gets angry at us for being late."

Malya walked up to the front door herself and knocked on it rather sharply, but as before, no one answered. She sighed and said, "Well, I guess you have a point. I can't honestly see Raya patronizing this place anyway, even though they have a lot of nice dresses."

"Can I help you two?" said an unfamiliar male voice nearby, causing Carmaz and Malya to look down the street in the direction it had came.

Strolling down the street, with a somewhat annoyed look on his face, was a middle-aged man in an orange and gray suit carrying what looked like a toolbox in his right hand. The man was clearly a katabans, because Carmaz didn't recognize him from the rest of the godlings.

"Are you Anwan?" asked Malya, stepping off of the front steps as the middle-aged katabans with squinting eyes approached them.

"That would be me," said the katabans, though he didn't sound very happy. "And I presume that you two are godlings, correct?"

"Yes," said Malya, nodding. She pointed at the shop behind them. "You are the same Anwan who runs Anwan's Tailoring, yes?"

"Of course," said Anwan. "The one and only. Why do you ask?"

"We're looking for a friend of ours and we thought she might have come here," Malya said. "We were just about to leave because we didn't see anybody and the place was locked up."

Anwan said a word under his breath in a language Carmaz didn't understand, though it sounded like a curse nonetheless. Then Anwan said aloud, in a polite tone, "Oh, I am so sorry for not being here. You see, a potential customer asked me to come to his house to fix up an old shirt of his, but when I got there, it turned out that none of his clothes needed any serious repair at all. I always lock up whenever I have to make house calls like that, but I apologize for not leaving a note that you could have read. While I can speak the human language well, I cannot write in it or even read it."

Carmaz glanced at the door. There was a sign on it, but the language was completely incomprehensible to him. Of course, all written languages were incomprehensible to him, considering how Carmaz could not read, but even he could tell that the words written on the sign were different from any human language that he knew of.

"I am sorry to hear that you had to waste your time like that," said Malya. "I understand because my husband back home has a job like yours, where he often has to travel to clients' homes to do work, and sometimes there is very little or nothing for him to do."

"Bad clients are bad clients no matter their species, it seems," said Anwan. "Anyway, you mentioned something about looking for a friend?"

"Oh, yes," said Malya, nodding. "We are looking for a young Carnagian woman with blonde hair. Her name is Raya Mana and she's a godling like us. Have you seen her?"

Anwan stroked his chin, then glanced at his shop and said, "Raya Mana … ah, yes. I do recall meeting her. A pretty girl, though hardly the most polite."

"Do you know where she is now?" asked Malya. "We are looking for her because we have not seen her in a while and don't know where she is."

"I do not know, sorry," said Anwan. "Princess Raya came to my shop in order to buy a dress from me, but we could not come to an agreement, so she left. I have no idea where she went or what she is doing at the moment, though if I did, I would definitely tell you."

Malya's shoulders slumped and she said, "All right. Well, thank you for your time. We must be leaving now, since the next sub-bracket challenge is about to start soon."

"Are you sure you want to leave right away?" asked Anwan. He gestured at his shop. "I have a wide variety of the best clothes in all of World's End. Why not buy some genuine World's End clothing that you could take back with you up north as a souvenir?"

"No, thank you," said Malya, shaking her head. "While I appreciate the offer, I don't have a lot of money with me nor am I interested in buying souvenirs. Sorry."

Anwan looked disappointed, but then he nodded and said, "That's fine. Well, I need to get back in the shop, anyhow, since it's still my work day and I still have a lot of work to get to. The life of a small business owner, you know."

"Oh, I completely understand," said Malya. She sounded like she had been wanting to talk about this with someone for a while. "My husband is always busy. He never seems to have time for me, even now that we're both older and he isn't working as often as he used to due to his age. We'll let you get to work. Carmaz?"

Carmaz stepped off the front steps. Anwan nodded at him in thanks and walked up to the front door of his store, which he unlocked with a simple silver key. When Anwan opened the door and stepped inside, he froze immediately, as though he had just seen something shocking, even though Carmaz hadn't seen anything strange or terrifying in there when he had looked inside.

"Anwan?" said Malya. "Is there something wrong?"

Anwan didn't turn around. He let out a deep, almost feral snort before he said, in a voice that sounded odd to Carmaz, "It's nothing. I just thought I saw something, but I think it was just the light playing with the shadows. Nothing to worry about."

"Nothing to worry about?" Carmaz repeated. "You sound worried."

"Worried? Oh, I'm not worried," said Anwan, shaking his head, though Carmaz noticed that he still hadn't turned around. "I'm rather old, you see, and I wasn't prepared for the shock. I'll be fine. You humans wouldn't understand."

Before either Carmaz or Malya could say anything else, Anwan raised his free hand and snapped his fingers. The door swung shut behind him all on its own, the sudden movement causing Carmaz to jump back in surprise. Through the door's window, Carmaz saw Anwan's head going deeper into the shop, still without turning to look at them to see if they had left yet.

Carmaz exchanged a puzzle looked with Malya. "He seems a

145

bit ... strange."

Malya shrugged. "He *is* a katabans. They have always seemed a bit strange to me. I'm sure it's nothing to worry about."

"You're probably right," said Carmaz. "But there's something about him that I'm not sure I like."

"He seemed like a perfectly polite individual to me," Malya said, "aside from his katabans strangeness, of course."

"Well, anyway, it looks like a dead end, just as I thought it would be," said Carmaz. "I mean, it's not a complete dead end, seeing as Raya was here, but Anwan doesn't know where she is now, so it looks like we're back to square one."

"And unfortunately, I don't think we have any time to visit any other tailor, seeing as the next sub-bracket challenge is starting very soon," said Malya. "That means we won't be able to find Raya until after the challenge is over, at least."

"Looks like it," said Carmaz. "But again, I'm sure she is just fine. I think we'd know if she was in any actual trouble. Most likely, Alira will send someone to find her and bring her to the challenge."

"Guess you're right," said Malya, though she didn't sound happy about that. "Let's head on over to the Stadium, then. If we leave now, we should be able to get there in time for the next sub-bracket challenge."

So Carmaz and Malya walked down the street in the direction of the Stadium. Even so, Carmaz looked over his shoulder one last time at Anwan's Tailoring. Anwan may have just been a normal katabans behaving in a normal katabans way, but Carmaz had a feeling that there was more to the tailor than met the eye.

I don't need to focus on that, Carmaz thought, shaking his head as he turned his attention to the street they walked upon. *At least I kept Malya from trying to visit Braim. Though now that I think about it, I wonder how the Ghostly God's studying of Braim is coming along. Maybe I'll hear back from him on it after this sub-bracket challenge is over.*

Chapter Thirteen

WATCHING THE GHOSTLY God's mansion explode was rather satisfying to Braim. He hadn't realized that it would be, but after what the Ghostly God had put him through, Braim found that he didn't feel at all sorry for the Ghostly God's loss.

But even so, Braim still had to duck to avoid the debris that was flung his way. So did Aorja, though she did it with a wild smile on her face even when one piece of flaming wood almost clipped her forehead. She looked like she had been waiting for this to happen for a long time, though most of Braim's attention right now was on the fight between the Ghostly God and Zeeree.

The Ghostly God had been taken by surprise by the explosion. He looked over his shoulder at the burning wreckage of the mansion, while Zeeree kept swinging his fists at the deity. Due to the fact that the Ghostly God was still intangible, however, Zeeree's fists continued to fail to hit him. The half-god didn't seem to notice, however, because his attacks were as ferocious as ever, even when a chunk of burning wood from the mansion flew through the intangible Ghostly God and struck him in the face.

"Zeeree!" Aorja shouted, her voice sounding much louder than usual, probably due to her using magic to increase its volume. "Come on! It's time to go!"

Zeeree immediately stopped trying to hit the Ghostly God and then ran toward Aorja and Braim faster than Braim expected a being of his size and weight to be able to move. With the light from the flames casting his front into shadow, Zeeree looked like a monster, though Braim stayed where he was rather than run away.

But before Zeeree could get very far, the Ghostly God materialized in front of him and slugged him in the face with one powerful punch. The blow sent Zeeree falling flat on his back, an impact which created a slight yet noticeable tremor in the earth.

"Zeeree!" Aorja shouted, this time much more fearfully than before. "No!"

Much to Braim's surprise, Zeeree actually got back to his feet. He swung his fists at the Ghostly God again, but as always, they hit nothing. The Ghostly God then responded by grabbing Zeeree and lifting him above his head. The half-god roared in anger and flailed his arms and legs, but he was practically powerless in the Ghostly God's hands.

"Foolish beast," said the Ghostly God, who did not sound like he was even putting any effort into holding Zeeree. "I am tired of wasting my time with you, especially now that I see that you were nothing more than a distraction to trick me while your mistress destroyed my mansion."

The Ghostly God hurled Zeeree into the burning and smoking debris of the mansion. Zeeree fell with an earsplitting *crash*, followed by a roar of pain from the fire, but before he could get up, the Ghostly God raised his hand and fired a burst of energy that caused the partially standing wall to collapse onto Zeeree with an almighty *boom*. Zeeree did not rise again.

"No!" Aorja screamed, her voice almost breaking. "Zeeree! Zeeree!"

Braim stood up and grabbed Aorja's arm. "Listen, Aorja, we got to run. There's no way we can defeat the Ghostly God on our own."

But Aorja was clearly not listening to a word he said. She looked as distraught as a mother watching her only child in pain. She wrenched her arm out of Braim's grasp and dashed out into the open, causing Braim to shout after her to come back, but again, she didn't listen.

The Ghostly God turned to face Aorja as she ran up to him. He merely smiled at her appearance, which Braim did not take to be a very good sign. "Aorja Kitano. I wondered when you—"

He was interrupted by Aorja pointing her wand at him and firing a burst of flame from it. The fire hurled through the air toward the Ghostly God, but he dissipated into mist before it and the fire flew past where he had been floating and struck the ground behind him, causing more flames to rise from the earth.

The Ghostly God rematerialized immediately, now wearing a bored expression on his face. "Is that how you say hello to your old master?"

"I wasn't saying hello," said Aorja, her voice shaky, despite the steady aim of her wand. "I was trying to kill you for hurting Zeeree."

The Ghostly God shook his head in disbelief. "Foolish girl, you *do* know that mortals can't actually *kill* gods, correct? Even the most powerful mage in the world could never hope to even harm me. I know you typically make decisions based on your emotions, but I thought that enough reason was left in you to remind you that taking on a god—especially a southern god beyond the Dividing Line—is a very *bad* idea."

"The only bad idea is messing with me," said Aorja. "Take this!"

Aorja teleported and reappeared behind the Ghostly God. The Ghostly God turned just in time to get blasted by a burst of electricity, which hit him in the chest.

But despite taking the blow head on, the Ghostly God didn't even flinch. He just grabbed Aorja by the neck and lifted her off her feet, knocking her wand out of her hand as he did so. Aorja kicked and punched, but her blows were even less effective against the Ghostly God than Zeeree's were.

"I should kill you right away, you little brat," said the Ghostly God. "You betrayed the gods twice, first by allying with Jakuuth Grinfborn and then by helping Uron escape the ethereal. The gods have a long memory for that sort of thing, you know. I'll tear you apart limb by limb for your crimes, which is far more merciful than what the others would do to you, given the chance."

Braim wasn't much of a fan of Aorja, mostly because she was a madwoman who didn't care much for him. But Braim also realized that Aorja was his only ticket off this crazy island, which meant that he would have to figure out how to save her no matter what.

But I don't have any magic, Braim thought. *I'm useless, especially against a god.*

Despite that fact, Braim decided to try his best anyway. He dashed out from the undergrowth, grabbing a large chunk of still-hot wood from the mansion's explosion, and then hurled it at the Ghostly God's back.

151

The chunk of wood sailed harmlessly through the Ghostly God's form, but it was enough to cause the Ghostly God to look over his shoulder at Braim. That gave Aorja the opportunity to act. There was a bright flash where Aorja's hands touched the Ghostly God's arm and the deity let out a shout of pain and dropped Aorja, who upon falling to the ground rolled over to her discarded wand and snatched it from the earth.

But Braim wasn't looking at Aorja anymore. He was looking at the Ghostly God, who was now behaving in a very strange manner.

The Ghostly God was gripping his arm. Or rather, where his arm had been moments before. It was now nothing more than a slightly misty metal stump. It wasn't bleeding or anything, but the Ghostly God held it like it was. Not only that, but the Ghostly God groaned and cursed in pain in a language that Braim didn't understand at all (though he guessed the meaning of the Ghostly God's curses quickly enough).

The Ghostly God looked at Aorja, who was now smirking at him with that same psychotic smirk from before.

"Oh, what's this?" said Aorja in a mocking tone. "You look like you're in pain. I didn't meant to hurt you that much. Just enough to make you let go of me."

"What ... did ... you ... do?" asked the Ghostly God. He actually sounded like he was in pain. "You shouldn't ... have even been able to so much as *touch* me ... how ..."

"Do you think I've spent the last month in hiding doing nothing but cowering and hoping that the gods don't find me?" asked Aorja.

"It would seem ... a logical conclusion to come to,

considering how easily frightened you mortals are," said the Ghostly God. "But clearly, you didn't."

"Of course not," said Aorja. "I've been studying the history of heathenism in this world, trying to find out how to hurt you gods. As it turns out, there are a variety of ways for us mortals to hurt gods. Still can't kill you, but we can still cause you a lot of pain if we want."

"I suppose … you aren't feeling charitable enough to explain exactly what technique you used to hurt me," said the Ghostly God.

"It's called magical overload," said Aorja. "I'm a Limitless, so all I did was channel my magical energy into your arm. Your arm couldn't take it, so it exploded."

The Ghostly God gritted his teeth. "Very clever, mortal girl, but cleverness won't save you by itself."

The Ghostly God raised the stump of his arm and focused on it. Mist came from nowhere and coalesced over his stump until it took the shape of his arm, which then solidified into a physical arm that looked just like the other one. He twisted his arm back and forth as if to test it before looking at Aorja again.

"So much for that," said the Ghostly God. "I am back to normal. That was a neat little trick that I will admit I didn't see coming, but that doesn't change the fact that I am going to tear you apart piece by piece, as I said before."

Then the Ghostly God shot Braim a dark look. "Don't think I've forgotten about you, either, Braim. I am simply taking this moment to deal with the more immediate threat."

"Hey, no one kills beautiful women while I'm around," said Braim, stepping forward, despite his fear. "Especially beautiful women who are my only way off this damn island."

"Talk all you like, but it won't convince me to let you go," said the Ghostly God. He turned his attention back to Aorja. "Now—"

Aorja waved her wand and a giant gray hand materialized out of nowhere around the Ghostly God. It clamped around him and tightened, causing him to gasp. He struggled against it, but to Braim, it looked like Aorja had the Ghostly God good and caught.

"Hand of Divinity," said Aorja without missing a beat. "Hand made of pure magical energy. Capable of holding down any god for as long as the Hand's summoner has the magical energy to power it. And lucky you, I am a Limitless, so I'll never run out of magical energy."

The Ghostly God continued to struggle against it, but it didn't even budge under his effort. Then the Ghostly God turned into a cloud of mist and flew up, which also caused the Hand of Divinity to vanish.

Rematerializing in the air, the Ghostly God pointed his hand at Aorja again, but Aorja matched his movement and aimed her wand at him. A loud *bang* made Braim cover his ears, while a purplish liquid shot from Aorja's wand and struck the Ghostly God in the chest.

The liquid rapidly covered the Ghostly God's surface, creating hissing noises wherever it touched and making the Ghostly God scream in pain. He tried to wipe the liquid off, but all his efforts seemed to do was spread it around even more.

"Anti-divinity acid," said Aorja. "Capable of eating through the skin of a god. Can't actually kill a god, obviously, but it certainly leaves its mark and is very hard to get rid of if you don't know how."

Braim had to admit that it was amazing to see the Ghostly God struggling with the anti-divinity acid. He actually rather enjoyed it, not because of any animosity he may have felt toward the gods, but because of how the Ghostly God had treated him. It felt good to see the southern god get what was coming to him.

But even as Braim stood there thinking this, he realized that this was the perfect opportunity for him and Aorja to escape. He ran over to her and, grabbing her arm, said, "Aorja, we have got to get out of here now!"

Aorja looked at Braim, but it was not in mere annoyance that she looked at him. She looked like she had completely lost her mind, because he didn't see any sanity left in her eyes at all. In fact, he was almost afraid to touch her or even talk to her, even though he wasn't sure that she was going to attack him.

"What are you babbling about?" said Aorja. "Let go of me or I'll do to you what I'm doing to the Ghostly God, only a thousand times worse."

"Because we have to leave before the Ghostly God recovers," Braim said. "I mean, you yourself said that you still can't kill the Ghostly God even with your magic. If we run now, we can get back to World's End without—"

"No!" Aorja shouted. She pointed her wand directly into his face, the craziness in her eyes making her look more like a wild animal than an intelligent human being. "I have waited too long to do this to him. And then he hurt Zeeree, which is unforgivable. Go away!"

Braim let go of her arm and staggered backwards, but Aorja swished her wand and pointed it at him again. Braim suddenly went flying backwards through the air, completely incapable of controlling his trajectory. He landed hard on the damp grass, the impact knocking his breath from his lungs. He then looked up to see Aorja turning her attention back to the Ghostly God, who was still struggling with the anti-divinity acid.

Braim scrambled back to his feet, feeling his chest hurt from where Aorja's spell had hit it, though he didn't think it was going to leave any lasting damage on his body. Thus, he was about to call out to Aorja again and see if he could reason with her (as doubtful as that was) when the Ghostly God—who had been frantically trying to wipe off the acid on his chest for the past few minutes—successfully got rid of the last of it.

As soon as he did, Aorja pointed her wand at him again, but then the Ghostly God pointed at her even faster. A beam of energy shot out from the Ghostly God's outstretched hand and struck Aorja's wand hand, sending her wand flying out of her hand and into the surrounding darkness and out of sight.

Yet that didn't stop Aorja from pointing her hands at the Ghostly God, even though using magic without a wand was generally a bad idea. But she didn't even get a chance to cast any spells that way, because the Ghostly God unleashed black lightning bolts from his own fingertips at her.

The black lightning bolts struck Aorja in the chest, sending her flying. She landed hard on the grass several feet away, but did not move or get up. Her eyes were closed.

The Ghostly God hovered toward her, the anger in his eyes as bright as the flames from the burning debris of his mansion behind him. He stopped over Aorja and looked down at her with disgust.

"Foolish mortal girl," said the Ghostly God. He raised one hand. "It looks like I will have to deal with you permanently."

Before he could kill her, Zeeree's familiar roar cut through the air. Braim looked over just in time to see Zeeree burst out from underneath the wall that had fallen on him and run toward the Ghostly God with murder clear on his face. The half-god's upper body was scarred and burned, while his legs were blackened and even melted in a few spots, though that didn't slow him down at all.

The Ghostly God turned around in time to receive a punch in the face from Zeeree. Surprisingly, it hit this time, causing the Ghostly God to stagger backwards, but he recovered quickly and started blocking Zeeree's punches just as quickly as Zeeree could throw them. He looked rather frustrated at this turn of events, like he was angry that Zeeree had survived and was trying to kill him again.

Braim considered running over and dragging Aorja out of the way. But both the Ghostly God and Zeeree were fighting too closely together for him to risk trying to save her. If he got caught in the middle of that fight, he'd probably get torn to shreds.

But what can *I do?* Braim thought, taking a step back involuntarily. *No magic, but can't get off the island without Aorja, either. And I can't help Zeeree much, if at all and the Ghostly God is too powerful for someone like me to even touch. There's nothing I can do to help.*

Braim hated standing around indecisively, so he decided that now was the perfect time to run while the Ghostly God was distracted. Even if Aorja had not been knocked unconscious, he still didn't trust her to actually take him off the island, much less take him back to World's End where he needed to go.

So Braim turned and ran into the surrounding jungle, ignoring Zeeree's roars and the Ghostly God's energy blasts behind him. He did not know where he was going or how he was going to get off the island, but he figured out what to do after he was safe from the Ghostly God's insanity.

Chapter Fourteen

RAYA ALMOST SCREAMED when she saw the corpse. But something about the darkness and secretive nature of this cave caused her words to get caught halfway in her throat, which made her scream come out as a tiny, rather pathetic yelp.

Even when Raya realized that the corpse was not going to move, she still had a hard time remaining calm. It was covered by a thick blue sheet, so Raya didn't know who it was, but the identity of the corpse didn't matter to her right now. What mattered more to her was how it had gotten here in the first place.

Oh my god, Raya thought, her hands shaking. *Oh my god. Is Anwan some kind of crazy serial killer? Is this the body of one of his victims? May Grinf have mercy on them.*

Raya felt so sick at the sight of the covered corpse that she threw up. She didn't want to—she hated throwing up—but her lunch came out of her mouth without her approval and splattered all over the floor and onto her shoes.

Raya leaned against the frame of the doorway, shuddering and heaving. She didn't think she was going to throw up again, but she didn't want to move, either, because she found herself morbidly curious about this room, even though her instincts told her to get out of there and find someone—*anyone*—and tell them about it.

Preferably one of the Soldiers of the Gods or maybe even one of the gods themselves if possible.

Despite all of that, Raya stayed where she was. She listened closely to the stairs behind herself, but did not hear anyone coming down. She assumed that Yag must have still been keeping Anwan busy, but of course she could not know for sure how long he could distract the tailor. It was entirely possible that Anwan was already on his way back, but Raya decided not to think about that because it made her panicky.

Aside from the covered corpse lying in the middle of a circle made of dried blood (or red paint, but it looked like dried blood to her), Raya noticed a few other strange things about this chamber. The walls were painted a deep black—the exact same shade as the darkness of the Void, disturbingly enough—but there was a single word written on them over and over again in white ink. Unfortunately, the word was not written in any language that Raya could read, but she was happy about that because she had a feeling that that word was not a good one.

Another thing Raya noticed was a desk in one corner that had papers written on it. And next to that desk, hanging off a rack built into the wall, was a black and gray cloak that looked almost like the robes of a mage, but somehow they looked much scarier than any mage's robes that Raya had seen.

But Raya did not feel like entering the room to find out more, because her nose was assaulted by the awful stink of death she smelled in this place, not helped by the fact that it was mixed together with the stink of her vomit. It seemed to be coming mostly from the corpse that lay underneath the blue sheet, but it also seemed to be coming from the room itself, as if many people had died here and been left to rot in the past.

That theory became more likely to Raya when she noticed a bucket in one corner full of bones. They did not look quite like human bones—probably katabans bones—but the mere sight of those bones was enough to make her stomach churn.

Okay, I've seen enough, Raya thought. *Time to get out. Must return to the Stadium.*

But despite telling her that, Raya didn't actually back out. She walked into the room, being careful to avoid stepping in her own vomit, and looked around at her surroundings. The entire place reminded her of the Temple of Grinf's Room of Justice back on Carnag, except that this place was a lot tinier and darker. It was like this room had been built as a place of worship, but Raya did not know which god was worshiped here or what kind of rituals that worshipers performed here.

Raya made her way to the back of the room, where the desk was (while also carefully avoiding looking at the corpse), because she figured that the desk would be where she would be able to find some answers. She almost stopped to peek under the blue sheet covering the corpse to see who it was, but just thinking about that corpse made her feel sick, so she didn't. She would let the Soldiers of the Gods or whoever look under it for her instead, after she told them about what she'd found.

It didn't take her long to reach the desk, but when she did, she was disappointed to discover that most of the papers were written in that same strange language as the lone word on the walls was.

Just what is *this language, anyway?* Raya thought, frowning as she lifted up a stack of papers and turned them around. *Looks like Godly Divina, but it seems different, too, as if it isn't.*

161

Although Raya could not read the words, she did see drawings on them. Not that that was very helpful, because most of the images made no sense to her. One drawing showed what might have been World's End, except it was engulfed by a large, tentacled beast that was unlike anything Raya had seen before. Another showed a skeletal hand carrying a large, jagged knife that appeared to be cutting through someone's chest. Most of the drawings were too faded and old for her to make out, but what she could see and understand made her sick to her stomach.

This is awful, Raya thought. *Absolutely awful. Who in the world would do such an awful thing and make such an awful place? Did Anwan do this or is someone else using this place without his knowledge?*

Raya's questioned was answered when she noticed the black Void metal knife on the desk, the one that she had found in Anwan's office earlier. She picked it up, along with its sheath because it was still sheathed, and looked it over once, but that was unnecessary because she had already known just from glancing at it that this knife was the same one from before.

The only way it could have gotten down here is if Anwan took it down here, Raya thought, trembling where she stood. *And Anwan could have only taken it down here if he knew about this place's existence. Which means ...*

Raya didn't know what that meant or what any of this meant. It seemed likely to her that Anwan was insane, a psychotic murderer who liked to hide the bodies of innocent people beneath his shop for his own ghoulish reasons. She wondered why the gods did not already know this, seeing as Anwan's Tailoring was right in the middle of World's End after all, but it didn't matter to her why that was. She just knew that she needed to get out of here now, before Anwan returned. She had a feeling that Anwan was not going to treat her well if he found her snooping around in his … whatever this room was.

"Hello, Princess Raya," said the familiar voice of Anwan behind her, before she could turn to leave. "I see you are lost."

Still holding Anwan's sheathed knife, Raya turned to face him. Anwan was standing in the doorway, still wearing that same tacky suit from before, but there was something about his body language that made him look far more threatening than before.

His eyes darted to the vomit at his feet. "Oh, dear. It looks like you must have gotten a little sick and couldn't help yourself. A perfectly natural response to what you just discovered, of course, but I can't help but feel *annoyed* that a grown woman like yourself couldn't clean up your own vomit. I guess you think you're a little too *good* for that, eh?"

Raya gulped. With Anwan in the doorway, there was no way that Raya could possibly escape. At least she didn't see any other escape routes out of here. She supposed there could have been a secret trapdoor somewhere, but the odds of her finding it were so low as to be nonexistent, so Raya focused on figuring out how to get past Anwan instead.

Anwan pulled his little string out of his pocket, which he began to play with like he had the first time Raya met him. It had seemed like a relatively harmless habit to Raya initially, but now Raya could hardly think of a more threatening gesture.

"Cat got your tongue?" asked Anwan. He scowled. "Or just too *good* to respond to a poor peasant like myself?"

Raya shook her head. "What … why are you here?"

"Well, princess, it might have to do with the fact that your stupid little friend—that uneducated wretch who can't even sweep streets all that well—succeeded only in wasting my time," said Anwan. "He wasn't very smart or clever. Almost as soon as I entered his apartment, I knew the idiot had lied to me. I thought about killing him—I was so angry I could have done it—but it would have been too risky, because there were other katabans nearby and I couldn't have killed him quietly or without getting blood all over my hands. That's why I decided to go back to the shop, but you know, I also realized that the idiot had perhaps been trying to distract me from something, probably put up to it by someone infinitely smarter than him. Looks like my intuition was correct."

Damn it, Yag, Raya thought. *You were supposed to keep him occupied until I was done.*

But Raya didn't say that out loud. Instead, she said, "You're right. I enlisted Yag's help so I could break in here without your knowledge."

Anwan chuckled. "Let me guess, was it for the red dress? I'm sure that it was. You wanted that dress more than anything else in the world. Don't try to pretend otherwise. I have decades of experience in dealing with fashion-conscious young women like you and I know when women like you really want a dress and will do anything to get it. It's rather silly, greed is, but I keep such thoughts to myself so I can make good money."

Raya unsheathed the knife and held it close to her chest. "Well, I have no idea what this place is or what your plans are, but if you don't let me out, I will stab you with your own knife and tell the gods about your horrible deeds."

Anwan twisted the little string in his hands, an amused expression on his face. "You're an awful liar for a candidate for the next Goddess of Deception. You couldn't stab me even if your life depended on it. You aren't that strong. Your hands are shaking, after all, and you look awfully pale."

Raya looked down at her hands. They were indeed shaking. She managed to stop them, but the fear and stress of the situation was still affecting her, making it hard to put on a brave face.

"Now why don't you put down the knife before you hurt yourself?" asked Anwan, gesturing at the desk behind her. "No need to play the brave hero when you are nothing more than a spoiled brat. And spoiled brats have a tendency to get themselves killed when they refuse to listen to their elders."

Raya, however, did not put the knife down at all, because she was painfully aware that it was the only reason Anwan had not yet killed her in cold blood. "If you want it so much, why don't you come and take it from me, you freak?"

"Freak? How am I a freak, when you are the half human, half katabans hybrid?" asked Anwan. "By all rights, you shouldn't even exist, because humans and katabans are never supposed to mix. That makes you similar to Braim Kotogs in some ways, although at least he's a pure human."

Anger shot up in Raya as she pointed the knife at Anwan and said, "Take that back, you foul little tailor. I am not a freak. I am the Princess of Carnag and I shall be treated as such."

"Royal titles mean as little to me as the mews of a kitten do to you," said Anwan. "All I see is the pathetic daughter of a traitor to our species, the daughter of a woman who joined the humans because she thought she was better than us and who shared our secrets with them. I would have drowned you as a baby and made sure that a freak like you wouldn't grow up to ruin the world with your unnaturalness."

Anwan's words bit deeply and sharply into Raya's mind, causing her to say, "How dare you say such evil things to me! If Father were here—"

"I have even less respect for your father, the king who helped bring Skimif into existence, than I do for you," said Anwan. "But please, freak, keep telling me what your father or your mother or your nanny or whatever would do if they were here. I might just remember to cower in fear and let you go, like a good katabans."

"I will still hurt you if you try to hurt me," said Raya. "Now let me go or else."

"You mean that you aren't the slightest bit curious about this place?" said Anwan, gesturing at the room in which they stood, though he didn't let go of his string as he did so. "I thought you were going to ask me to explain to you what I do down here."

"I don't need to know that," said Raya, shaking her head. "All I know is that you are up to no good. I will let the gods figure out what you were doing down here. My job is to make sure that the world knows about your wickedness."

"Again, you assume I am just going to let you go when you have no proof to back up that assumption," said Anwan. He tugged his string twice. "Had you simply gone into the back room, I would have let you go without any issue. Unfortunately, you have seen far too much, so I will have to make sure you never leave alive."

Anwan sighed and looked at the ceiling. "And that means I will need to come up with a convincing reason for your disappearance. I've had to do it before, of course, but it is always an unpleasant and grueling task for me, because my mind is good at putting together material into beautiful or functional clothing, not at putting together elaborate lies and deceptions to deflect suspicion off of myself."

Raya didn't see how Anwan could kill her, because he was unarmed and she was not, but she needed time to come up with a way to get past him, so she said, "I don't understand. If you katabans serve the gods, then why are you threatening to kill me? I thought that the katabans on World's End were supposed to protect me and the others or at least leave us alone for the duration of the Tournament."

"You are assuming that I serve the gods at all," said Anwan. He laughed. "I haven't truly served them with my heart for decades. I have thrown in my lot with another group, one not quite as powerful as the gods, but who serve a master much greater than they."

"And who might they be?" asked Raya. She realized that her hands were shaking again, causing her to consciously focus on them to make them stop.

"They're a group of katabans known as the Empty," said Anwan. "They've existed for years now, but have not been able to operate in the open due to the identity of the force that they worship. I count myself among them because I can tell the way that history is turning and I would rather not find myself on the losing side, if you catch my drift."

"Who is their master?" asked Raya.

Anwan tied his string into a little knot before undoing it entirely. "She goes under many names, as beings of her stature tend to, but the one she is known best under—the one you mortals are most familiar with—is the Void."

Raya's eyes widened. "You mean to say that there is an entire cult of katabans who worship the Void?"

"Correct," said Anwan. "We are a minority, have always been a minority, but that has not stopped us from existing against both the persecution from our fellow katabans and the divine mandates of the gods. Despite our name, we are far from empty, I hope you understand."

Raya gestured at the room in which they stood. "So what is this place, then? Some kind of worship site where you freaks worship the Void?"

"Of course," said Anwan, nodding. "But this isn't the only one of its kind on World's End. We have worship sites for the Void everywhere. We have to, because every time one is discovered, it's always destroyed and the people who worshiped in it are usually killed. Mine just happens to be one of the most well-hidden, because not even the gods would think to check for a Void worship site inside the shop of a tailor, particularly the shop of the most famous tailor on the whole island."

Anwan sounded quite pleased with himself, while Raya felt more disgusted than anything. She was also starting to feel sick to her stomach, but she didn't have anything else to throw up, so she just ended up feeling very ill.

Raya gestured at the corpse under the blue sheet. "And who is that and why are they here? Do you Void followers eat the dead?"

Anwan made a disgusted sound. "Eat the dead? Honestly, princess, I thought you had a higher opinion of me than that. No, we do not eat the dead. We normally do not even have the dead at our gatherings. This corpse has a grander purpose than being someone's lunch, I can assure you."

"What is that 'grander purpose,' then?" said Raya. "And why couldn't it have been placed inside a coffin, at the very least?"

"A coffin would have gotten in the way," said Anwan. Then he frowned. "But what am I doing, giving away our secrets to you? The Void would be rather angry if she learned that I was revealing all of our secret plans to a known enemy like you. Not that there's much you can do about them, of course, but you still shouldn't be allowed to know them, because knowledge is power, after all, and the Void does not want anyone to have more power than her."

"I guess you aren't going to tell me who is under the sheet, then," said Raya. "Let me guess: It's just some random dead person, right?"

"Actually," said Anwan, a devious smile crossing his lips, "showing you the corpse actually *is* something I can show you. Look and tell me whether you recognize this person at all."

Anwan stopped playing with his string long enough to snap his fingers. The top of the blue sheet folded open, probably due to Anwan's telekinesis, which revealed the face of the corpse lying on the floor.

It was the face of Saia, Carmaz's friend, except with darker, grayer skin that was almost black. His eyes were closed, his chest still.

Then the blue sheet went back over Saia's face, blocking it from view. Yet Raya still saw Saia's face in her mind's eye, because it was too striking of a mental image for her to forget.

"Was that ..." Raya tried to find the words, but it was hard because even her body was shaking now. "Was that Saia?"

"Indeed it was," said Anwan, nodding. "Or *is*, I should say, since that is his body, the very same one that the Void consumed after her first attack on World's End a week ago. She gave it to me for safekeeping."

"I thought that the Void had destroyed it," said Raya. "I mean, isn't that what the Void always does? Isn't that why we say that it 'consumes' people?"

"The Void does not have to destroy what she takes if she does not want to," said Anwan. "The Void can spare the bodies of those she kills if she wants. Ultimately, all is meant to be consumed by the Void, but she can put off consuming completely if she has a greater plan for it."

"And why is it in a circle of blood down here?" asked Raya. She inched to the right, though she hoped that Anwan didn't notice. "What does the circle of blood mean?"

"It has a purpose, but I am not at liberty to divulge that purpose to you or anyone else," said Anwan. He looked at Saia's covered body. "What matters is that the Void has her reasons for what she does and I am not to question them, only to follow her orders to the best of my ability."

"Why don't the gods know about this?" asked Raya. She thought she saw an opening—Anwan seemed distracted by his string, so if she ran at him quickly, she might be able to take him by surprise. "I can't see them tolerating this sort of behavior from one of their subjects, especially on their own island."

"The gods may be powerful, but they are not all-knowing," said Anwan. "The Empty have worked for ages to hide ourselves from the gods' watchful eyes. Besides, the gods are so arrogant that they would never suspect that anyone would dare attempt to create such a place right under their noses. And by the time they realize the truth, it will be too late for them and for Martir in general. All shall be consumed by the Void."

Now Raya was certain that Anwan would not expect her to charge at him with his knife. She just needed to gather the courage to attack him, but it was difficult due to a combination of her empty stomach and her tiredness from opening that ethereal portal earlier.

But maybe I don't need to attack him at all, Raya thought. *Maybe all I need to do is open another ethereal portal and escape.*

But Raya shot down that idea as soon as it came to her mind. Aside from the fact that she was too tired to open another portal, there was the simple fact that Anwan was also a katabans and likely had decades, maybe even centuries, worth of experience in opening those types of portals. Even if she managed to open one, Anwan might just go after her and drag her back here, where he'd finish the job.

Looks like I need to stab the bastard in the face, Raya thought. *Not that that frightens me, of course.*

"Now, then," said Anwan, still twisting his little string. "I think we are about done here. You and I have talked long enough. It was unpleasant knowing you, Raya, knowing you and your mother, who I imagine will scream once she sees your mutilated corpse."

Anwan took a step forward, but Raya said, "Wait!" causing him to stop, much to her surprise.

"Wait for what?" said Anwan.

Raya had to steady her hands again, which seemed to shake every time she stopped paying attention to them, and then said, "Well, I was going to ask you about the red dress. Do you still have it? I didn't see it when I was looking through the backroom, so I thought that you might be able to tell me where it is."

Anwan looked at her in disbelief. "You are seriously asking about the location of a petty, insignificant dress when your own life is on the line?"

"I was just asking," said Raya, "to distract you."

Moving as quickly as she could, Raya threw the Void metal knife at Anwan. But Anwan opened an ethereal portal behind himself and stepped into it. As soon as he did, the portal closed and the knife flew harmlessly into the darkness of the staircase behind him.

Seeing her chance, Raya ran around Saia's corpse, heading for the now unblocked doorway, before another ethereal portal opened up in front of her. Raya skid to a stop as Anwan stepped out of the portal, a vicious snarl on his face. He grabbed Raya by the shoulders and shoved her to the floor. The back of her head smacked against the floor, causing her to cry out in pain, but before she could do anything else, Anwan stepped on her chest and pinned her to the floor. Despite his aged appearance, his foot held her down with surprising strength, even when she grabbed his ankle and tried to shove him off.

Then Anwan jabbed his arm to the left and the Void metal knife flew out of the shadows and into his hand. He then raised the knife above his head, a gleam of madness in his eyes.

"Don't worry about your clothes, Raya," said Anwan with an evil smile on his face. "I promise not to get too much blood on your clothes, but I cannot promise that your death will not be painless."

Chapter Fifteen

CARMAZ SAT DOWN in the back row of the Stadium box. To his right was Malya, who still seemed worried about Raya, even though there was no reason at all to assume she was in trouble. Upon arriving at the Stadium, he and Malya had told Alira that Raya was missing, but the Judge had assured them that she was going to send someone to locate Raya and that the next sub-bracket challenge was going to begin with or without her. That had assuaged Malya's fears somewhat, but Carmaz still noticed how Malya kept glancing toward the exit, as if she thought that Raya was going to walk in any minute now and join them. Carmaz understood Malya's worries, but he found it hard to care because he was enjoying the lack of Raya's annoying and unwanted flirtation.

He tried to focus purely on the vision bubbles before them that showed the participants in the Spider Goddess Sub-Bracket Challenge. In particular, he focused on the vision bubble that showed Tashir, who was competing with another aquarian, a female who had a squid-like head.

From what Carmaz understood of this challenge, it required the two challengers participating in it to climb up a gigantic spider web to a platform near the top of the ceiling, with the first person to reach the platform being declared the winner of the challenge and going on to the main bracket challenge later on. That sounded like a simple challenge in theory, but the webbing was quite sticky and unstable, which meant that the challengers could not simply rush up as quickly as they could. Speed was still a necessary part of the challenge, of course, but they also had to be careful, lest they get stuck or accidentally fall off (as happened to one unfortunate challenger, who had almost reached the top before he made the wrong move and fell all the way to the ground, although he thankfully survived the fall due to the fact that the floor had been replaced with a soft, spongy substance).

Tashir and his opponent were neck and neck with each other. They were scaling the webbing with special gloves and boots given to them by Alira prior to the start of the challenge so that they would not get their hands and feet caught on the webbing. Tashir didn't have his sword with him, probably because he didn't need it for the challenge, although Carmaz realized that the sword would have also weighed him down unnecessarily, which would have made it harder for him to reach the top.

In any case, Carmaz was convinced that Tashir was going to win. The makhimancer displayed a certain proficiency with his climbing abilities that told Carmaz that Tashir was a good climber, much better than his opponent, even though the two were currently equal. But even Carmaz could tell that Tashir's opponent—whose name he did not know, although he had seen her before—was a lot more hesitant about the climb than Tashir was, like she was not used to this kind of physical feat.

Sitting back, Carmaz once again thought about the Ghostly God and Braim. He wished that the Ghostly God would contact him with even a vague update on how his experiments with Braim were progressing. Carmaz especially hoped that the Ghostly God returned Braim right away. He knew that it was only a matter of time now before someone went to check up on Braim and discovered that he was missing.

I doubt anyone would suspect me of having anything to do with it, but I bet that the Ghostly God will put all of the blame on me so he doesn't have to deal with the inevitable outrage from the rest of the gods, Carmaz thought. *But would that result in me being kicked out of the Tournament?*

Carmaz eyed Alira. She was watching the vision bubbles as well, but he knew just how easily she would disqualify Carmaz if she found out that he had broken the rules. The idea of being kicked out of the Tournament made Carmaz feel a little ill, but he told himself that if the Ghostly God could figure out how to bring Saia back to life, then it would be worth it.

Besides, the Ghostly God said he'd wipe Braim's memory clean after he was done with him, Carmaz thought. *And replace them with fake memories of his sickness. That way, no one ever has to know the truth about what happened to Braim, not even Braim himself, except for me and the Ghostly God, of course.*

Still, Carmaz's conscience ate at him, because he knew that what he was doing was wrong. And under ordinary circumstances, he would never do such a thing to anyone, not even to his worst enemy.

Not like these are ordinary circumstances, though, Carmaz thought. *I'm in line to become a god, the Void is actively seeking to destroy us, and I am actually working with a god. There is nothing ordinary about my current situation, no matter how you look at it.*

To Carmaz's right sat the young mage known as Yoji. This would have annoyed Carmaz, because Yoji had an annoying tendency to drone on and on about the various obscure branches of knowledge that he was a master of to anyone who would listen. It was one of the reasons why he usually avoided the mage, because Carmaz didn't have a lot of patience for that kind of nonsense.

But today, Yoji was very quiet, sitting in his seat and watching the vision bubbles with interested eyes. His wand was on his lap, but he didn't seem like he was going to be casting any spells anytime soon.

Yoji being silent was normally a good thing, but today Braim found it even harder to ignore than the mage's incessant blabbering about this or that subject. He wondered if there was something wrong with Yoji.

Thinking that he was going to regret asking, Carmaz said, "You sure seem quiet today, Yoji."

Yoji looked at Carmaz, then looked back at Tashir's vision bubble. "You don't happen to be a mage or in any way magical, do you, Carmaz?"

Carmaz scratched his right ear. "No, I'm not. Why?"

"Because I prefer to speak only with other mages, of course," said Yoji. He looked at Carmaz again, except this time with youthful arrogance etched on his features. "Not that you are an idiot or anything, but I know that non-mages typically struggle to understand the things that we mages speak of. So I am just going to sit here and watch the challenge instead of talk to you about issues that you are obviously ignorant of."

Carmaz wasn't sure if he should be offended by what Yoji

said or not. On one hand, Yoji was correct that Carmaz was not a mage and was not interested in magic or discussion about magic. On the other hand, Carmaz was pretty sure that Yoji was implying that he was an idiot, even if he said otherwise.

Shaking his head, Carmaz just returned his attention to the vision bubble showing Tashir's challenge before Malya said, "Carmaz?"

Carmaz looked at her. "Yes?"

"Do you sense anything?" asked Malya. "Anything … off?"

"Off?" Carmaz repeated. "I don't understand."

"Well, it is hard to describe," Malya said. "But when I say 'off,' I mean that something feels like it shouldn't be."

Carmaz was annoyed by Malya's vague concerns, so he said, "Such as what, exactly? You aren't being very specific."

Malya rubbed her hands together and said, "I am thinking in particular of Raya and Braim. No one knows where Raya is—"

"She's fine," Carmaz interrupted her. "Why do you keep worrying about her?"

"Because it isn't normal for a godling to vanish like this," said Malya. "Especially one like her. I am fearful for her safety."

"Alira said she has someone looking for her," said Carmaz. He glanced at the Judge, who like the rest of the people in the room was not paying him or Malya any attention. "I bet Raya just got lost. World's End is a huge city, after all. She'll turn up eventually."

Malya nodded, though she still looked concerned. "What about that Anwan fellow? The one who said he didn't know where Raya was?"

"What about him?" asked Carmaz. "He seemed like a

perfectly normal person to me. Or as normal as a katabans can be, anyway."

"Yes, but there was something about him that I didn't like," said Malya. "Didn't you feel it? It was like a threatening darkness was about him."

Carmaz thought about it. "Well, now that you mention it, I did sense something off about him, but I do not like jumping to conclusions based off feelings alone. I prefer to act based on evidence and facts."

"The facts are that that was the last place that Raya is known to have visited," said Malya. She looked around, as if afraid that someone might be eavesdropping, then leaned in and whispered, "Do you think it's possible that Raya might still be there and Anwan was lying to us about not knowing where she is?"

"Why would he lie to us?" asked Carmaz, keeping his voice as low as hers. "He didn't seem like the type of person to do that."

"I don't know," said Malya. She shook her head. "Maybe you're right. Maybe I am worrying too much. My husband always tells me that I am a worrywart. It's in my nature, I suppose. Still, I think we should have at least checked out the area around his shop for clues, if nothing else."

"Perhaps we can do that after the challenge is over," said Carmaz, gesturing quickly at the vision bubbles. "Right now, I doubt Alira would let us go anywhere, even for a reason like that."

"I know," said Malya. "But maybe if we tried, we could convince Alira to let us go. It's not like our presence here determines the outcome of each challenge, after all."

"You have a point," said Carmaz. "But you still haven't

explained to me why Raya would still be in that shop. Are you implying that Anwan might be holding her against her will?"

Malya shrugged. "Again, I don't know. All I know is that I am still worried for Raya's safety."

Raya's probably safe, Carmaz wanted to say. *It's Braim you should be worrying about. I don't know what the Ghostly God is doing to him, but I doubt it's pretty.*

But knowing that saying that aloud would get him into an infinite amount of trouble—trouble that he had been studiously avoiding for the better part of a day—Carmaz simply said, "As I said, Raya will be fine. The Soldier looking for her will find her insulting some katabans peasant somewhere and we'll all have a good laugh."

The skepticism on Malya's face was obvious, but then Malya nodded in resignation and said, "I guess you're right. Whatever happens, Raya will be fine, I'm sure."

Relieved, Carmaz said, "Glad you agree. Now let's sit back and support Tashir. He needs our—"

Carmaz felt a hand tap on his shoulder. He looked over his shoulder quickly, expecting to see someone, but he saw nothing except for the back wall. That and a folded piece of paper on the shoulder of his chair, a piece of paper that he was absolutely certain had not been there even one second ago.

Taking the piece of paper off the chair's shoulder, Carmaz looked at it in confusion. Then he looked at Malya and asked, "Is this yours?"

"No," said Malya, shaking her head. "I have never seen it before. Where did it come from?"

"I have no idea," said Carmaz. He looked over his shoulder

again, but still didn't see anyone. "Did you see anyone standing just behind me, per chance?"

Again, Malya shook her head. "No, I did not. Why?"

Carmaz wasn't sure if he should tell Malya about the hand he had felt—or thought he felt, because if Malya had not seen the person who had touched him, then it was possible that he had just been imagining things. He certainly didn't want to worry her with his own concerns.

Instead, Carmaz unfolded the paper and looked down at it. He could tell that there were words written upon it, but unfortunately he could not tell what those words said because of his illiteracy. There weren't many words, but that didn't make them any easier for him to read.

Looking at Malya, Carmaz said, "Can you read it for me?"

Malya nodded as she took the paper and looked at it closely. Then she gasped. "By the gods ..."

"What?" said Yoji, who was leaning forward to look around Carmaz at Malya. "Did you see something?"

"It's not what I saw, but what I just read," said Malya, her eyes still locked on the letter. Then she looked at Carmaz and the look in her eyes told him that all of her worst fears had come true. "If what this letter says is true, then we have no time to waste."

"What does it say?" asked Carmaz. "You're speaking vaguely again."

Malya looked Carmaz directly in the eyes. "According to this letter, Raya's life is in great danger at this very moment. And if we do not go to Anwan's Tailoring right away, then we might never see her alive again."

Chapter Sixteen

BRAIM TORE THROUGH the undergrowth of the dark jungle of the Ghostly God's island, running as fast as he could. He didn't hear the Ghostly God chasing him, but that didn't make him slow down or relax. He wasn't even sure how far he had run. He might have covered half the island at this point, or close to it.

As he ran, Braim kept wondering how he was going to get off Zamis without Aorja's help. No magic, no boat, no airship, nothing. He could swim, but he knew that Zamis was too far away from World's End to make that practical.

The jungle just seems to go on forever, Braim thought as he jumped over a fallen tree. *Either this island is huge or I'm imagining things.*

Or maybe … he was still in the Mind Chamber.

Oh gods I hope not, Braim thought, dread creeping up his spine as he ran. *Aorja, Zeeree, the Ghostly God's mansion … maybe everything I've experienced since Aorja freed me is nothing more than a realistic illusion created by the Ghostly God as part of his bizarre experi—*

Braim lost his train of thought when he tripped over a root and fell flat on his face on the jungle floor. The impact almost stunned him, but he recovered and got up onto his hands and knees as soon as he could.

But Braim was too tired to keep running, so he instead crawled into the hollow of a nearby tree. He tossed a handful of dirt inside just to make sure that there weren't any animals in there, before he crawled inside and lay down on the cold dirt and leaves, panting and sweating.

Must rest, Braim thought, curling into a fetal position. *Or at least take a moment to think about what to do next.*

Unfortunately, Braim was so exhausted from the events of the day that he couldn't remain conscious long enough to think of his next course of action. His eyelids fell shut and soon he drifted off into sleep from which he was unlikely to awaken again anytime soon.

But Braim's dreams were not blank. He found himself walking in a dark, unknown place that he didn't recognize. It looked like an underground cave, but somehow he could tell that he was deep underground, as in so deep that he couldn't dig to the surface even if he wanted. How he knew that, he wasn't sure, though he wrote that off as being nothing more than his subconscious at work.

Despite the darkness of the cave, Braim could perfectly see his surroundings. On the walls were images of strange humanoid beings that appeared to be made out of rock. They resembled an army marching into battle, though against what Braim didn't know.

Not that Braim tried to make sense of anything he saw. This was a dream, after all, and dreams rarely made any sense. The way he saw it, it was just his subconscious showing him strange images that it came up with. If Braim had been an oneiromancer, he might have thought about his dream a bit more seriously, but for now he intended to take the entire thing in stride, no matter what strange developments might arise here.

That was when Braim heard voices from up ahead. At first they sounded like they were speaking nothing but gibberish and nonsense, but the closer Braim got to them, the clearer their words became, until he could now understand what they were saying.

"...yes, they are almost ready to awaken," said one of the voices, which sounded as conniving and trustworthy as a snake. "It won't be long now, I can promise you that, my lady."

"How can you be so sure?" said another voice, this one feminine and harsh. "They have slept for eons and you have promised to awaken them several times already."

"Understand, my lady, that I cannot control all circumstances and that even I am sometimes blindsided by things I did not see coming," said the male voice. "I have done my best to try to awaken them in the past, but as you no doubt know, things have not always worked out according to plan."

"You have made that excuse to me before," said the feminine voice. "The only reason I haven't yet killed you is because you are the only one who can do this. But I am even starting to question that fact about you, considering how slowly you have been about putting this plan into action."

"Patience is a virtue, my lady," said the masculine voice. "I know how hard it is to wait for the thing that you want more than anything else in the world, but you must still be patient, though not for much longer, I hope."

Braim realized that the masculine voice wasn't saying 'my

lady' to show respect to the feminine voice. It was a sarcastic insult, which made Braim realize that the two speakers were probably not as close as he thought they were. Though if the feminine voice had been as annoying to the masculine voice in the past as she was now, Braim could understand his sarcasm.

"How long is 'not for much longer'?" asked the feminine voice in a sharp tone. "Days? Weeks? Months? Years? Centuries?"

"Days, I believe," said the masculine voice. "Or possibly a couple of weeks. It all depends on how the next phase of the plan goes, which is currently outside of my control. But I am confident that it will go well. The dominoes have been set and will fall in the way that I have set them up to fall. That I promise to you from my stone heart."

Suddenly, Braim could see two figures standing at the end of the tunnel. At first, he could not see them well, but his every step took him closer and closer to them. By that, he meant that every step seemed to cover at least ten steps, though he didn't question how that was possible because this was a dream and in dreams all things were possible.

The two figures were strange and looked nothing like anyone Braim knew. One of them was a thin, though obviously strong, woman with harsh skin that looked like it was made out of stone. The other, a short man with similar skin, although his was colored like midnight in contrast to the woman's diamond-colored skin. Neither of them wore clothes, but because they did not appear to have genitalia, Braim didn't feel awkward about looking at them.

"You are as indecisive as ever," said the stone woman. "Days or weeks, pick one already. One or the other."

"D-Days," the stone man said. "Yes, that is when they will

awake and the world above will be ours."

The world above? Braim thought. *What is he talking about?*

"And no one will see it coming?" asked the stone woman. She looked at him quite severely. "Are you certain of it?"

"I am one hundred percent certain, my lady," said the stone man, nodding. "The gods know of us, but they do not suspect that we will attempt to attack them. They think of our sleeping brothers as nothing more than a minor curiosity. They will not see it coming."

"I certainly hope they do not," said the stone woman. "Not that I think they will be able to stop us, but it would be so satisfying to attack them when they least expect it."

"Agreed, my lady," said the stone man. "Especially now that they believe the Void to be the real threat. And by the time they do realize who the real threats are—namely, us—it will be too late for them to stop us."

Even though Braim wasn't trying to hide or be stealthy, neither of the two strange beings seemed to notice him approaching. He wondered if they were ignoring him, but it seemed unlikely because he was fairly certain that he had not been invited to be a part of this conversation.

Just what are they, though? Braim thought as he continued walking toward them. *I've never seen anything like them before. Not humans, gods, half-gods, aquarians, or katabans. What species do they belong to?*

"Unless the awakening is delayed yet again," said the stone woman, bitterness in her voice. "I must ask once more: Are you *certain* that they will awaken?"

"Of course I am," said the stone man, a hint of annoyance in his voice. "How many times must I tell you that? Have I not won your trust over the centuries? I thought that you understood that I never lie."

"You may not lie, but you often make promises you cannot keep," the stone woman pointed out. "But this time, I think there is a real possibility that you will succeed here. I am still doubtful, but at the same time, we have never had an opportunity quite like this at all in the past and I do not wish to lose it because of my doubt."

"Then stop needling me and start trusting me," said the stone man. "No one even knows what we are about to do. The Tournament and the Void have both proven to be very good distractions, but even if they didn't distract the gods, the deaths of so many of their siblings was fortune in itself, taking their attention away from the depths of the earth to the surface above."

"Indeed," said the stone woman. Then she froze. "Do you feel that?"

Braim also froze. He knew that the stone woman wasn't addressing him, but he tried to feel what she felt. Of course, he felt nothing, because this was all a dream and he usually didn't feel anything in dreams.

The stone man shook his head. "No. What am I supposed to feel?"

"Another presence," said the stone woman. Her voice had dropped to a whisper. "Not one of us."

"One of the gods?" asked the stone man. His tone became very tense.

"No," said the stone woman, though her body language and tone didn't relax. "A human."

187

Braim took a step back. *Uh oh. She senses me.*

Then the stone woman looked in his direction. She had burning red eyes that reminded Braim of molten lava ... and she was looking directly at him.

"There," the stone woman said, pointing at Braim. "Someone is watching us and listening to our every word."

The stone man looked at Braim as well. His eyes were shiny and green, like emeralds, and he said, "Then allow me to get rid of him."

Braim took another step back, but before he could run, the stone man lunged at Braim. Braim just managed to raise his arms in front of his face before the stone man was upon him, his massive rocky fists rushing through the air toward him.

Then Braim awoke suddenly. He awoke so suddenly that he sat up and smacked his forehead straight against the rough wood interior of the tree. The blow caused him to see stars and let out a yell of pain before he silenced himself quickly and listened hard to the jungle outside. It was hard to listen, however, because he was also focused on the strange dream that he had just experienced, which had seemed far more real than any dream he had ever had before.

After a minute or two of hearing nothing but silence, Braim sighed and sat back against the tree's interior. Rubbing his forehead, which was bruised from where he had smacked it against the tree's interior, Braim did not know what to make of that dream or of the stone people he saw in it.

What were they talking about? Braim thought. *It sounded to me like they were talking about awakening something, or a lot of somethings in this case.*

Braim wanted to dismiss it as nothing more than a very strange, if vivid, dream, but he understood that he hadn't actually been dreaming at all. What he had seen was an actual scene occurring somewhere in the world today. Somewhere in Martir—perhaps *under* Martir, if their reference to 'the world above' meant what Braim thought it meant—were two strange individuals discussing something sinister and deadly for the gods and the world in general. Braim only wished that the two had been more specific in what they were discussing, because then he would know exactly what they were planning.

I should probably tell the gods what I saw when I get back to World's End, Braim thought. *It will probably make more sense to them than it did to me.*

Shaking his head, Braim decided to put that dream aside for now. At the moment, he had more urgent things to worry about, like getting his magical abilities back and returning to World's End. Of course, he wasn't sure if he could do the first, but the second at least was somewhat realistic.

Or is it? Braim thought. *Aorja and Zeeree are probably—hopefully—still fighting the Ghostly God, keeping him distracted and all that. And again, I don't have any way to get off this island by myself, so if the Ghostly God kills them, then I'm screwed unless everyone on World's End realizes that I'm missing and tries to find me.*

Braim peeked his head out of the tree and looked around at his environment quickly, just to make sure that there was no one around here. He didn't see anyone, but he didn't feel like getting up and walking around, at least not yet. He estimated that he had gotten maybe ten minutes of rest, if that, which was hardly enough time for him to gather the strength he needed.

If only I had a friend with me, Braim thought, pulling his head back into the dank air of the tree's interior. *Someone like ... like Carmaz. Ruwa has a jungle, I think, so he probably knows how to survive out in this kind of environment. He'd be really useful at the moment.*

Unfortunately, Braim knew that desiring Carmaz's help was mere wishful thinking more than anything at the moment. The fact was that he was on his own, but he still didn't want to leave his little hideaway just yet.

I wish I knew how the battle between Aorja and Zeeree and the Ghostly God went, Braim thought, wiping the sweat off his forehead. *If the Ghostly God won, then he's probably looking for me even now. And I doubt it will take him long to find me. After all, this is his island, so he probably knows it better than anyone. Certainly knows it better than me, at least.*

But sitting here didn't seem like a smart move, either. He was safe, but also trapped. If the Ghostly God found him, he'd have nowhere to go. He had to leave. At least by leaving he increased his chances of escape, even though he still wasn't sure how he was going to get out of here.

Crawling out of the tree's nook, Braim stood up to his full height and looked around again. The jungle was dark and thick and he didn't have a sword or machete with which to cut through it, so he'd just have to be a lot more careful about where he stepped. While the jungle seemed to be devoid of all life, Braim knew enough about jungles to know that it was silly to assume that they were completely devoid of life. For all he knew, there could be some kind of dangerous animal watching him even as he stood there.

Gotta stop thinking and worrying, Braim thought, shaking his head to clear his thoughts. *Thinking and worrying isn't action. But walking is.*

So Braim decided to resume walking in the direction that he been running in before. He would keep going until he found the beach. After that, he'd figure out what to do next.

Walking much more carefully than before, Braim headed in what he assumed was the south (although without the sun overhead he could not confirm that). He did his best to avoid walking into the bushes and vines, carefully brushing them out of his path as he walked.

But Braim didn't take more than five steps from the tree's nook before he heard rustling in the trees above. He looked up and caught a glimpse of yellow in the leaves, followed by a loud, echoing *whoop whoop!* sound that caused him to jump.

"What in the gods' names was that?" said Braim aloud, still looking up at the treetops.

He heard more rustling in the treetops and then several yellow blurs fell down around him. Braim's head whipped back and forth as he tried to follow the blurs, but then something slammed into his back and he fell onto the ground face first. He felt something on his back, something heavy and large, its claws digging into his clothes, but Braim rolled over, causing the creature to jump off his back.

Scrambling back to his own feet, Braim looked at the yellow creatures that surrounded him. They looked like monkeys, except larger, at least as tall as he, and far bulkier. There were six in all, but that small number didn't make Braim feel confident he could beat them when they all looked like they could tear him apart piece by piece individually if they wanted. And they all smelled like a mixture of wet fur and mud, their fur damp, as if they had been caught in a sudden rainstorm.

"What …" Braim looked around, trying to keep an eye on all of them at once. "What *are* you creatures?"

Braim didn't expect any of them to answer, mostly because they didn't seem intelligent enough to, but then without warning, one of the yellow monkey-like creatures said, "You pathetic mortal. Did you really think you could escape me so easily?"

The yellow monkey was speaking in the Ghostly God's voice.

Chapter Seventeen

NWAN'S JAGGED VOID metal knife came flying down at Raya's face. Raya screamed, but was unable to move. She just watched the knife coming closer and closer to her face, now more certain than ever that she was going to die here.

But then, when the knife was about halfway between Anwan and Raya, a thick, armored hand grabbed Anwan's arm, stopping it in midair. Both Raya and Anwan stared at Anwan's stopped arm in surprise.

"What the hell?" said Anwan. He looked to the right. "Who the hell are you?"

Raya also looked in the direction that Anwan was. Standing to her right was a large, armored figure that Raya had never seen before in her life. He wore a thick helmet in the shape of a skull, which would have frightened Raya to death if she hadn't already been scared out of her wits at this point. She could not see his eyes, nor could she see his skin. The armor seemed to cover him up very well, as it left no part of his body exposed from what she could see.

"I am the Princess's protector," said the large figure. His voice was monotonic, yet there was a hint of a threat in it as well. "And you have stepped over the line."

My protector? Raya thought. *I don't have a protector.*

Anwan scowled. "Let go of my arm or else I will—"

Anwan was interrupted by a loud *snap* that made Raya wince. A second later, Anwan dropped the Void metal knife—which thankfully fell next to Raya's head and not on it—and began screaming in pain, wrenching his arm from the armored figure's hand and staggering backwards. Raya noticed that his arm was hanging in a rather unnatural position now, which explained the source of the *snap* quite well.

"By the Void!" Anwan screamed, gripping his broken arm as he staggered against the wall. "What ... what was ..."

The armored figure grabbed Raya and hauled her up to her feet, but far more gently than a being of his size should have been able to. He then put one massive arm around her shoulders and said, "How are you, Princess? Did Anwan harm you?"

Raya, still dazed from everything that had happened, shook her head and said, "Not much."

The armored figure nodded his large head and then looked at Anwan, who was still screaming over his broken arm. "Then allow me to finish him."

"But wait," said Raya, grabbing the figure's body, which was cold to the touch. "Who are you? Where did you come from? Why are you protecting me? Are you ... are you my guardian spirit?"

"Princess, I will explain more later," said the armored figure. "At the moment, your safety is paramount. I must get you out of here before Anwan can cause you any more harm."

The armored figure then scooped Raya up into its arms rather expertly. But Raya—taken aback by this sudden move—clung to his large chest even though she realized that he wasn't going to drop her.

Anwan, on the other hand, had already recovered from the pain, or at least had learned to tolerate it, because he had stopped screaming and was now glaring at both Raya and her savior with hatred in his eyes. He held his broken arm, which still looked unnatural at his side.

"I cannot ... cannot allow either of you to escape," said Anwan. His voice was ragged. He sounded close to collapse. "If you escaped now, then you would be able to tell the gods about what the Void is planning and that ... would not be good."

Anwan pushed himself off the wall and stood in the armored figure's way. He was quite scrawny and weak in comparison to Raya's savior, especially with his broken arm, but Raya clung to the armored figure for her own safety anyway.

"Step aside," the armored figure said, his voice even more threatening than before. "Or I will be forced to harm you."

"You don't scare me," said Anwan, shaking his head. He gritted his teeth. "I have peered into the Void and seen true horror. You are nothing more than a being in a tin can."

Raya smirked, despite still being quite afraid of Anwan, and said, "Oh, what are you going to do, knit us an ugly, ill-fitting dress? We are so frightened."

"I can do far worse than make ugly clothing, Princess," said Anwan. "But perhaps I should show you, since you seem so clearly skeptical of my power."

An ethereal portal appeared behind Anwan and he stepped into it. The second he did, the portal vanished, but before either Raya or her armored savior could move, another ethereal portal opened up in front of them and Anwan jumped out of it. He then slammed into the armored savior as hard as he could. And despite his small size, he managed to make Raya's savior stagger backwards.

Then Anwan jerked his good hand forward and another ethereal portal open behind Raya and her savior. They almost fell through it, too, but the armored savior managed to regain his balance in time to stagger away. Just in the nick of time, too, because when the portal closed shut, it almost closed on the armored savior's head.

"Tricky one, you are," said Anwan. "Why don't you treat yourself to some *real* darkness?"

Anwan held out his hand and unleashed a dozen thick black tendrils that darted through the air toward Raya and her savior. Her armored savior turned around in time to block the tendrils, which stabbed into the back of his armor ferociously, but despite that, the armored savior didn't so much as flinch, even though it looked to Raya like the tendrils had stabbed straight through his armor and, by extension, his body as well.

Raya yelped as the armored savior whirled around again, causing the tendrils to snap and fall to the floor, where they dissipated into harmless gas. The armored savior then moved Raya over into his left arm and aimed his right arm at Anwan, who was looking at him in astonishment and fear.

"How did you survive being stabbed in the back like that?" asked Anwan in horror. "That isn't possible."

"I cannot feel pain, Void worshiper," said the armored savior. "But I am afraid that I cannot say the same for you."

The tips of the armored figure's fingers unfolded, revealing tiny gun barrels. It was such an unexpected thing to see that Raya at first did not hear the armored figure when he said, "Cover your ears, Princess!"

But when Raya realized what he'd said, she slammed her hands over her ears just in time for the bullets to start shooting out of the armored figure's fingers. The armored figure's body vibrated as he fired bullet after bullet after bullet at Anwan, which Raya looked up at in order to see what was happening exactly.

The bullets were riddling holes in Anwan's chest, making him stagger backwards with each blow. Blood oozed from the bullet holes in his chest, yet Anwan somehow managed to remain standing despite the terrible pain he must have been in. And still the armored figure shot at him, which made Raya briefly wonder just how much ammunition he had and when he would ever run out.

After what felt like hours of shooting, the armored figure suddenly stopped firing. He lowered his right arm, the tips of his fingers now smoking, his expression as neutral as ever.

Anwan, on the other hand, was a bloody mess. His tacky gray and orange suit had been torn to shreds, its tatters just barely clinging to his body, and that only because of the blood making his clothing sticky. His chest had taken the brunt of the shots, leaving little hidden, although his arms and his legs had a few bloody bullet holes in them as well.

Yet Anwan still stood, despite all of the shots he had taken. That made Raya worry that her savior's bullets hadn't been enough—a frightening enough thought in itself—before Anwan gave one final, shuddering gasp and fell forward onto the ground and he stopped moving.

Raya let out a sigh of relief, which she hadn't even realized that she had been holding in. She looked up at the armored figure, although he was still looking at Anwan as if he thought that the tailor might rise again. Her savior now smelled vaguely of gun powder, which was a smell that Raya didn't like and which made her feel a little sick.

"Is he … is he dead?" asked Raya.

"He should be," said the armored figure. The threat had vanished from his tone. It was now quite monotonic again. "Most living beings cannot survive having so many bullets shot into them, unless they also happen to be gods. Anwan was a mere katabans, so he is most likely dead."

Raya sighed again. "Oh, thank the gods. I thought for sure I was a goner there. And I would have been, if it hadn't been for you."

"That is true," said the armored figure. "But I wish I had not saved you like this, because now you know about me, even though I was given clear instructions to keep my existence a secret from you for as long as possible."

Raya looked up at the armored figure's helmeted face in puzzlement. "Who ordered you to keep your existence a secret from me?"

"I would rather not say," said the armored figure, still not looking at her. "I am not *supposed* to say. But it seems utterly pointless for me to keep up this secret now. I am only concerned that my creators will be displeased with me, but I am sure they will understand once I explain the situation to them."

"Well, then get on with it," said Raya, folding her arms across her chest. "It's not like I have anything else to do right now, after

198

all."

"I would rather tell you after we leave this place," said the armored figure, gesturing at the dark room in which they stood. "I want to get you to safety first, but if you need a name, call me Keeper. It is the name I was given because I am supposed to keep you safe."

"Keeper, huh?" said Raya. "All right, Keeper. But I don't see why you can't just tell me while we're down here."

Keeper sighed, a rather hollow and metallic sound coming from him. "All right. I'll give you the brief version: I am an automaton created by your parents to protect you without your knowledge."

Raya blinked. "An automaton? You mean like the ones that the Mechanical Goddess has?"

"Yes," said Keeper, nodding. He tapped his chest. "I am made entirely of metal. I can think like an organic being, but cannot feel emotion or pain or get hungry or tired."

"Oh," said Raya. "But when did my parents make you? And why didn't they tell me about you? Why did they think I'd need your protection?"

"Your parents, the King and the Queen, did not think that anything bad would happen to you on World's End, but they wanted to ensure that you would be safe without their watchful eyes," Keeper said. "Thus, they commissioned Carnag's greatest mechanics to build me using the designs of the automatons created by the Mechanical Goddess, which your mother had access to from years of her serving her."

"Are you the one who saved me when I first entered the ethereal?" asked Raya.

Keeper nodded. "Yes."

"So you can enter the ethereal, too?" said Raya. "I thought that only the gods and katabans could enter it."

"Your mother granted me that ability when I was created," said Keeper. "I spend most of my time in the ethereal in order to remain hidden from you and from everyone else."

"Really?" said Raya. "Then where were you when Ragao first attacked me? Remember that?"

"Unfortunately, I was not available to rescue you at the time," said Keeper. "I had returned to the ethereal to recharge my energies, because I had thought that you would be safe while in the Stadium. I did not think you would intentionally stomp out of the Stadium and run into that half-god."

Keeper, despite allegedly lacking emotion, certainly sounded like he regretted that mistake of his. Raya still felt rather annoyed about it, but because he seemed sincerely regretful, she decided not to hold it against him.

Instead, she said, "That still doesn't explain why my parents didn't tell me about you, though."

"They didn't want to worry you," said Keeper. "They knew you would be offended if they gave you a bodyguard, so in order to avoid offending you, I had to keep my entire existence a secret from you and everyone else. It was rather easy, I will admit, because you are not very perceptive of your surroundings."

"Hey!" Raya said in annoyance. "Are you my bodyguard or my critic?"

"Just an observation, Princess," said Keeper. "I mean no harm by it."

If Keeper had not been a ten-foot-tall hulking machine and if

200

they had been on Carnag rather than on World's End, Raya would have had him kicked out of Carnag Hall for that remark.

But Raya could not do that, so she just folded her arms over her chest and pouted. "Well, from now on, keep your observations to yourself unless I explicitly ask for them. Clear?"

"Crystal clear, Princess," said Keeper, though Raya had a feeling that he was just humoring her. "Anyway, I do not trust this place, even with Anwan dead. It is too dark and frightening. It has been tainted by the Void and I fear that—"

Keeper suddenly stopped speaking. He looked down at Saia's covered corpse as if it had spoken. Raya also looked at it, even though she wasn't sure what Keeper was looking at.

Then Raya saw it. A tiny bit of movement under the blue sheet. It was so small as almost imperceptible, but it was definitely real and definitely there.

And then, before Raya's startled, fearful eyes, Saia's corpse sat up.

Chapter Eighteen

CARMAZ RUSHED THROUGH the streets of World's End, trying to make every stride longer than the last. Around him ran several Soldiers of the Gods, carrying swords and shields, as well as Malya and Yoji, who had also volunteered to come with Carmaz to Anwan's Tailoring in order to help find Raya.

As Carmaz ran, doing his best to keep up with the quick Soldiers, he remembered what had happened after Malya read the note on his seat. She had given it to Alira, who had taken the note and read it herself before declaring that it was worth investigating and that she was going to send any Soldiers of the Gods that she could find to Anwan's Tailoring in order to investigate the letter's claim about Raya's fate.

Malya had managed to convince Alira to let her go with them and had also roped Carmaz in. Perhaps 'roped' wasn't the correct word to use, because Carmaz, despite his antipathy toward Raya, didn't want her to be killed or hurt, so he had agreed to go and help however he could. One of the Soldiers of the Gods had given him a crystalline sword to carry, which felt a lot more natural in his hands than the sword he had used during the Human God Sub-Bracket Challenge earlier that day. Still, Carmaz knew that he was no master swordsman, so he would have to rely mostly on the combat prowess and experience of the Soldiers around him in case he found himself in a fight.

As for the other godlings, Alira had told them all to stay in the Stadium where they would be safely under her eye. The only one who had managed to convince Alira that he should go with Malya and Carmaz was Yoji, who had claimed that they would need a mage such as him to help deal with any possible magical threats to Raya's life. But when they left the Stadium, Yoji had simply informed Carmaz that he was bored of watching Tashir easily beating his opponent and that he hoped that rescuing Raya would be a lot more fun.

Not sure what is 'fun' about saving a woman's life from whatever monster has her, Carmaz thought as he turned the corner with the Soldiers. *But it's good that we have Yoji with us anyway. I have a feeling that we're gonna need all the help we can get.*

Up ahead, Carmaz saw the sign for Anwan's Tailoring. The streets around the place were empty, but that made sense because it was now a little later in the day and most katabans had probably gone back to their homes by now. Yet as they drew closer to the building, Carmaz felt an overwhelming sense of evil emanating from it, as if there was some kind of wicked spirit haunting the place.

Carmaz thought that he was the only one to feel that when Malya looked at him and said, "Do you feel something off about Anwan's Tailoring, Carmaz?"

Carmaz nodded and said, in a voice that was somewhat short of breath due to how fast he was running, "Yes. What do you think it is?"

"Not sure," said Malya, shaking her head. "But we are about to find out."

Upon reaching the building, the lead Soldier knocked loudly on the front door, shouting, "Mr. Anwan! This is the Soldiers of the Gods. Please open your doors. We are here to investigate a claim that one of the godlings in the Tournament of the Gods is in your shop."

There was no response. Carmaz tried to look through the display windows of the shop, but he didn't see anyone on the inside, which made him wonder if Anwan was out again or if he simply did not want to open the door for the Soldiers.

"No answer," said the lead Soldier, looking over his shoulder at the others. "Prepare your weapons. We are going in."

The other Soldiers held up their swords and shields, while Malya drew her blades, Carmaz redoubled his grip on his sword, and Yoji flipped his wand into the air before catching it again.

The lead Soldier nodded when he saw that they were ready and then turned and slammed into the front door with his shoulder. It must not have been a very strong door, because he managed to knock the door in with only one blow. The lead Soldier entered right away, followed by the other Soldiers, all of whom moved as quickly and efficiently as if they were invading an enemy fortress.

Carmaz, Malya, and Yoji also entered, though the front room was now crowded with the dozen or so Soldiers plus the three godlings. It was also quite hot and dark and Carmaz saw no sign of either Raya or Anwan until Yoji pointed over the heads of the Soldiers and shouted, "Look over there!"

Following Yoji's finger, Carmaz saw a back door at the other end of the room that appeared to lead to the storage room. The Soldiers immediately began making their way over to it, but as they made their way through the piles and racks of clothing, Carmaz thought he heard movement in the clothing around them, movement that did not belong to him or anyone else. He stopped and looked at a nearby pink skirt hanging off a rack, causing Malya to grab his arm and say, "Carmaz, what are you standing around for? We have to go and save Raya."

"I know," said Carmaz, though he didn't take his eyes off the skirt, because he was pretty sure that he had heard something moving behind it. "Did you hear that?"

"Hear what?" asked Malya, who now sounded annoyed.

Before Carmaz could answer, a gloved hand shot out from between the skirt and the dress to its left and grabbed Carmaz's throat. He gasped as the hand's fingers constricted, cutting off his air supply, but then Malya raised her left sword and brought it down on the arm. Before her sword could cut through the arm, however, it let go of Carmaz's throat and vanished back into the dress rack.

"What was—" said Malya, but she was interrupted by the sound of a Soldier screaming, causing her and Carmaz to look over their shoulders.

Though it was hard to see amidst all of the piles and racks of clothing everywhere, Carmaz saw one of the Soldiers lying on the floor of the shop bleeding from his chest. It looked like his chest armor had been stabbed straight through, leaving a gaping, bloody hole that bled profusely. A couple of his fellow Soldiers were trying to perform some healing magic on him, though it was hard to tell whether it was working or not.

"What's going on here?" said Yoji, pointing his wand this way and that as he looked around. "Who's attacking us?"

Then Carmaz heard movement behind the clothes pile to his left and, without hesitation, he turned and stabbed his sword straight through the pile. He felt his sword stab into flesh and a second later a figure in a gray cloak materialized on the other side of the clothing pile. The figure's face looked almost human, save for the furry cheeks and the blue hair that pegged him as a katabans.

The figure gasped from the pain, but that was all he managed to do before Carmaz pulled is sword out of his gut. The figure then collapsed face-first onto the clothing pile, the blood from his gut staining the clothing he had fallen upon.

"Anyone know who this is?" asked Carmaz, gesturing with his now-bloody sword at the obviously dead katabans before him.

One of the Soldiers ran over, jumping over a pile of clothes, and bent over the dead katabans. The Soldier examined the dead katabans with scrutiny before standing up again and looking at Braim, his eyes serious and grim.

"I don't know the identity of this katabans, but I recognize his robe," said the Soldier. "It is the same color and design of the robes worn by members of a cult known as the Empty."

"The Empty?" Carmaz repeated. "What's that?"

"A cult of katabans that worship the Void as the ultimate goddess," said the Soldier. There was obvious disgust in his voice. "But that doesn't explain what some of them are doing here in Anwan's shop, unless Anwan is one of them."

"Maybe they're holding Anwan and Raya hostage," said Carmaz. He looked around. "If that one is there, then the could be more anywhere."

"Agreed," said the Soldier, nodding. He then shouted to the rest, "Everyone! Keep your guard up. It appears that we have been ambushed by members of the cult known as the Empty. We don't know how many members of Empty are in the shop, but to be safe, don't hesitate to attack if—"

The Soldier was interrupted when a large, bearish katabans wearing a gray Empty cloak burst out from underneath another nearby pile of clothes, sending shirts and dresses flying everywhere. Carmaz, Malya, and the Soldier ducked to avoid getting hit by the flying clothes, but as they did that, the bearish Empty follower slashed at the Soldier with claws that looked like they could rip through steel.

The Soldier, however, managed to raise his shield in time to block the claws, but the impact was enough to knock him down. The bearish Empty follower tried to swipe at him again, but Carmaz intervened this time, putting his crystalline sword between the Soldier and the Empty follower in order to block the blow.

The impact of the Empty follower's claws on his sword almost knocked the blade out of Carmaz's hands, but he retained his grip on it and forced the Empty follower's claws back. The Empty follower pulled back, but rather than attack Carmaz, it immediately vanished into thin air, as if it had never existed at all.

"Where did it go?" said Malya, looking around the rather cramped shop in alarm. "Did it leave?"

"No," said the Soldier who had been knocked down by the Empty follower, shaking his head as he got back to his feet. "He turned invisible, most likely. Members of the Empty cult are known to be masters of invisibility magic, which is what makes them so dangerous to fight."

Just as those words left his mouth, another Soldier on the left side of the room suddenly lost his sword, which now floated in the air seemingly of its own free will. The sword then moved in and slashed its original owner's throat before the Soldier could even cry out and the Soldier collapsed immediately.

The floating sword then swung through the air toward two nearby Soldiers, but they managed to raise their own shields in time to block it. But just as they did that, another Empty follower, this one with skin like that of a snake, materialized behind them and jabbed them both in the back with two quick hits. The blows must have been more painful than they appeared because the two staggered forward, lowering their shields and allowing the sword from the invisible killer to swoop in and behead both of them with surprising speed.

The snake-skinned follower vanished into thin air again, while the sword clattered to the floor along with the now-headless bodies of the Soldiers. One of the surviving Soldiers fired an ice bolt at the spot where the sword had been floating, but his ice bolt simply flew through the air until it struck the wall on the opposite side of the shop, where it stuck like an arrow through a target.

Carmaz looked around the shop's interior, but with the Empty followers being invisible amid the piles and racks of clothing, he knew that he and the others were sitting ducks. He glanced at Yoji and Malya, who were both also looking around quickly, but they looked even more panicked than he felt.

Carmaz tried to listen for any sounds that the Empty might have made. He heard movement above him and looked up in time to see an Empty follower, clinging to the ceiling, strike with a scorpion-like tail directly at his head.

Without thinking, Carmaz ducked. But he just barely missed the Empty follower's scorpion-like tail, which whistled through the air above his head, barely grazing the tips of his hair. He heard Yoji yell and then saw a burst of fire strike the Empty follower's tail.

The Empty follower let out a shriek of terror and fell off the ceiling onto Carmaz. The Empty follower, despite being rather thin, was heavier than he looked, because his weight almost crushed Carmaz, although the follower rolled off him quickly. Then the Empty follower tried to turn invisible, but then Malya appeared and stabbed it in the back with both of her glowing swords.

The Empty follower then let out a yell of pain before suddenly collapsing when Malya drew her swords out of his back. But before any of the others could celebrate this victory, an earsplitting screech assaulted the ears of everyone in the small shop.

Carmaz slammed his hands over his ears, but then he saw movement in the clothing rack to his right, causing him to jump forward instinctively. Just in the nick of time, because the long claws of the bearlike Empty follower from earlier tore through the clothes and would have ripped him to shreds if he hadn't moved.

Carmaz turned to slash his sword at the Empty follower, but the lead Soldier was already on him. The lead Soldier jabbed his own sword through the clothing, causing the bearish Empty follower to let out a howl of pain before slashing at the lead Soldier again. This time, the claw tore through the lead Soldier's arm, causing him to let go of his sword and stagger backwards from the pain.

The Empty follower, however, still had the sword stuck in its abdomen. It tried to remove the blade, but it must not have been very smart, because it didn't turn invisible again or try to escape. This allowed Yoji to point his wand at it and shout, "Take this, you foul creature!"

The clothes around the bearish Empty follower suddenly rose around it and then constricted around its neck like a snake. The bearish Empty follower gasped for breath and tore at the makeshift cloth snake, but in seconds it gave up and crashed over backwards onto a clothing rack behind it. The lead Soldier's sword rose from its stomach like a tree rising from a hill, though the bearish Empty follower was clearly down for the count now.

But even as the bearish one fell, that same loud screeching from before grew even louder and then, without warning, a dozen Empty followers materialized in every corner of the room. Without waiting for the Soldiers and the godlings to realize what was going on, the Empty followers jumped into their midst, attacking and slashing and yelling, forcing the Soldiers and the godlings to fight back just as viciously in order to survive.

Carmaz, however, managed to stay out of it. It wasn't that he didn't want to help the Soldiers win, but he realized that if these Empty followers were trying to stop him and the others from going any deeper into the shop, then that meant that Raya was definitely here and was probably in even more danger than they were at the moment.

So Carmaz slashed and jumped his way through the clothing in order to reach the open door at the other end of the room, which he believed led to the storage room, which was probably where Raya was being kept. It was slow-going due to all of the clothing, but he kept at it anyway and did not allow the fighting all around him to distract him from what he was trying to do.

But when he almost reached the door, another Empty follower appeared in his path. This one wore gloves, which meant that it was the same one that had tried to strangle him earlier. This time, however, it carried a knife in its hand, which it tried to stab him with almost too quickly for him to dodge or block.

Almost. Carmaz managed to move to the right, barely dodging the Empty follower's sharp blade, and then, in one smooth motion, stabbed the follower in the chest. The follower gave a shriek of agony, but collapsed the second Carmaz pulled his even bloodier sword out of its chest. Carmaz stepped over the corpse and then ran into the open doorway into a longer and stuffier room that did in fact appear to be the storage room, if all of the clothing in here meant anything.

"Raya!" Carmaz shouted as he ran, looking this way and that for any sign of the Princess. "Are you there? Can you hear me? Raya!"

But he received no response. So Carmaz kept running as fast as he could toward the back of the storage room, which seemed to go on forever, but he didn't let that discourage him. As long as he could save Raya, he was willing to do almost anything at this point.

Then Carmaz saw yet another door at the end of the storage room. It was different from the last door. It was black and appeared to be made out of solid stone. It was cracked open, like someone had just recently entered it, maybe even Raya, so

Carmaz decided to enter and find out what was behind the door.

But before Carmaz reached the door, yet another Empty follower appeared in front of the thick stone door and shoved it closed. The door slid shut with a loud *whomp*, causing Carmaz to skid to a stop as he looked at his new opponent.

This Empty follower was much taller and skinnier than the others. A hood covered his face, but he could see green eyes in the shadows of the hood that looked both pleased and annoyed. The Empty follower had no weapon, but that didn't mean he was not dangerous.

"Move out of the way," said Carmaz, brandishing his sword before him. "Or I'll *make* you move."

"You are a tricky one, I will give you that, and quite deadly as well, considering how you have already killed two of my brothers," said the Empty follower with a chuckle. "But I will not let you pass. Right now, Brother Anwan is ensuring that the ceremony is complete and I must make sure that no one interferes with it."

"What ceremony?" said Carmaz. He shook his head. "It doesn't matter. What matters is that I am going to take you down."

"Do what you will to me, but I will not die easily," said the Empty follower. "Or at your hands."

The Empty follower raised his hands and two thick black tendrils shot out of his wrists at Carmaz. Carmaz slashed them with his sword, cutting the tendrils in half, and then dashed toward the Empty follower, who conjured his own sword made of the same black stuff and charged at Carmaz.

The two met halfway, slashing and slicing at each other with their swords. Carmaz blocked every one of the Empty follower's blows, while the Empty follower blocked every one of his attacks as well.

What Carmaz found so shocking about the Empty follower was the ease with which he blocked all of Carmaz's attacks. It was like he wasn't even trying. His sword appeared wherever Carmaz swung his, blocking his blows without effort, but whenever his opponent attacked Carmaz, Carmaz struggled to block it. He almost got stabbed once because of his own slowness, which made him wonder how the Empty follower was able to move so quickly.

Not that Carmaz had any time to think about the situation in depth, however. He was too busy keeping up with the Empty follower to think. He just had to survive.

Then Carmaz noticed that the Empty follower was driving him back to the rest of the shop. He hadn't realized it, but already they were a few steps farther from the thick black stone door than they were moments ago. He realized that the Empty follower wasn't trying to kill him, but instead keep him as far away from the door as possible.

I have no idea what that ceremony is, but something tells me that Raya is a part of it, Carmaz thought.

Then Carmaz slipped on a piece of clothing on the floor and staggered. It was not a big slip, but it was enough for him to lower his guard for only a second, giving the Empty follower an opening. His opponent tried to stab him in the stomach, but Carmaz managed to dodge it. Then his opponent slammed the flat of his blade against Carmaz's stomach, causing Carmaz to stagger backwards, almost out of breath.

"Well, well, well, godling," said the Empty follower, his tone mocking. "How does it feel to get a taste of your own medicine? Is it painful? If it is, don't worry, because the Void will consume you soon enough, and when she does, you will not feel pain—or anything else—ever again."

Carmaz gritted his teeth. If he had struggled to fight against the Empty follower earlier, when he had been uninjured, he was certain that he was not going to be able to win now. All the Empty follower needed was one more good blow like that and Carmaz was certain that he'd go down for good.

And if I do, then I will never get to bring Saia back to life, Carmaz thought. *And Raya will also die.*

Those two thoughts, as horrible as they were, gave Carmaz the strength he needed to stand his ground. He raised his sword, but found it incredibly difficult because of the pain in his stomach where the follower had struck him.

"You can still stand and fight?" said the Empty follower in surprise. "Where do you mortals keep finding this strength to go on? Is it because you are a godling?"

Carmaz shook his head. "No. It's because I am not going to let you win. That's why."

The Empty follower raised his own black sword again. "I guess it doesn't matter. You'll go down in one more blow, most likely, so I'll make this quick."

The Empty follower then rushed at Carmaz. Carmaz staggered backwards again, making himself look weaker than he was. He waited for the right opportunity to strike, mentally counting down the seconds for the perfect opportunity to show itself.

Then Carmaz grabbed a dress off the pile of clothing to his

right and threw it at the Empty follower. The Empty follower—who clearly did not see that coming—did not dodge it. The dress flew into his face, causing the Empty follower to stop and almost trip. He reached for the dress on his face, giving Carmaz an opening. Carmaz then dashed toward the Empty follower, his sword level and aimed for his enemy's chest.

The Empty follower must have heard Carmaz approaching, because he slashed wildly with his sword. But Carmaz dodged it and then slashed at the Empty follower's chest. His sword carved a path down the follower's chest, causing his opponent to yell in shock and pain as blood shot out, but Carmaz followed it up with a kick that sent the unnamed follower falling flat on his back on the floor.

Then Carmaz tried to bring his sword down on the follower's chest, but before his blade struck, an ethereal portal opened underneath the Empty follower and he fell into it. A second after the follower disappeared into it, the portal closed and Carmaz's sword struck the stone floor, making a loud *clang* that made Carmaz wince.

But Carmaz quickly raised his sword again and looked around, expecting the Empty follower to reappear and try to kill him at any moment. He panted and felt the sweat rolling down his forehead, smelled the blood on his sword mixing with the heat of the storage room, but the Empty follower did not reappear.

Is he gone? Carmaz thought, looking around again. *Maybe he doesn't think he can beat me.*

Shaking his head, Carmaz ran over to the closed stone door. He grabbed the door's handle and pulled it as hard as he could, expecting the door to be extremely heavy. But much to Carmaz's surprise, the door opened as easily as any.

So Carmaz wasted no time in dashing through the open door into the dark staircase below, hoping against hope that he would save Raya from Anwan. He even found himself praying to the gods for her safety despite himself, though that did not make him feel any more trusting of the gods in general than he normally was.

Chapter Nineteen

AT THIS POINT, Braim was pretty much convinced that the yellow simians were just another illusion that the Ghostly God had created. That was the only explanation for why he had just heard one of them speak in the Ghostly God's voice.

Nonetheless, Braim tried to put on a brave face. He said to the lead monkey, "How did you find me? What happened to Aorja and Zeeree?"

The yellow monkey stared at him rather blankly. Then it said in the Ghostly God's voice, "Foolish katabans. How dare you question me. To the Mind Chamber with you!"

Braim looked around at the other monkeys surrounding him. None of them appeared likely to explain that non sequitur. They all did, however, look rather hungry, like they wanted to eat him for lunch.

Braim then looked at the lead monkey again. "What?"

"You mortals always ask such stupid questions," the lead monkey said. "That is one more reason I am glad to be a southern god. Otherwise, I would have to deal with these kinds of dumb questions all the time."

Braim was now faced with two possibilities: One, that the Ghostly God was indeed speaking through this monkey but had completely lost his mind and was repeating random non sequiturs that made him look like a mad man. Or two, the Ghostly God was not in fact speaking through this monkey and it was merely repeating things that it had heard the Ghostly God say at one point.

Now Braim had never heard of any sort of monkey-like creature that could mimic the words and voices of people, but then, he was in the southern seas, after all, where many strange creatures and things existed.

Doesn't make it any less freaky, though, Braim thought. *But it does mean that I can't just reason with it. Damn.*

The question, then, was how he should get away from these monkeys. While Braim was not physically weak, he was in no condition to fight these monkeys in a brawl. He was tired, sweaty, dirty, and without any magic. These monkeys, on the other hand, looked strong enough to wrestle a baba raga, which meant that he'd have to use his brains to figure out how to escape them instead.

Not that that's much better, Braim thought in annoyance. *'Using your brains' isn't easy when you're worn out like I am.*

Yet Braim was in no mood to die today, so he tried to think of a plan to escape from them. It was hard to do, though, due to how the monkeys stared at him like he was going to be their next meal. They also smelled like … well, like wild animals that never bathed.

Unfortunately, it was hard to plan an escape without knowing anything about these creatures except that they were obviously mimics. He guessed also that they were probably physically strong and incapable of more than the most rudimentary of thinking. If they were like most animals, then they were probably easily spooked by bright lights and sudden, loud sounds.

Too bad I can't make either, Braim thought, wiping sweat off his forehead. *At least without magic. But I don't even have any non-magical ways to do that.*

Braim did briefly wonder why these monkeys were not already tearing him apart, but maybe this was part of their strategy. They would try to throw him off-guard with their uncanny mimicry and then attack him. Or maybe they actually did work for the Ghostly God and were simply trying to make sure that Braim was easy for the Ghostly God to find.

Whatever the case, Braim observed the monkeys' group dynamics a bit more closely to see if he could find any clues that could help him. He noticed how all of the other monkeys were, in one way or another, always either looking at or facing their leader. They seemed to be looking to their alpha for guidance, which meant that these creatures were pack animals.

And pack animals always follow the leader, Braim thought. *If so, then I think I see my way out.*

Braim bent over and grabbed a large stick off the ground. It was thick and heavy, but he found that he could hold it well enough. He pointed at the lead monkey, which looked at him in surprise.

"Hey, monkey," said Braim. He focused more on making his tone hostile and challenging because he wasn't sure that these monkeys could understand words. "I could beat you in a fight so fast that you wouldn't even realize it was over until next week."

The alpha monkey must have sensed the hostility in his voice, because it let out a menacing growl before stepping forward, a clear sign that it had accepted his challenge. Its underlings stepped back, as if to give them more room in which to fight.

"Guess you're not a coward after all," said Braim. "Of course, that doesn't mean you'll be able to beat me, but you can at least make yourself look tough."

The alpha monkey's tail swished through the air as it eyed Braim, which made him wonder what it was going to do. He kept his guard up, however, because he was pretty sure that this creature could kill him easily if he wasn't careful.

Then Braim heard something running behind him and looked over his shoulder in time to see one of the other monkeys rushing toward him. It swung its fists at his face, forcing Braim to jump to the side to avoid the blow, but then that monkey's tail swung out of nowhere and slammed into his gut.

It was like getting hit by a sledgehammer. The blow knocked Braim's air out of his lungs and sent him staggering, though he managed to retain his grip on his large stick. Still, the pain made it hard for his eyes to focus, and by the time his focus returned, the alpha monkey was running at him with a look of rage on its primitive features.

Braim swung his stick at the alpha monkey and hit it in the face. Unfortunately, the alpha monkey must have been much stronger than it looked, because Braim's stick broke against the side of its face, leaving him with a tiny stump of wood that was hardly good for anything.

But the impact of the blow did cause the alpha monkey to stagger away from him, though the second monkey caught the alpha and helped him regain his balance. The two then rubbed their noses together, a sign of affection if Braim had ever seen one.

That was when Braim realized that the second monkey wasn't just a random member of the pack coming to the aid of its leader. It was the alpha's mate.

Great, Braim thought. *Looks like his girlfriend is trying to help him out. What a great relationship those two have.*

As if they could hear his sarcastic thoughts, the two monkeys looked at Braim and started walking toward him. Braim stepped back, but he couldn't step back very far because there were a couple of other monkeys behind him. He doubted they would participate in the fight, but they probably wouldn't leave him, either, at least until the alpha couple were finished with him, anyway.

Gotta think fast, Braim thought. *How the hell am I going to get out of this alive?*

Braim looked down at the stick in his hand, or what was left of it, anyway. It was sharp and pointy, but there was no way he could get close enough to stab either of the couple without endangering his own life needlessly. He wished that he had a better weapon, but unfortunately he didn't.

Braim took another step back, but stopped when he heard the growls and snorts from the monkeys behind him. He thought about praying to the gods for aid, but considering that the only reason he was in the situation at all was because of one of the gods, he decided he could save himself.

Time's a wasting, Braim, he told himself. *Just act!*

So Braim threw the stick at the alpha couple. They must not have expected that, because the stick struck the alpha himself in the forehead, sending him staggering backwards, while his partner turned to make sure he was okay.

Seeing an opportunity, Braim ran up to the female and kicked her as hard as he could. His blow, however, only glanced off the female's backside, but despite that, she whirled around and roared at him with far more anger than he had seen in any of the monkeys yet.

The female body-slammed him, which sent Braim flying. He flew a few feet and hit the ground hard, the landing knocking his breath out of his lungs again, his entire body aching from the powerful blow. He looked up to see that one of the other members of the pack was standing over him, but it didn't look like it was going to help him. It just grinned, as if it enjoyed seeing Braim getting beaten up by its leaders.

Shaking his head, Braim stood up in time to see the alpha couple stomping toward him again. Only this time, both looked beyond angry. He wasn't sure if they were angry that he had dared to attack the female or if it was because he had hurt the alpha male or both, but it didn't matter. He was now certain that neither the alpha nor its mate were going to hold back.

Run, damn it, run, Braim told himself, but he didn't have anywhere to run to because the rest of the pack had tightened their circle around him and the alpha couple, cutting off all possible avenues of escape.

Then Braim noticed a vine hanging from the thick and heavy-looking limb of a nearby tree. It was rather high off the ground, well-above the heads of the apes, but an idea occurred to him. It was a crazy idea, one that would result in his death if he didn't do it right, but he had to try it because it was the only option he had left.

So Braim, steeling himself for what he was about to do, charged the alpha couple, yelling loudly as he did so. The alpha couple actually stopped. They now looked confused as well as enraged, as if they were wondering why this scrawny, unarmed human was charging at them like a wild bull.

But their confusion was precisely what Braim had counted on. When he got close enough, he jumped as high as he could and landed on the head and shoulders of the alpha male, who let out a snort of shock and anger, but Braim didn't stay on the alpha long. He jumped one more time, taking advantage of the alpha male's height to give him more air.

As he flew through the air, Braim reached for the vine. He almost missed it, but then his fingers wrapped around it and he pulled down with all of his weight, swinging forward away from the alpha couple underneath him.

A second later, a loud *snap* followed and Braim fell along with the thick tree branch to which the vine had been attached. Braim hit the ground first, landing flat on his bottom, but he was followed less than a second later by the branch itself ... which fell directly on the heads of the alpha couple, who only had time to let out one last cry of shock before they collapsed underneath the weight of the branch.

Panting and sweating, Braim scrambled to his feet and turned to look at the alpha couple, hoping that his plan had worked.

There, lying underneath the heavy tree branch, were the alpha couple. The male had placed his arms over the female to protect her, but it obviously hadn't helped, because the two were quite clearly out cold. They weren't dead—he saw their chests rising and falling in tandem—but he had no doubt that they would not recover for quite a while.

Straightening up, Braim looked around at all of the other monkeys. They stared at Braim with pure shock. Clearly, they had not expected their potential lunch to take out their leaders. Braim found that he enjoyed their shocked expressions. It made him feel far more powerful and even authoritative than he had in a long time.

Braim pointed at the unconscious alpha couple underneath the branch. "See that? I want you all to take a good, long look at your leaders. If any of you bastards try to kill me, I'll do to you what I did to them, only *much* worse."

Of course, the monkeys did not seem to understand his words, but they clearly understood his tone, because not a single monkey looked like they were going to attack him. In fact, Braim thought that the monkeys were now looking at him with respect, as if he was their new pack leader now.

And then all of the monkeys bowed around Braim. This surprised Braim, but he hid his surprise because he didn't want the monkeys to view any weakness on his part. He tried his best to look as aloof and leader-like as possible.

Of course, Braim couldn't help but wonder what he was supposed to do next. He had not planned on becoming the leader of a pack of whatever these creatures were. He had only intended to beat their leaders so he could escape and figure out a way off of Zamis.

But I guess having a pack of my own monkeys isn't such a bad thing, Braim thought, looking around at the bowing creatures. *At least they aren't going to kill me, anyway.*

"They won't," said a familiar voice in his ear, making the hairs on the back of Braim's neck stand on end. "But I might."

Braim turned around to see the Ghostly God floating behind him with a scowl on his face. Without hesitation, The Ghostly God grabbed Braim by the neck, wrapping his cold metallic fingers around Braim's windpipe, and raised the godling above the ground even as the monkeys fled shrieking into the jungle.

"Now, Braim," said the Ghostly God, the rage in his voice barely disguised. "Why don't we finish what we started earlier? Of course, this time, I am going to make my next experiment on you as painful as possible and you won't escape."

Chapter Twenty

WATCHING SAIA'S CORPSE sit up was the most terrifying thing that Raya had ever seen in her life. He sat up jerkily and unnaturally, like a puppet, the blue sheet falling into his lap as he did so. His back was to her and Keeper, but that didn't make the spectacle any less frightening.

Raya looked up at Keeper. As an automaton, he didn't seem to be afraid. He did, however, hold Raya a little closer to his armored body as if to protect her from Saia's strange movements.

Saia twisted and turned his neck sharply and in ways that a normal person shouldn't have been able to. He looked down at his hands and then threw the blue sheet off. When he stood up, Raya noticed that Saia wore a dark robe that reminded her of mage robes, except they looked unnaturally black, as if they had been woven out of midnight.

Then Saia turned to face Raya and Keeper. Raya screamed when she saw his face.

His face was pure black, with only two red slits to show his green eyes. It didn't seem to have a nose, didn't seem to have a mouth or any other features. It was nothing but a dark, endless void, one which made Raya want to run away forever and never look back. Yet it was still somehow recognizable as Saia's face.

Then Saia waved his hand at Raya and she immediately shut up, even though she still wanted to scream. So she just clung to Keeper more tightly than ever, hoping against hope that this was all just one terrible nightmare and that she would awaken any minute now.

Keeper, however, merely said, in his usual monotonic voice, "Who are you?"

Saia tilted his head to the side in an unnatural way. "Who am I? I am the Void, or a part of the Void, given a body that allows me to bypass the limitations placed upon the Void by the gods."

"What does that mean?" said Keeper. "I have never heard of this before. I thought that the Void could not take on physical bodies."

"It can, but does not want to," said Saia. "It is … inconvenient, but sometimes you need to take on temporary measures in order to achieve long-term goals. This body is one such temporary measure, but in the long run, I will dispose of it."

"What are you talking about?" asked Keeper. "How is this even possible?"

"It is possible because of the ceremony, of course," said Saia. He—or she, if it was the Void controlling him—gestured at the blood circle on the floor. "To bond part of my soul with a body, I had to perform this most ancient of ceremonies. You might have heard of it, though I doubt it, considering how obscure this ceremony is."

"I would listen to your explanation of it, but I am afraid that you are a threat to Princess Raya and thus must be eliminated," said Keeper. He raised his gun hand again. "Good bye."

Keeper unleashed round upon round at Saia again, the sound

of bullets as loud and earsplitting as ever in the tiny chamber. Raya covered her ears again, but she didn't take her eyes away from Saia, even though she wanted to.

Because the bullets did not penetrate Saia's body. Where they struck, they simply vanished into his skin, as if they had not hit him at all. They did not pass through Saia's body or bounce off it. It was like they had been absorbed, like water being absorbed by a sponge, and Saia didn't even flinch, which told Raya that the bullets didn't even hurt him at all.

Then Saia raised a hand and a shadow tendril shot out from his wrist and slashed Keeper's gun arm off. Keeper let out a shout of surprise as his gun arm fell to the floor with a loud *clunk* and he almost dropped Raya in surprise, but the protector managed to redouble his grip on her, thankfully.

"That didn't really hurt me, but it was annoying," said Saia or the Void or whatever was speaking through the corpse. "Very annoying, in fact. Now can I explain how the ceremony worked or are you going to try to kill me again?"

Raya looked up at Keeper, who was looking at the spot where his arm had been sliced clean off. Raya wondered how Keeper was managing to remain operational at all, considering how damaged he was. Then again, he was an automaton, so he couldn't feel pain even if he lost an arm like he did now.

"All right, then," said Saia. He gestured at his face. "You see, in the beginning, before either Martir or Harnum existed, there was the Void. It has no beginning and it has no end. It simply *is* and it will simply always be, long after Martir ends."

Saia's voice sounded similar to how it had in the past, but there was also something off about it that Raya didn't like at all.

She could hear undercurrents of the Void's own voice, albeit not as obvious as it normally was. Still, Raya wished that Keeper's bullets actually had killed him, because just hearing Saia's distorted voice was enough to make her want to run and hide.

"But despite my agelessness, the ceremony only worked because of a certain mortal who came back to life recently," said Saia. "The one known as Braim Kotogs. Remember him? His resurrection truly shattered the rules of this world. The gods have done their best to keep the damage checked, but in the end, they cannot stop the Void, no matter what."

Saia sounded incredibly gleeful, as if he was delivering the greatest news in the world. But to Raya, his words sounded as nice as being told that she only had a few more hours in which to live, and then she would die a horribly painful death.

"But why a body?" asked Keeper. "I thought that the Void could travel without one."

"The Void can," said Saia, nodding. He grinned. "But the gods expect that and will fight against the Void's attempts to enter Martir the normal way. The gods would never expect the Void to take on the form of a mortal, much less directly underneath their noses like I am doing now. They are fools, the whole and utter lot of them, but like everything else, they, too, will be consumed."

Then Saia looked directly at Raya and his grin grew even larger. "I remember you, Princess Raya. I remember how you escaped me the first time. But don't worry. Unlike some, I *learn* from my mistakes, so I am not going to let you escape me again."

Raya immediately raised her hand in order to open an ethereal portal, but just as she did so, another black tendril emerged from the ground and slashed through her wrist.

Raya watched in shock as her hand fell onto the floor; in fact, she was too numbed by the shock to even feel the pain that should have followed her hand being cut off.

But then the shock wore off soon enough, causing Raya to scream in pain as Keeper shouted, "Princess!"

"As I said, I learn from my mistakes," said Saia. "That is why I will consume you, you and everyone else in this world. But don't worry. I will make it quick and painless."

Chapter Twenty-One

ARMAZ REACHED THE bottom of the staircase in only a few minutes. But it was a hard few minutes, because the closer he got to the bottom, the more the primal fear in the pit of his stomach made him want to turn and run away. It was that same primal fear he had felt back when the Void had consumed the Stadium, only this time it was even worse, probably because he had run directly at it today.

But Carmaz had fought the fear because he wanted to save Raya more than he wanted to run away. He didn't necessarily want to save Raya because he liked her. He did it because she was another human being and a fellow godling and, despite her annoyance, had actually not done anything to deserve to be consumed by the Void, which he figured was what her ultimate fate was going to be if he didn't save her.

Now Carmaz stood before the door to the chamber. It was just as black as the door above, although this one was made out of wood rather than stone. He reached for the doorknob, but as soon as he touched it, he pulled away instinctively.

The doorknob had felt cold, but not just cold, icy cold, as cold as a cold winter day in the jungles of Ruwa. Granted, Ruwan winters were not terribly cold, but that was the closest thing he could compare the doorknob's temperature to, as he had never been anywhere colder than that before.

But this wasn't ordinary cold. It was the coldness of the Void, which meant that the Void was keeping the door shut. That thought made Carmaz want to turn and run, but he stayed where he was. He thought about running back to go and get the others, but as far as he knew they were still fighting the Empty followers. Besides, even if he could go and get them, by the time he did, there was no guarantee that Raya would even still be alive.

Guess I'll just have to knock the door down, then, Carmaz thought.

He took a couple of steps back to put some distance between him and the door, and then charged at it with his shoulders. Carmaz slammed into the door with his shoulder as hard as he could, putting all of his strength into the blow, and without warning the door flew open and he staggered inside, though he managed to regain his balance quickly enough to hold up his sword to protect himself from any possible attacks by whoever was on the other side.

The sight Carmaz saw perplexed him. Lying on the floor to the right was Anwan, who looked like he had been shot dozens if not hundreds of times. In fact, his body was in such poor condition that Carmaz almost didn't recognize the tailor until he noticed that the bloody mess on the floor wore a suit with a color scheme similar to that of Anwan.

Then Carmaz noticed a dark figure standing in the center of a ring that appeared to be made out of blood. And standing opposite the figure was a one-armed mechanical giant who carried Raya in his other arm, only Raya was crying and screaming for some reason, like she was in severe pain. He noticed blood on the mechanical giant's arm, which he thought must have meant that the giant had harmed Raya, but then he noticed Raya's bloody, detached right hand lying on the stone floor, which made him feel ill as soon as he spotted it.

But Raya suddenly stopped screaming when she saw Carmaz. She then smiled, but it was a very weak smile that she was did not seem likely to sustain for very long.

"Carmaz!" Raya said. Carmaz wondered at how she was apparently no longer bothered by the fact that she had lost one of her hands. "You're here!"

Carmaz nodded and pointed his sword at the dark figure. "I am. And I am here to save you from this person. The Void, I presume?"

The dark figure chuckled. It was a familiar chuckle that reminded Carmaz of Saia, though he dismissed the thought as pointless. "Correct. But not entirely."

The dark figure then turned, and when Carmaz saw the dark figure's face, he was certain that he had gone insane: It was the face of Saia, albeit cloaked in shadow and much more sinister-looking than normal. Still, there was no way Carmaz could ever mistake that face for the face of anyone else in the whole world.

"Carmaz Korva," said the Void, though her voice sounded closer to Saia's than her normal voice. "Aren't you happy to see your friend again? The one you thought was dead?"

Carmaz, still shocked by the dark figure's appearance, shook his head and said, "You aren't Saia."

"I may not be, but this body is—or rather, was—his before I took control of it," said the Void. She patted her chest. "It is every bit as solid as the day I consumed it."

"You …" Carmaz was so filled with rage that he could barely find the words to describe his anger. "You are a monster, irredeemable and vile, just as I always thought."

"Insults do not harm me," said the Void. "My power is above yours in every single way. But do go and keep insulting me. It just makes you look that much more pathetic."

Carmaz had no idea how the Void was controlling Saia's body. He didn't know who the mechanical giant was or why Anwan had this dark chamber underneath his shop. He didn't even know whether to believe the Void's claim about controlling Saia's body. Or what to say in response to what she just said.

Carmaz charged at the Void with his sword, yelling as he did so. He didn't care if he was no match for the Void. He was going to tear her apart piece by piece for disrespecting Saia's memory. It was the only thing he could do, the only thing he *wanted* to do, and he was going to do it no matter what the Void threw at him.

The Void hardly looked surprised at his attack. She just extended Saia's hands and two black tendrils shot from them, hurtling through the air toward Carmaz.

Carmaz, however, rolled forward underneath the tendrils, allowing them to pass him by overhead. He then rolled to a crouch and slashed at the tendrils with his sword, cutting through them as easily as if they were butter. Half of the tendrils fell to the floor and the other half returned to the Void, but Carmaz was already up and running toward the Void even before the tendrils hit the floor.

The Void didn't even flinch. She just raised her hand again and summoned another shadow spike from the ground, which went straight for Carmaz's chest.

But Carmaz dodged it, spinning to the right to avoid it. Even so, the spike did graze his arm, although it was barely enough to wound him, much less slow him down, and soon Carmaz was in front of the Void.

With another yell, Carmaz slashed the Void in half. His sword passed through her body—*Saia's* body—with ease, but no blood or anything came out. In fact, the Void didn't even blink when he did that, as if he hadn't hurt her at all. Still, attacking her felt good, so Carmaz raised his blade and brought it down on her again.

This time, however, the Void caught the blade with one hand and tore it out of his hands. She then snapped the sword in half and threw both halves away, where they clattered to the stone floor outside of Carmaz's reach.

"Enough," said the Void. The amusement in her voice had vanished, replaced by a deadly seriousness that made Carmaz hesitate. "I am sick of playing with you. The Void desires to consume everything, so allow me to consume you, just as I consumed the soul of your friend."

The Void's arms turned into pure shadow and then wrapped around Carmaz's body before he even realized what was happening. He struggled against the shadow tendrils, but they were so cold and so draining that he gave up soon enough.

Then Carmaz felt what might have been little teeth biting at his body. Carmaz had once, as a child, been bitten by a large rat. It had not been the most painful injury he had ever sustained, but the rat had had unusually sharp teeth, so the pain of that injury stood out in Carmaz's memory even years after the fact.

That was how Carmaz felt now, with the Void constricting

him the way it was. It was like a hundred of those large rats, with teeth twice as sharp as the rat's had been, were biting away at his body. Even worse, Carmaz was starting to become tired and lose consciousness, even though on an intellectual level he was aware that he was going to die if he gave in to the rest his body so mightily desired.

His eyes drooping, Carmaz looked the Void in the eyes. The Void's eyes were green, a different color from Saia's. Despite that, it was hard not to see Saia's face in there, even though he was absolutely certain by now that Saia's soul was gone. Seeing his friend's face, even if he knew that the soul behind it was gone, weakened his resistance to the Void's grip on him.

"Yes ..." said the Void, her voice far more soothing than it had been before. "Allow the Void to consume you. Don't fight. Don't resist. Just let oblivion claim your consciousness. You do not need to exist. Don't be afraid of the darkness beyond. It is the natural home of all living creatures. Sleep ... sleep ..."

Carmaz found himself starting to nod off. Of course, he knew that he had to stay awake, that he had to fight off the Void's influence, but all he wanted to do was rest. The exhaustion of the day was starting to catch up with him now. In fact, he couldn't remember the last time he had taken a nap. He decided that he could close his eyes for a second ... maybe two seconds ... three seconds ... all right, half a minute, but no more. Then he would wake up and be ready to fight the Void once more.

But before he could close his eyes, an ethereal portal opened up behind the Void. Surprised, the Void looked over her shoulder and said, "What in the world—"

She was interrupted when the ethereal portal actually *fell* on her, cutting off the tendrils that she had wrapped around Carmaz. The tendrils dissipated into shadows moments before they hit the floor, while Carmaz staggered back as all of his energy returned to him. He was still tired, still exhausted from the fighting, but now he didn't feel like taking a nap or resting at the moment.

But Carmaz, as it turned out, didn't even need to do anything else, because the portal slammed shut on the Void and then vanished with a loud *pop*. When it did, the Void—and Saia's body—were gone, leaving only Carmaz, Raya, and the mysterious mechanical giant in the room, plus Anwan's corpse, though Carmaz paid no attention to that.

Instead, Carmaz looked at Raya and the mechanical giant. Raya held her other hand out, the one that was still attached to her arm. Her face was pale and she looked close to fainting, but incredibly, she was also smirking, as if she had gotten the last laugh on some joke that Carmaz didn't know about.

"Take … that, you bitch," said Raya, her voice so weak that she sounded close to death. "Ha … ha."

Then Raya suddenly collapsed in the mechanical giant's arm. The giant, however, managed to keep her from falling out of the crook of his arm, though with the way Raya was bleeding, she obviously needed medical attention right away.

The giant must have had the same idea as Carmaz, because he looked up at Carmaz and said, "Carmaz, we must get the Princess to the nearest healer immediately. She has already lost far too much blood and opening the ethereal portal like that took out what little energy she had. Her parents are going to shut me down when they learn of this."

Carmaz still had no idea who the mechanical giant was or

237

what he meant by that last sentence, but the giant was clearly an ally, so Carmaz nodded and said, "All right. But what about the Void?"

The giant strode forward, though Carmaz wasn't sure how the giant intended to leave the room, because he looked too tall to go underneath the doorway. "I believe Raya managed to temporarily banish the Void to the ethereal. Or at least that part of the Void that was possessing Saia's body or whatever it was."

"Will it come back?" asked Carmaz.

The giant shook his head. "Not certain. It was cut off from the source, so it will probably simply die in the ethereal, but whether it will return or not, we must get Raya to help. Come with me."

The giant strode past Carmaz and actually managed to fit through the open doorway, though he had to bend over to do it. Carmaz turned and followed, trying to avoid stepping in the drops of blood from Raya's hand-less arm.

"What is your name?" asked Carmaz, following the giant up the steps.

The giant, who took the steps two or three at a time, said tersely, "Keeper."

"Well, Keeper, we might not be able to get Raya to a healer fast enough," Carmaz said as they walked quickly up the stairs. "Right now, there are about a dozen or so Soldiers of the Gods, plus Malya and Yoji, fighting against an equal number of Empty followers in Anwan's shop above."

"Then we will slaughter anyone who tries to stop us from getting Raya the medical attention that she needs," said Keeper without missing a beat. "Are you prepared to kill?"

Carmaz, taken aback by Keeper's words, nonetheless managed

to say, "I actually have already killed a couple of people today, so —"

"Good," said Keeper without looking at Carmaz. "But enough talking. For now, we must walk and, if necessary, fight and kill. Nothing else matters."

Carmaz nodded. He didn't want to talk much to this strange 'Keeper,' if that was his actual name. Having seen the Void use the body of his deceased best friend, he didn't want to do much of anything except see Raya to safety. At least then he might be able to prevent the Void from taking over *her* body in the future, anyway.

Chapter Twenty-Two

I AM TEMPTED," said the Ghostly God, his voice deep and threatening, "so very, very tempted, to rip your head off and feed you to the mimic monkeys that you just fought."

Braim said nothing in response because he couldn't even speak. He could barely even breathe. In fact, he was pretty sure at this point that he wasn't going to be breathing again any time soon. The darkness was gathering in the corner of his eyes and his throat burned from the pressure applied to it by the Ghostly God. He flailed his limbs about wildly, but neither his feet nor his fists hit the Ghostly God.

"But I won't," said the Ghostly God. "I may be insane, lacking in what your mortals conventionally think of as 'morality,' and even lack some basic social skills that the other gods tell me I need, but I am not stupid enough to kill the one being whose body and soul could show me everything I have ever wanted to know about the afterlife, and so much more."

The Ghostly God's grip actually lessened on Braim's neck, allowing him to breathe better. But the Ghostly God still didn't let go and soon Braim stopped flailing his limbs about entirely.

"Of course, just because I won't kill you doesn't mean I cannot experiment upon you so painfully that it might accidentally kill you anyway," the Ghostly God continued. "Look at this."

The Ghostly God held up what appeared to be a wand, only Braim noticed that it had a sharpened tip coated in metal. It looked sharp enough to stab through Braim's chest.

"This is an invention of mine," said the Ghostly God, "which I call the Soul Collector. Do you know what it does?"

Braim could not answer or shake his head. He just stared at the Ghostly God in annoyance.

"It collects souls," said the Ghostly God. "By that, I mean that all I need to do is stab it in your body and it will draw your soul from your body. Your body will continue to function on a basic level, but only for a little while, and it won't be able to do anything else like walk or talk or even eat."

The Ghostly God brought the tip of the Soul Collector close to Braim's chest. "I would prefer to study you whole, but it is sometimes necessary to dissect creatures in order to understand how they work. Perhaps I will discover the secrets to resurrection by separating your soul from your body. Of course, it might also end up killing you, but I have used it before on some of the mimic monkeys around here and, aside from removing their soul from their body, has not had any real negative effects. Though now that I think about it, one monkey did end up exploding, but I have worked out all of the kinks and I am confident now that that won't happen to your body."

The Ghostly God pulled the Soul Collector back. "Just one stab ought to do it, and then your soul will be mine."

Alarmed, Braim struggled against the Ghostly God's grip again, but as before, his struggles were useless. He continued to struggle anyway, however, at least until the Ghostly God slammed the tip of the Soul Collector into his chest.

The sudden penetration of the Soul Collector into his chest made Braim scream. Or he tried to, but the Ghostly God choked off his scream quickly enough. Yet that did nothing to get rid of the pain that followed the stabbing of the Soul Collector into his chest, or the intense pain that followed immediately afterward.

'Intense' was a severe understatement. The pain ripping through his body—that ripped through his very soul—was beyond anything Braim could ever remember feeling before. It felt like someone was trying to pull him in half while also picking out his eyeballs with spoons. His skin became white hot and it became impossible for him to think. His insides boiled, while his hair felt like it had caught fire.

Braim couldn't even scream, because his tongue felt like it had melted to the roof of his mouth. Pain and pain alone dominated his mind and that pain was almost enough to drive him hopelessly insane.

Just when Braim was certain that he couldn't take it any longer, however, the Ghostly God suddenly said, "What in the world is—" before he interrupted himself with a loud scream that almost shattered Braim's own eardrums.

Then Braim suddenly fell to the ground and landed flat on his back. The fall jarred him from his reverie and he became aware of the muddy ground and wet leaves underneath him. He looked at his chest but no longer saw the Soul Collector there, though there was a hole in his chest where it had been. Before his startled eyes, the hole began to heal itself, until soon Braim's chest was whole once more. His skin and hair and inner organs no longer felt quite so painful as before, and he could now feel the pain rapidly retreating from his body, save for the pain on his neck where the

Ghostly God had choked him.

Before Braim could spend too much time marveling at this sudden and unexpected turn of events, he heard the Ghostly God yell and looked up to see the deity had dropped the Soul Collector. The Ghostly God was looking at his own hand, which looked like it had been burnt, but Braim did not know what was going on and he wasn't sure that he even wanted to know.

"My hand ..." said the Ghostly God, his voice full of pain as he grabbed his wrist. "Why does it burn? Why did the Soul Collector rebound?"

Braim scrambled to his feet and, for good measure, snatched the Soul Collector away from the Ghostly God. Yet he also held the little device as far from his body as he could, even though he knew that the Soul Collector only worked when it was actually stabbed into someone, not merely by being in the same vicinity as a person.

"Rebound?" said Braim, though he found it hard to talk because his throat hurt from where the Ghostly God had choked it. "What do you mean?"

The Ghostly God, through gritted teeth, said, "I meant that the Soul Collector cannot separate your soul from your body. As a result, the energy it expended had to go somewhere, and thus it went to—harmed—me. In other words, you got lucky."

"Looks like I did," said Braim. "Always did think that the luck of Dranyx was with me. But I guess it wasn't with you, huh?"

"My sister and I never have gotten along very well," the Ghostly God said. "But I doubt she saved you. Likely it was your strange nature that prevented the Soul Collector from doing its job. But it is no matter. The pain will leave me soon and then I will think of some other way to study you."

Braim stepped back, thinking he could run, but then he looked down at the Soul Collector in his hands and an idea occurred to him.

Raising the Soul Collector like a sword, Braim said, "No, you aren't. You are going to take me back to World's End right away."

"And why, pray tell, would I do that?" said the Ghostly God. "There is still plenty of time before the day is over, plenty of time before everyone realizes you're missing. That is still plenty of time for me to study you. Even if there wasn't, you have no power over me."

"Oh, don't I?" said Braim. "I wonder what would happen if I stabbed you with your own Soul Collector. If it really does collect souls like you said, then I wonder if that means it can collect the soul of a god as well."

The Ghostly God's face became even paler, if that was possible. Still gripping his wrist, he said, "It doesn't work on gods. Divine beings such as myself have souls that are completely different from the souls of mortals such as yourself. Stabbing me with my Soul Collector would do nothing, even if I let you do it."

"If that's the case, then why do you look even paler than normal?" asked Braim. "Might it be because I have a point and you're just trying to deny it so I don't try it on you?"

The Ghostly God rubbed his wrist. He looked away and said, "Fine. I have not actually tested it on a god. None of my siblings would ever consent to participate in such an experiment and I have not tried it on myself because I am not that kind of fool. I believe it will do nothing to me or to any of the other gods, but I do not know for sure."

Braim stepped forward, still holding the Soul Collector before him. "Then why don't we test it? Weren't you the one telling me earlier that sometimes you have to make sacrifices for the greater good or whatever? Granted, I'm not sure how useful knowing how to separate a god's soul from a god's body would be, but I think it'd be worth investigating just the same, don't you? For the greater knowledge of Martir, at least?"

To Braim's satisfaction, the Ghostly God floated backwards slightly. It was slight enough that someone else might have dismissed the movement as meaningless, but Braim understood it to mean that he was getting to the Ghostly God and that he just needed to keep pushing the point until he got what he wanted.

"Not all sacrifices are worth making," said the Ghostly God. His tone was level, though Braim caught a hint of worry in it. "Some areas of knowledge even we gods must remain ignorant of, for that is the way that the Powers have ordained it."

"You're just afraid I'll stab you with it and it will remove your soul from your body," said Braim. "It's okay if you admit it. I won't look down on you any more than I already do for your fears."

"I fear nothing," said the Ghostly God. "Besides, you are assuming that I will even let you touch me. Remember that I am a god and you are a mortal. If I so desired, I could remove your head from your body and obliterate you from this world with a single thought."

"But you won't," said Braim. "You want to be able to study me. If you killed me off, you wouldn't be able to understand anything about me. Right?"

To Braim's satisfaction, the Ghostly God did not answer that charge. He just looked furious, which was all the answer Braim needed.

"And anyway, if you killed me, you'd piss off Alira and the rest of the gods," said Braim. "Remember, I'm still in the Tournament, so killing me off would probably get you the same treatment as Diog. Speaking of Diog, I wonder how he's doing."

"Diog's status is irrelevant," said the Ghostly God. Then he sighed. "But I must, for once, concede the point to you. I would rather not, but even I must admit when I am defeated. And you, Braim Kotogs, have certainly caught me in a trap that I cannot easily think my way out of."

Braim sighed in relief, though he didn't lower the Soul Collector yet. "So you will take me back to World's End, then?"

"It appears that I have no choice in the matter," said the Ghostly God. His shoulders slumped. "I will still have to answer to my siblings for my actions. That is not going to be fun."

"Well, getting kidnapped and then mentally tortured by a psychotic deity like you wasn't exactly my definition of fun, either," said Braim. Then a thought occurred to him and he looked to the left and to the right briefly. "Say, where'd Aorja and Zeeree go? Did you—"

"They escaped," said the Ghostly God in a voice of pure disgust. "They ran away. To where, I don't know, but Aorja recovered and then used her magic to teleport herself and Zeeree from my grasp."

Braim smirked. "Looks like today just isn't your day. I almost feel sorry for you."

"I do not need your pity, mortal," said the Ghostly God. Then

246

he shrugged. "Oh, well. I will find Aorja and her oversized pet one of these days and kill them both. I suppose that for now, I should return you to World's End."

Braim eyed the Ghostly God carefully. "You aren't actually going to put me in the Mind Chamber, are you?"

"Of course I won't put you back in the Mind Chamber," said the Ghostly God. "At this point, it would be useless for me to do that to you. I will instead return you to World's End, just as I promised."

Then the Ghostly God held out his hand. "But first, return my Soul Collector to me. It is mine, so you cannot keep it."

Braim brought the Soul Collector close to his chest. "No. I don't trust you or anyone else with something this powerful, even if you did make it yourself. Besides, I'm going to need proof that you tried to steal my soul and I think that this Soul Collector ought to quell any doubts about that."

The rage of the Ghostly God's face was so great that Braim almost thought that the Ghostly God was going to break the agreement and kill him there and then. There wasn't much of anything that Braim could do to stop him, after all, given the power disparity between him and the Ghostly God.

But then the Ghostly God nodded and said, "Very well. I can wait until after you lose the Tournament. By then, the other gods should not care about what I or anyone else does with you. Just keep it safe for me until then."

"Unless I win the Tournament and become the God of Martir," said Braim. "Then you won't even be able to touch me."

"True, but I doubt you have what it takes to become the God of Martir," said the Ghostly God. "You do not even have magic anymore. How do you expect to compete with your fellow godlings, many of whom *do* use magic?"

Braim frowned. "You mean you can't give me my magical powers back?"

"No, I cannot," said the Ghostly God, shaking his head. "The bracelet you wear can only take away powers, not return them. The only entity I know of that can restore magical powers is the Mysterious One, and he's currently far away from Martir."

Braim cursed this complication under his breath, but then said aloud, "All right. I can live with that for now. Looks like I'll just have to figure out how to contact the Mysterious One, then. I'm sure he'd be more than willing to help me, since he knows me and all."

"Good luck with that," said the Ghostly God sarcastically. "No one knows how to contact him, not even us gods. I suggest that you should learn to adjust to your magic-less state. It should hopefully make you a little more humble."

"Says the most arrogant god in all of Martir," said Braim. "Anyway, I'm done talking about this. Just send me back to World's End. I'll take it from there."

The Ghostly God looked very reluctant to do so, but he nodded once more, raised his other hand, and said, "Then go, Braim, and do your best to win the Tournament. If you fail ... I will be waiting for you."

Then the Ghostly God snapped his fingers and Braim suddenly found himself back in his room in the inn he was staying at on World's End, standing all alone next to his bed. He heard the sounds of some kind of commotion going on outside, but with the curtain drawn over his window, he could not tell what was happening out there.

No strange white creatures or tiny wooden villagers with sharp teeth anywhere, Braim thought, looking around his room and noticing the box on his dresser that the bracelet had been inside earlier. *Guess he must have actually teleported me back to my room. Good on him.*

Braim took one step forward, with the intent of finding Alira and tell her what had happened to him, when the Ghostly God suddenly reappeared next to him. Braim jumped to the side and raised the Soul Collector, but the Ghostly God held up his hands defensively.

"Watch where you point that thing, Kotogs," said the Ghostly God. "I just have one last thing to tell you. You will learn it sooner or later anyway, but I thought you should hear it from my own lips first."

"All right," said Braim, although he didn't lower his guard at all. "What is this thing that you want to tell me about? Can't be that important."

"Actually, it is," said the Ghostly God. "Haven't you wondered who helped me to kidnap you in the first place? Remember, it was not I who placed that box in your room. I had an accomplice. A mortal accomplice, to be more specific."

"A mortal accomplice?" said Braim. "Amazing. I thought you considered yourself too good to work with a mortal."

"Very funny, but even us gods occasionally need the aid of a mortal, especially a mortal who no one would ever suspect of helping me," said the Ghostly Gods.

"Then get on with it," said Braim, folding his arms across his chest.

"All right, all right," said the Ghostly God. "I just wanted you to be prepared for the revelation, but I won't delay it a second longer."

The Ghostly God leaned forward, a far too happy smile on his lips, as he said, "My accomplice—the one who helped, albeit indirectly, put you through all of what you just experienced—is Carmaz Korva, your friend and fellow godling. And he helped me without regret."

Chapter Twenty-Three

WHEN CARMAZ AND Keeper emerged from the dark staircase and into the main area of Anwan's Tailoring, they discovered that the fight between the Empty followers and the Soldiers was over. The Soldiers had won. Most of the Empty followers had either been killed or run away. Both Malya and Yoji had survived. In fact, it was Yoji who used his magic to temporarily heal Raya's hand by staunching the bleeding (though he complained that it was difficult because the Void's darkness seemed to have infected Raya's wound somehow and that it would probably require divine magic in order to heal it perfectly). But Raya would live, at least long enough for them to find a proper healer to finish the job.

It wasn't long after that that nearly every Soldier of the Gods in the city descended upon the shop. Captain Garvan took Carmaz, Malya, and Yoji aside and questioned all three of them about what they knew about this attack, while the other Soldiers worked on either moving the corpses of their fellow Soldiers and dead Empty followers out or investigating the shop itself and the dark chamber beneath it. The streets were also closed off and any katabans bystanders kept away until the Soldiers could confirm that Anwan's Tailoring was no longer a threat to the general well-being of the population.

As for Keeper and Raya, Captain Garvan ordered about a dozen of the Soldiers to escort them to the nearest healer's station. While Yoji's magic had prevented Raya from dying, the fact was that she needed the kind of medical attention that even Yoji could not provide for her. Keeper was allowed to continue to carry her because Carmaz had assured the Soldiers that the automaton was on their side.

Still, Carmaz wanted to go with Keeper and Raya, but he couldn't because Garvan grilled him on every possible detail of the Void's presence in the chamber below Anwan's Tailoring. Carmaz answered the questions to the best of his ability, but there were several times where he shrugged because he did not know the answer to that question. Malya and Yoji received questioning as well, although they were not questioned as deeply as he was.

Once Captain Garvan finished questioning Carmaz and the others, he gave orders to another set of Soldiers to escort Carmaz, Malya and Yoji back to the Stadium. He also gave them a note to give to Alira, though Carmaz didn't know what the note said. He guessed that it was probably an explanation of what had happened, although with the way Captain Garvan gave it to him rather surreptitiously, he had a feeling that it was probably something more important than that.

But regardless, Carmaz didn't dwell on it much. As he walked with Malya and Yoji back to the Stadium, his focus was rather scattered. Part of him worried about Raya, who, despite being the most annoying person in the world, he still didn't want to die. This was the worst condition he had ever seen her in and he would honestly be shocked if she survived. Carmaz knew that she was probably going to be okay—magic could do all sorts of things he didn't understand, especially katabans magic—but that still didn't stop him from worrying about her anyway.

Another thing that occupied Carmaz's mind was the fact that the Void had taken Saia's body. It infuriated him greatly. Just thinking about it was enough to get his blood boiling. In fact, Carmaz wanted to swim across the ocean that separated World's End from the Void and teach the Void a lesson. It was an irrational thought, to be sure, but Carmaz didn't care.

The Void truly is an evil entity, Carmaz thought, shoving his hands into his pockets so that neither Malya nor Yoji would notice them balled into fists. *Taking Saia's body and desecrating it like that ... I cannot think of a more evil thing for a person to do. And she knew it would get to me. That's why she did it. She knew it would demoralize me and that it would make me easy to crush. And she almost succeeded.*

That's what bothered Carmaz the most. It was his own weakness in the face of the Void's overwhelming power. Had Raya not saved him at the last minute, he would almost certainly have been consumed by the Void. He had not mentioned that particular fact to Captain Garvan, Malya, Yoji, or anyone else. Nor had Keeper said anything about it, though that was probably because Keeper had been so intent on getting Raya to safety that he saw no point in mentioning it.

I just did not know how ... alluring the Void's words could be until I heard them myself, Carmaz thought. *And that is what makes me weak. The Void now* knows *I am weak. She knows I was too weak to save Saia and too weak to resist her. Some god I'll* make.

These thoughts and others like them swirled in Carmaz's head during the entire walk back to the Stadium. He heard Malya and Yoji talking to each other. It sounded like they were talking about the fight and how awful it had been, but Carmaz didn't join in the conversation, nor did they ask him anything. That was all right by him, because right now all he wanted to do was get back to the Stadium, tell Alira what happened, learn who won the Spider Goddess Sub-Bracket Challenge (which he was certain had to be Tashir), and then go back to his apartment and get ready for the next couple of sub-bracket challenges.

It wasn't long before the Stadium came into view, but when it did, there was something going on at the entrance. From what Carmaz could see, it appeared that all of the godlings were standing around and talking to each other at the entrance to the Stadium. Even Alira was standing near them, though she was talking with a tall, red-haired man with green—

Carmaz froze in his tracks. He blinked several times, certain that his eyes were playing tricks on him, but no matter how much he blinked, Braim Kotogs—whose clothes looked rather dirty and ragged—still stood there talking to Alira about something.

"Oh, look," said Malya, pointing at the entrance to the Stadium. "It looks like Braim is feeling well enough to walk around again. At least one good thing happened today."

"But why are his clothes so dirty?" asked Yoji, scratching his bald head. "He looks like he was playing in the mud."

"And which god is that floating there with him?" asked Malya, squinting. "He's rather hard to see."

Of course, Carmaz had zero problem identifying the Ghostly God, who was floating near Braim and Alira. He was nodding his head with every word that Braim said, which all but confirmed

Carmaz's worst fears.

Then the Ghostly God looked in their direction, smiled a chilling smile, and vanished into mist. Alira and Braim looked at the mist that floated where the Ghostly God had been, but only for a moment. In the next, the two were back to their conversation, but Carmaz now wished that he could also turn into mist, because he knew exactly what was going to happen next.

But maybe I can slip away before Braim notices me, Carmaz thought, taking one step backwards. *He's still talking with Alira and doesn't seem to have noticed us yet. So if I am careful, I might—*

"Hey, Braim!" said Malya in an unnecessarily loud voice, waving in his direction. "How are you feeling? I haven't seen you all day!"

Carmaz wanted to punch Malya to make her shut up, but he didn't. He just stood there as Braim looked in their direction, already prepared for whatever Braim's reaction was going to be.

Braim at first looked quizzical, as if he was not sure what he was looking at. But the longer he stared, the angrier his face became, until Braim turned his whole body and started walking over to Carmaz and the others. He walked quickly, not wasting even one step, and Carmaz knew that his days were numbered.

"Braim?" said Malya, who must not have been as smart as Carmaz thought she was, because she genuinely did not seem to notice Braim's anger. "What's the matter? Did you see something that—"

Braim stormed past her without another word. He also stormed by Yoji, who stepped aside silently and didn't even look at his fellow mage or at Carmaz.

Carmaz raised his hands and said, "Braim, I can explain. I only did what I—"

Braim punched him in the face. Though Carmaz was strong, even he was unprepared for the strength of Braim's punch. It was enough to send him falling on his behind, but before he could do anything else, Braim kicked his jaw. That, too, hurt, and far more than the punch, because Braim wore very thick, heavy boots with thick toes. Carmaz even felt a little bit of blood leak out from the side of his mouth from where Braim had struck him.

The nearby Soldiers of the Gods moved to break up the fight, but one look of warning from Braim caused them to stop. Then Braim bent over, grabbed Carmaz by the collar, and forced him up to his feet. Braim's eyes burned with anger, angrier than Carmaz had ever seen them before.

"Braim!" said Malya, who sounded shocked at Braim's actions. "What are you doing to Carmaz? He hasn't done anything to you. In fact, I'd say he's a hero, because he helped save Raya from being killed."

"Hero?" said Braim, though he didn't look at Malya when he said that. His breath was hot against Carmaz's face. "Then why did he work with the Ghostly God to have me kidnapped and tortured?"

"What?" said Malya. "What are you talking about?"

But Braim seemed to be ignoring Malya now, because he said to Carmaz, "Do you even *know* what I've been through over the last day because of your idiocy? I was mentally and physically tortured. I almost went insane and almost lost my very soul. Do you feel *proud* of yourself for that?"

Carmaz's jaw hurt too much for him to speak, so he said

nothing. He just met Braim's gaze as firmly as he could.

"I should beat the living crap out of you for what you did to me," said Braim. He pulled back his right hand, which was balled into a fist. "And maybe I will. I thought I could *trust* you, but I guess this teaches me not to trust people so easily, huh?"

Then a hand wrapped around Braim's pulled back arm, causing him to look over his shoulder. Alira stood behind Braim, but Carmaz had not noticed her approach. She was holding his arm, but she wasn't looking at Braim. She was looking at Carmaz, though unlike Braim, she looked more disappointed than angry.

"Let him go, Braim," said Alira. Her tone was sharp. "I'll deal with Carmaz."

"But—"

"If you hit him again, I will disqualify you from the Tournament," said Alira, without changing her tone. "The Rulebook says that Tournament participants are not supposed to fight outside of the Tournament. The only reason I have not yet disqualified you is because of what you have been through recently, although I will not hesitate to do so if you continue to refuse to listen to me."

Braim looked like he was going to punch Carmaz anyway, but then he let go of Carmaz's collar. Alira let go of Braim's arm and Braim stepped aside, although he didn't leave. He just stood there with his arms folded over his chest and watched as Alira stepped toward Carmaz.

"Carmaz Korva," said Alira. There was no kindness in her voice. "According to the Ghostly God, you worked with him to kidnap Braim and take him away from World's End. Is that true?"

Carmaz almost denied the charge, but then he realized that it would be pointless to do so at this point. He looked at Malya and Yoji briefly. The two looked as shocked by this question as if Alira had asked Carmaz if he had murdered a bunch of children.

Then Carmaz looked up at Alira again. His jaw still hurt from Braim's kick, but he managed to say, "Yes, I did."

Malya actually gasped when she heard that, while Yoji looked like he couldn't believe his ears. Braim looked like he wanted to punch Carmaz in the face again, but he must have had great self-restraint, because he didn't move an inch from the spot where he stood.

"Then you are disqualified from the Tournament," said Alira.

Carmaz blinked. "Wait, you aren't going to ask me *why* I did it?"

"Your motivations are irrelevant," said Alira simply. She held up the Rulebook. "It says in the Rulebook that any attempt by one participant in the Tournament to endanger the life of another Tournament participant—whether inside or outside of the Tournament itself—is grounds for immediate disqualification. It does not matter why you did it. All that matters is that you did it. You broke the rules. Therefore, you must suffer the consequences."

Carmaz had suspected that this would happen, but he was still so shocked that he wasn't even sure how to react. All he could think about was how he had failed his people back on Ruwa … and how he had failed Saia as well.

"Soldiers, please escort Carmaz back to his apartment," said Alira, looking at the Soldiers standing around them. "He may gather whatever possessions he owns before we send him back to Ruwa for good."

The Soldiers nodded and moved in closer to Carmaz, surrounding him on all sides. Alira, meanwhile, turned and walked back to the Stadium. She gestured for the other three godlings to follow her, which they did, but not without looking back at Carmaz. Malya had shock and disappointment on her face, Braim looked pleased, and Yoji looked confused.

Carmaz didn't say another word to any of them, however. He just turned and walked back up the street, Soldiers of the Gods all around him, his shoulders slumped and his head down.

I've failed, Carmaz thought. *And now, Ruwa truly is doomed to remain little more than a wasteland for the distraught. And it is all my fault.*

Chapter Twenty-Four

DEEP BENEATH THE surface of the earth, the figure who called himself Stalac stood over the legions of resting beings that stretched out for as far as the eye could see. They were all as still as stone, but he could feel their hearts beating and sense their dreams, the same dreams that they had dreamed for eons, ever since they were cast into this endless slumber.

But now, Stalac could feel something a little different about them. Their dreams were becoming vaguer and weaker. Occasionally, he even saw movement among the resting. The twitch of a finger or toe, a yawn, the turning of a head. It was the most movement that he had seen in centuries. More than that, however, it was proof that they were indeed about to rise again.

Then Stalac heard someone walking behind him. Turning around, Stalac saw his mistress, Lady Dia, walking up the slope toward him. She looked as radiant as ever, with her diamond-colored skin and her ruby eyes, but she also looked angry, as if she had just heard bad news that had put her in a bad mood.

"My lady," said Stalac, his voice tinged with sarcasm. "What are you angry about now? Do you think we won't be able to handle the surface dwellers?"

Lady Dia shook her head and stopped a few feet from him.

"No. I am angry about that human who saw us. He knows that we exist and he might tell his fellow humans about us. If so, then that will take away the element of surprise that we have worked so hard to cultivate."

"My lady, I sincerely doubt that that human will tell anyone anything," said Stalac. "He seemed as confused and shocked at seeing us as we were at seeing him. Likely he will dismiss it as nothing more than a fevered dream brought on by his mushy brain. I see nothing to worry about."

"It doesn't matter whether you worry about it or not," said Lady Dia. "What matters is that we may need to revise our plans ... *again*."

"There will be no need for that," said Stalac hastily. "Our brothers and sisters are about to awaken. And once they do, we can begin the invasion right away, before the surface dwellers are able to come up with a counterattack against us."

"I suppose you are right, Stalac," said Lady Dia. "But even if you are, that does not change the fact that at least one of the surface dwellers knows of us."

"Nothing is perfect, my lady," said Stalac with a shrug. "If that human knows, then he knows. Besides, you have been nagging me about starting the invasion for ages, and now that it is actually about to begin, you are starting to have second thoughts?"

"I am having second thoughts about *nothing*," Lady Dia said flatly. "I am only concerned that the invasion will not be as successful as I hoped."

"Only if you believe that one human really can make a difference against our forces," said Stalac, "which I hope you do not, because your people need your unwavering confidence if they are going to be a successful invading army against the surface dwellers."

To Stalac's satisfaction, that seemed to rile Lady Dia, because she said, "Of course my confidence is unwavering. I will not let a pitiful human deter me. I will lead the invasion like any great leader and we will crush the surface dwellers without hesitation."

"Good," said Stalac, nodding. "Very good, my lady. I estimate that the first of the golems will awaken within the next hour. Why don't we prepare their welcome party and get them up to speed on everything that has happened since they were cast into sleep? An ignorant army is not an effective army, after all."

Continued in:

Invasion of the Chosen

After the events of the last book, Braim Kotogs now wants to move up in the Tournament of the Gods in order to secure his own safety from the beings who want him dead. To win his sub-bracket challenge, Braim must defeat his opponent—a shy, unassuming woman with a mysterious past and agenda—in battle, but when Braim learns of a terrible secret about his true nature, he will have to do more than simply win the sub-bracket challenge in order to survive.

Raya Mana finds herself kidnapped by a violent and insane mage who intends to use her for her own vile ends. But when Raya escapes the mage, she must now work with the mysterious Hermit of the Swamp in order to return to World's End, although with the violent mage and her half-god pet chasing her, Raya will have to use all of her wits and intelligence to make it back alive.

Shunned and hated by his people, Carmaz Korva now lives alone in the Ruwan wilderness when he stumbles upon a plot by a mysterious race of golems to invade the surface and kill everyone on his home island of Ruwa. Carmaz must work with a legendary —and insane—mage and his son in order to stop the golems' invasion before it begins, because if he does not, then everyone and everything he loves will be destroyed.

Available in ebook and trade paperback wherever books are sold!

Glossary:

Aorja Kitano. A former student at North Academy who specialized in musical magic. Though she is good at pretending to be kind and intelligent, in truth she is insane and violent and is currently on the run from the authorities for her crimes against Martir. She has a 'pet' half-god called Zeeree who she managed to tame. She is also a mage known as a 'Limitless,' which means that she has access to unlimited magical energy (although that does not make her invincible).

Aquarians. A species of fish-like humanoids that live in the Undersea, which is the name for the part of Martir underneath the Crystal Sea. Like humans, aquarians worship the northern gods and can use magic, although they have different names for the gods and also do magic differently from their human counterparts. They have a variety of different appearances and races, much like humans, although their differences tend to be even more dramatic than the ones between humans.

Automatons. Mechanical beings created by the Mechanical Goddess to carry out her will, although the Carnagian Royal Family has been experimenting with making automatons of their own in recent years.

Darek Takren. The adopted son of Jenur Takren and a graduate of North Academy. He specializes in pagomancy, or ice magic, and is currently the leader of the Xocionian Monks. He was the protagonist in the Mages of Martir novels and is a good friend of Braim Kotogs.

Diog. The God of the Grave. Aquarian name: Hamafa.

Godling. Name for human beings who are destined to become gods.

Half-gods. The prototypes of the gods that the Powers abandoned in the Void after finishing Martir. Half-gods, while stronger than mortals, are not quite as strong as gods, although they can give the gods a good fight. They also tend to be more animalistic and lack some of the higher reasoning functions of the gods themselves due to their incompleteness, which makes it possible for beings who are weaker than them to control or manipulate them. The most well-known half-god is Zeeree, the Half-God of Poison, who serves Aorja Kitano.

Harnum. The world that existed before Martir. It was destroyed by Uron, one of its inhabitants, and everyone who lived there was killed off. The Powers arrived many years later and used Harnum's remains as the foundation for Martir, although some Harnumian buildings and objects can still be found deep beneath Martir's surface.

Jenur Takren. A native of Ruwa and current Magical Superior of North Academy and adoptive mother of Darek Takren. Like Malock, she was a major character in the Prince Malock World novels. In her youth, she was a member of the Dark Tigers Guild, an assassin's guild based in Ruwa, but eventually left it when she became disgusted with the Guild's mission. She adopted Darek Takren when he was only five years old after his birth mother was murdered by an enemy of hers.

Katabans. A species of intelligent beings who exist to serve the gods. 'Katabans' means 'minor spirit,' as katabans are spirits who often take on physical forms in order to follow the gods' commands. Their appearances range from human to beast, depending on their preferences, personality, and what they need to complete whatever mission given to them by the gods.

King Tojas Malock. The son of Queen Markinia and King Halock of Carnag. Current King of Carnag. He was the protagonist of the Prince Malock World novels and is married to Queen Hanarova. He is a fair and just ruler, although he spoils his daughter too much.

-Mancy. A suffix usually attached to Latin prefixes that denotes the name of a magical discipline. For example, hydromancy means 'water magic,' pyromancy means 'fire magic,' panamancy means 'healing magic,' and so on.

North Academy. The most prestigious and most difficult to get into magical school in the world. It is located in the northernmost reaches of the Great Berg and can only be reached with great difficulty. It is run by Jenur Takren, who is the current Magical Superior of the school.

Northern Isles. A region of the world located on the northern half of the Dividing Line that consists of thousands of island nations of various sizes. It is where almost all of Martir's human population is located, as well as many aquarians.

Northern Pantheon. The gods who rule the northern half of Martir. In contrast to their southern siblings, the northern gods are kinder and more respectful to mortals. They also tend to take mortal names (for example, Grinf), rather than titles translated from Godly Divina (for example, the Loner God).

Ooka. The God of Knives and Shadow. Aquarian name: Ooka.

Queen Hanarova. The katabans wife of King Malock and mother of Princess Raya Mana. Like Malock, she was a major character in the Prince Malock World novels. While not a bad person, she has a fierce rivalry with Jenur Takren that started in their youth and continues to this day.

Rock Isle. The most secure prison in the Northern Isles. Home to many of the most dangerous criminals in the Northern Isles.

Silver spoon. A slang term, common in the Northern Isles, usually applied to princesses, especially spoiled or bratty ones. The male equivalent is gold blood and the terms come from the folk song *Princess Silver Spoon and Prince Gold Blood.*

Skimif. The previous God of Martir. He was once an aquarian farmer who was chosen by the Powers to announce their return to Martir back in the Prince Malock World series. The Powers eventually made him into the God of Martir, but he was killed by Uron thirty years after his ascension.

Southern Pantheon. The gods who rule the southern half of Martir. In contrast to their northern siblings, they hate mortals and see them as no different than any other kind of animal. They tend to be more vicious and animalistic and don't understand humans as well as their northern siblings do.

The Almighty Ones. A group of four beings who live in the Spirit Lands and are responsible for judging and guiding the spirits of the dead. Originally consisted of the Dark Lady, the Arbiter, the Great Snake, and the Mysterious One before the Arbiter and the Great Snake were killed. They are far more powerful than the gods, but typically do not directly interfere with the physical realm, preferring to focus instead on the Spirit Lands where they rule.

The Dividing Line. The exact line that divides the northern and southern sides of Martir. This line can be crossed by any god or mortal, but if a southern god crosses it, then this god cannot kill any mortals on the northern side.

The gods of Martir. Super-powerful and immortal beings who each control a particular domain of Martir, such as the elements or even abstract concepts. The gods used to be one united force, but after the Godly War, they were separated into the Northern Pantheon and the Southern Pantheon and have remained that way ever since.

The Godly War. An ancient conflict that took place shortly after the creation of Martir eons ago. The War started over a disagreement between the gods over how to treat mortals. Half of them wished to use mortals for sport and food, while the other half wanted to have them as worshipers and followers. The two sides waged a war that killed many gods and countless mortals before the Powers stepped in, ended the conflict, and wrote up the Treaty to govern relations between the two sides.

The Ghostly God. The God of Ghosts and Mist. A southern god. Highly intelligent, but cruel and antisocial. Has an intense fascination with studying the dead and where ghosts go after their bodies die.

The Mechanical Goddess. The Goddess of Machines. A southern goddess. She is the creator of the automatons. Queen Hanarova served her in her youth.

The Mysterious One. One of the Almighty Ones. Originally pretended to be the mythical God of Mystery and Magic before revealing his true identity at the end of the Mages of Martir series. Strange and enigmatic, he nonetheless cares about Martir and does what he can to help protect it.

The Powers. A group of six powerful and ancient entities who created Martir, the gods, humanity, and everything else within Martir. Their exact nature is a mystery, but it is known that they are currently creating other worlds beyond the Void. They have only visited Martir once since creating the world but otherwise are not actively involved in the world's day-to-day functions, which are instead regulated by the gods themselves.

The Spirit Lands. A land where all spirits go when they die and where they are judged by the Mysterious One for their deeds in life. Those who are judged as righteous go beyond the Gates to rest eternally, while the ones judged wicked are banished to the Unknown to be tortured forever.

The Thief's Way. A magical discipline generally practiced by followers of the late Hollech, the former God of Deception, Thieves, and Horses. Practitioners of the Thief's Way can travel through shadow and also detach body parts and have them emerge from the shadows to attack someone or steal from them. Most practitioners of the Thief's Way are scorned by their fellow mages and generally treated as criminals even if they do not actually commit any crimes.

The Treaty. A document that governs relations between the Northern and Southern Pantheons, written by the Powers themselves.

The Void. A powerful and evil force that exists beyond the edge of Martir. Its sole purpose is to destroy and devour everything that exists. While the Void does not technically have a gender, it is usually referred to with female pronouns.

Tinkar. The God of Fate and Time. One of the oldest gods and a northern god. Aquarian name: Seyar.

Uron. A powerful being who existed in the world before Martir, where he was a bitter scientist who was hated by everyone. He allowed the Almighty One known as the Great Snake to possess him so he could get back at his people, but due to a series of unforeseen events, Uron and the Great Snake ended up banished to the physical realm without a body for centuries. After Uron got a body, he then attempted to destroy Martir, but was ultimately destroyed by Braim Kotogs and now no longer exists as a spiritual or physical being.

World's End. Also known as the Throne of the Gods. The final island in the southern seas and home to most of the katabans on Martir.

About the Author

Timothy L. Cerepaka writes fantasy as an indie author. He is the author of the Prince Malock World fantasy novels, the Mages of Martir fantasy novels, and the Two Worlds science-fantasy series. He lives in Texas.

Find out more at his website at www.timothylcerepaka.com.

Other books by Timothy L. Cerepaka

Prince Malock World:

The Mad Voyage of Prince Malock

The Return of Prince Malock

The New Era of Prince Malock

The Coronation of Prince Malock

Mages of Martir:

The Mage's Grave

The Mage's Limits

The Mage's Sea

The Mage's Ghost

Two Worlds:

Reunification

Alliance

Allegiance

Retaliation

Desinence

Tournament of the Gods:

Gathering of the Chosen

Betrayal of the Chosen

Invasion of the Chosen

Standalones:

The Last Legend: Glitch Apocalypse

All of the above books are available in ebook and trade paperback wherever books are sold!